Halfhyde
and the Guns of Arrest

Historical Fiction Published by McBooks Press

BY ALEXANDER KENT
Midshipman Bolitho
Stand Into Danger
In Gallant Company
Sloop of War
To Glory We Steer
Command a King's Ship
Passage to Mutiny
With All Despatch
Form Line of Battle!
Enemy in Sight!
The Flag Captain
Signal–Close Action!
The Inshore Squadron
A Tradition of Victory
Success to the Brave
Colours Aloft!
Honour This Day
The Only Victor
Beyond the Reef
The Darkening Sea
For My Country's Freedom
Cross of St George
Sword of Honour
Second to None
Relentless Pursuit
Man of War

BY DOUGLAS REEMAN
Badge of Glory
First to Land
The Horizon
Dust on the Sea

Twelve Seconds to Live
Battlecruiser
The White Guns

BY DAVID DONACHIE
The Devil's Own Luck
The Dying Trade
A Hanging Matter
An Element of Chance
The Scent of Betrayal
A Game of Bones

On a Making Tide
Tested by Fate
Breaking the Line

BY DUDLEY POPE
Ramage
Ramage & The Drumbeat
Ramage & The Freebooters
Governor Ramage R.N.
Ramage's Prize
Ramage & The Guillotine
Ramage's Diamond
Ramage's Mutiny
Ramage & The Rebels
The Ramage Touch
Ramage's Signal
Ramage & The Renegades
Ramage's Devil
Ramage's Trial
Ramage's Challenge
Ramage at Trafalgar
Ramage & The Saracens
Ramage & The Dido

**BY ALEXANDER
FULLERTON**
Storm Force to Narvik

BY PHILIP MCCUTCHAN
Halfhyde at the Bight
of Benin
Halfhyde's Island
Halfhyde and the
Guns of Arrest
Halfhyde to the Narrows

BY JAMES L. NELSON
The Only Life That
Mattered

BY V.A. STUART
Victors and Lords
The Sepoy Mutiny
Massacre at Cawnpore
The Cannons of Lucknow
The Heroic Garrison

The Valiant Sailors
The Brave Captains
Hazard's Command
Hazard of Huntress
Hazard in Circassia
Victory at Sebastopol

BY R.F. DELDERFIELD
Too Few for Drums

Seven Men of Gascony

BY DEWEY LAMBDIN
The French Admiral
Jester's Fortune

BY C.N. PARKINSON
The Guernseyman
Devil to Pay
The Fireship
Touch and Go
So Near So Far
Dead Reckoning

BY JAN NEEDLE
A Fine Boy for Killing
The Wicked Trade
The Spithead Nymph

BY IRV C. ROGERS
Motoo Eetee

BY NICHOLAS NICASTRO
The Eighteenth Captain
Between Two Fires

BY FREDERICK MARRYAT
Frank Mildmay OR
The Naval Officer
The King's Own
Mr Midshipman Easy
Newton Forster OR
The Merchant Service
Snarleyyow OR
The Dog Fiend
The Privateersman
The Phantom Ship

BY W. CLARK RUSSELL
Wreck of the Grosvenor
Yarn of Old
Harbour Town

BY RAFAEL SABATINI
Captain Blood

BY MICHAEL SCOTT
Tom Cringle's Log

BY A.D. HOWDEN SMITH
Porto Bello Gold

The Halfhyde Adventures, No. 3

Halfhyde and the Guns of Arrest

Philip McCutchan

MCBOOKS PRESS, INC.
ITHACA, NEW YORK

Published by McBooks Press, Inc. 2004
Copyright © 1976 by Philip McCutchan
First published in Great Britain by George Weidenfeld & Nicolson Limited

Cover painting: *Coaling a Battleship* by Claud Shepperson in *Practical Coal-
mining,* 1907. Courtesy of Mary Evans Picture Library.

Library of Congress Cataloging-in-Publication Data

McCutchan, Philip, 1920-1996
[Guns of arrest]
Halfhyde and the guns of arrest / by Philip McCutchan.
    p. cm. — (The Halfhyde adventures ; no. 3)
ISBN 1-59013-067-7 (trade pbk. : alk. paper)
    1. Halfhyde, St. Vincent (Fictitious character)—Fiction. 2. Great
Britain—History, Naval—20th century—Fiction. 3. Espionage,
German—Great Britain—Fiction. 4. British—Africa—Fiction. 5.
Traitors—Fiction. I. Title.
PR6063.A167G86 2004
823'.914—dc22

                                                                    2004002294

Distributed to the trade by National Book Network, Inc.,
15200 NBN Way, Blue Ridge Summit, PA 17214
800-462-6420

Additional copies of this book may be ordered from any bookstore
or directly from McBooks Press, Inc., ID Booth Building,
520 North Meadow St., Ithaca, NY 14850. Please include $4.00 postage
and handling with mail orders. New York State residents must add
sales tax to total remittance (books & shipping). All McBooks Press
publications can also be ordered by calling toll-free
1-888-BOOKS11 (1-888-266-5711).
Please call to request a free catalog.

Visit the McBooks Press website at www.mcbooks.com.

Printed in the United States of America

9 8 7 6 5 4 3 2 1

Chapter 1

IT WAS A LONG WAY from the sea and the lash of bright silver spray over the plunging bow of a warship: as the sun climbed high above the fells, bringing to a rich bronze the autumn tints on wood and grassland, Lieutenant St Vincent Halfhyde shaded his eyes and looked towards the spectacular immensity of Whernside in the distance. His gaze travelled south-easterly next, towards the long summit of Ingleborough between Greta and Ribble. After the sea, Yorkshire was his first love, though he had seen little of it in the past few years: during the gall of unemployment on the Admiralty's half-pay list, he had seldom made the long train journey north to his father's farm in Wensleydale; the seedy poverty of life as an officer without appointment had made him prefer the anonymity of London and the motherly ministrations of Mrs Mavitty, his landlady in Camden Town who always treated him as a gentleman no matter what. Not that the good people of Wensleydale would have treated him any differently; but he would not sponge upon his parents nor feel unable to buy beer for beer in the hostelries of Hawes. Now, however, he was no longer on half-pay: after a commission afloat that had ended the wilderness years he was on leave and awaiting appointment, which was a totally different kettle of fish. A sovereign or two jingled loose in his pocket, uncommitted except for his pleasure, and once again he could afford whisky in place of beer . . .

He turned to his companion. "I've a mind to anchor for a spell, Reuben."

The old man clicked his tongue. "Y'aren't at sea now, Master Vinny. But we'll rest. I'm not so young as I was."

"I dare say the sheep can wait for us." Halfhyde slid the canvas haversack from his shoulder, took off his cloth cap, and lowered his body to the soft, springy earth of the fellside. He glanced at Reuben Rumbelow's face: it was large and square, with a full white beard, and what skin was visible was weatherworn to a leathery brown. Halfhyde smiled to himself: old Reuben, his father's shepherd these last forty years, would be a mere passenger on the heaving wet decks of one of Her Majesty's ironclads at sea, and he, Halfhyde, was equally ignorant, despite his rural background, of the foibles of the Yorkshire Lonk or any other breed of sheep; yet much more than facial toughness linked the men of the sea with the men of the hill farms. Each faced wind and weather, scorching sun and driving sleet. Each was steeped in the lore of his own calling to such an extent that his reaction to events was instantaneous. Each was watchful for the safety of his charge, be it vessel or animal. Each was hardened to a lonely life and to the self-reliance that was an essential part of his work. Between old Reuben and "Master Vinny" there was a strong bond: Reuben Rumbelow had been part of High Farm for many years before Halfhyde's birth.

Halfhyde brought out a flask of whisky, unscrewed the stopper, and handed the flask to Reuben.

"It's early, Master Vinny."

"Damn it, look at the sun! It's noon. And the sheep won't mind."

"If they put a foot in a pothole, they'll mind."

"It'd take more than the whole flask to stop you pulling them clear. Have a mouthful, Reuben: wet your whistle."

No further argument: the shepherd took his mouthful, a meagre one, and wiped his lips with the back of his hand. Bread and cheese were brought out and eaten in friendly silence as a light wind chased streaks of white cloud across the sky to bring a dappled effect to dale and fell. Behind them the first of the autumn fires smoked from the chimneys of the market town of Hawes between Ribblesdale and Swaledale. It was the shepherd who broke the silence after a couple of mouthfuls.

"You've not said much about what you've been up to . . . and you've been back at t'farm a week now."

"There's little to tell, Reuben."

Reuben made a gesture of impatience, met the eye of the collie lying full stretch a few yards away, head between paws, feathery tail outstretched behind. "That's nobbut modesty!"

A grin touched Halfhyde's mouth. "I sank a Russian fleet."

"Never!" The shepherd stared. "All by thissen?"

"With the assistance of my captain," Halfhyde said in acknowledgment of modesty, "and a good ship's company."

"Is that true, Master Vinny?"

"It is."

Reuben scratched his head. "I'll be buggered. I've never known you to tell owt else, I'll say that. But by gum! It's a wonder you didn't start a bloody war!"

"That's what Their Lordships said to my captain. But in the

end, Reuben, honour was satisfied all round and some good was done. For various reasons Their Lordships were able to regard the damage to the fleet as a self-inflicted wound. Anyway, the Russians are lying very low now, and I'll say no more about it."

"They told you not to, did they, these Lordships?"

Halfhyde grinned again. "Something like that, Reuben. So tell it only to your sheep." He got to his feet and stretched, tall, slim, and agile. He called to the fell dog who, grinning back at him from behind a mat of hair, waved his tail and stood up, coming towards Halfhyde who bent to rumple his ears. The shepherd looked on with indulgence: the young master, whom he could never quite think of as a full-fledged officer of Her Majesty's fleet, had always got on well with animals and children, and to Reuben that was praise enough. But it seemed he did not get on with the Russkies! To sink a fleet of great warships was both a wonderful and terrible thing to do, and indeed in the peace and tranquillity of the Pennine fells was an impossible thing for a man to visualize who had never so much as seen the sea . . . Reuben thought of death, and broken bodies, and fire, but was unable to see the whole picture or to appreciate the dramatic horror of the last moments of a great ship.

The two men carried on with the day's work, Reuben communicating with the collie in the manner known only to the shepherd-brotherhood of the fells, a skill that Halfhyde knew he would never learn. Even here, even today, his thoughts were with great waters and the race of men who went down in danger to the sea. His very gait rolled to the imagined heave of a slippery deck with life-lines rigged fore and aft in a sea-way. After Reuben's question his thoughts had gone back across the world to the China seas, and the task of the gallant old *Viceroy,* Captain Henry Bassinghorn in command, to plant the British flag on the volcanic island that was now to go down on the Admiralty charts as Halfhyde's Island: Bassinghorn himself had insisted on this on their return to report to Their Lordships of the Admiralty. The Hydrographer of the Navy had been pleased enough to concur with orders from the First Sea Lord, and Lieutenant St Vincent Halfhyde, though still very much alive, had passed into history. The shattering roar of the eruptions that had laid Admiral Prince Gorsinski's flagship almost vertically upon an upthrust mountainside halfway between Hong Kong and San Francisco exploded in his ears again. The work, strictly speaking, had perhaps been God's! In those terrible eruptions, due to the forcing of God's hand by the impact of gunfire from the Russian cruiser, an arm of solid land had been lifted and thrown across the anchorage; the Russian squadron was in there still, and would remain there until the metal rusted away and the great gun-batteries fell to pieces, stark memorials to the frustrated ambitions of the Czar of All the Russias.

Walking the fells with his mind elsewhere, answering old Reuben's occasional questions absently, Halfhyde was scarcely aware, as the sun went down the sky towards Kendal and the lakes behind, that they had turned homeward. Coming down a little to the east of Hawes and meeting the road running through Wensleydale to Leyburn, they began to walk the last mile to High Farm on the road's hard, rutted surface. They had gone no more than a couple of hundred yards when from behind came the urgent tinging of a bicycle bell; and they moved to the left in single file to allow free passage to the cyclist.

They were hailed. "Well, I'll be damned, sir, if 'taint Master Vinny hissen." The cyclist braked, skidded in a shower of dust and stones, and dismounted: he was the postman from Hawes. "A good afternoon to you, sir."

"And to you, John." Halfhyde shaded his eyes with one hand. "What's the hurry?"

"I was going up to t'farm. There's a telegram from London." The voice was hoarse with import. "From t'second Sea Lord o' t'Admiralty, for thee."

"A telegram, indeed!" Halfhyde held out his hand. "Let's have it, and its dictates!"

The envelope was passed across: Halfhyde slit it quickly. It was brief enough: *Lieutenant St Vincent Halfhyde, Royal Navy, from Second Sea Lord. You are to report to Commander-in-Chief Plymouth forthwith on appointment as lieutenant for special duties in Her Majesty's Ship* Prince Consort, *Captain Henry Bassinghorn, Royal Navy, in command.*

Halfhyde caught his breath. "Bassinghorn again!" he said aloud. "He must have asked for me. That's an honour, at all events!" He put a hand on the postman's shoulder. "Thank you, John. You've brought me good news, though you'll prove a Job's comforter to my unfortunate mother and father. Off you go back to Hawes."

"A safe journey to you, Master Vinny." The postman saluted, almost standing at attention, feeling his position as a link in the chain of momentous communication: not often did one speed a naval officer upon his duty. True, the great houses of the district provided their quotas of officers for the regiments—the West Yorkshires, the Green Howards, the Duke of Wellington's, the King's Own Yorkshire Light Infantry—but Her Majesty's

Navy was a rarer flower. As the harbinger swung his machine round and pedalled off back to Hawes, Halfhyde took Reuben Rumbelow's arm. "Dinner tonight must lack my company, old friend. Forthwith means what it says—at once if not sooner! I'll pack my gear and then my father must drive me in the trap to the railway station at Hawes."

The long journey was made even longer by the disappointment in the faces at High Farm. From Hawes Junction Halfhyde went to Northallerton and caught the Edinburgh–London express stopped for him on telegraphed orders from the stationmaster at Hawes. In London next morning, after changing into uniform at the station hotel at King's Cross, he caught the train out of Paddington for Plymouth.

When his uniform cases had been removed from the guard's van, Halfhyde took a cab to Devonport and the dockyard gates in Fore Street, to be immediately absorbed into the atmosphere of the Navy. Devonport, like Portsmouth, like Chatham in the Nore Command, was a sailor's town. Here the fleet was everything, the military garrison a thing of the second rank. The libertymen from the ships in port filled the streets, overflowing from the public houses in carousing groups. Some of the men wore sennit hats, others round caps, and others again the peaked caps of petty officers. There were gnarled able seamen with faded blue collars and a full quota of gold good-conduct badges on their left arms; men with beards, men clean-shaven, men with years of service behind them, and youngsters starting their first commission afloat. Looking from the dark interior of the cab, Halfhyde noted the ship-names on the black, gold-lettered cap ribbons: *Inflexible, Agincourt, Calliope*—known to the fleet as "Hurricane Jumper" after making out to sea from Apia in Samoa into the jaws of a hurricane to seek safety in open water while less prudently commanded ships succumbed—*Arethusa, Trafalgar, Royal Oak,* and many more, honoured names that over the years had carried the White Ensign across every ocean of the world. Some of the roistering sailors had women on their arms; others, alone, stopped occasionally in their lurching progress to take a swig from a bottle. As Halfhyde's cab swayed on, police appeared, supported by the military: they blew whistles and shouted for the roadway to be cleared; and from the distance behind him Halfhyde heard the skirl of the pipes and the beat of the drums. He ordered the cabbie into the roadside, to wait. Past him came a Highland regiment, proud men in hackled bonnets with kilts aswing around weather-hardened knees. The air was filled with the sound of the pipes and drums playing "The Campbells Are Coming." Carried proudly aloft behind them were the Queen's and regimental colours, the latter bearing the battle honours. When the rearguard had gone past down Fore Street and under the dockyard gate, Halfhyde ordered his cabbie to proceed again, past Miss Agnes Weston's Royal Sailors' Rest by the dockyard gate. At the gate he gave his name and that of his ship to the constable on duty and was saluted through to the offices of the commander-in-chief. Before moving on, he leaned out of the window again.

"The Scots—are they embarking for foreign service?"

"Yessir. Bombay, sir, and the North-West frontier. The *Malabar's* lying off in the Sound, sir, to take them from tenders."

Halfhyde nodded and signalled the cabbie to move on. After the troopship sailed out of Plymouth Sound, there would be many seasick Scots and the pipes would lie silent—to the delight of the Sassenachs among the *Malabar*'s crew. Bowling over the dockyard cobbles, Halfhyde sniffed the smells appreciatively— the tar and the rope, the canvas that still lingered from the old sailing navy, the salt of the sea blown inshore from the Sound and the Hamoaze—the waters sailed by Drake when he went out to sweep the Channel clear of the great Armada and save England as surely as Nelson had, later. Halfhyde hummed to himself:

Take my drum to England, hang et by the shore,
Strike et when your powder's runnin' low;
If the Dons sight Devon, I'll quit the port o' Heaven . . .

The cab stopped: port had been reached, but it was not heaven. Emerging from the cab, Halfhyde was saluted by a sentry of the Royal Marine Light Infantry and by the sergeant of the guard, to whom he gave his name and errand. Inside the commander-in-chief's building he was met by the flag lieutenant.

"Mr Halfhyde?"

Halfhyde gave a slight bow. "At your service. Am I to report to the commander-in-chief in person, or to the chief of staff?"

"The former, who shall see you presently. My office is at your disposal meanwhile."

Halfhyde nodded his thanks, and followed the immaculate flag lieutenant along a green-painted passage. In the flag lieutenant's office Halfhyde asked the question he had been dying to ask ever since he had received that urgent telegram: "Do you know what this is all about? I refer to the fact of my special duties."

"I do, but I must leave the telling of it to the admiral." The flag lieutenant, who gave his name as Newton-Andrews, smiled understandingly. "You've had a damned long journey from Yorkshire, and you've been speculating."

"I have, very busily. And then there's the ship herself. The *Prince Consort* has a poor reputation in a sea-way. I'm pleased enough to have an appointment afloat, but—"

"But you can think of more modern battleships?"

"You have it precisely, Mr Newton-Andrews. I know the *Prince Consort's* reputation, as I say. Apart from anything else, she's said to be dangerous when in company with other ships if she should be so unwise as to exceed ten knots. Ten knots is not fast . . . and speaking of reputations, I have my own to consider."

"Your reputation for insubordination, Mr Halfhyde?" The flag lieutenant's eyebrows shot up. "I should hardly think *that* worth preserving."

"No. My reputation as a seaman and a ship-handler."

"Not a reputation famed for its tact."

"I am not a tactful man. God failed to grant me that grace," Halfhyde said, half mockingly.

"Nevertheless, I would advise tact with the admiral, and some concealment of the irritation which is said to afflict you when in the presence of senior officers—"

"Only some senior officers, not all. I have the greatest respect for Captain Bassinghorn, and to that extent I am delighted to be joining his command." Halfhyde stared into the flag lieutenant's eyes, coolly. "Mr Newton-Andrews, you appear to know a great deal about me."

"You are not precisely a retiring officer, Mr Halfhyde."

"Only a half-pay one, from time to time—as, it seems, you know."

"Yes," the flag lieutenant said, rather coldly. "As to the speed and performance of the *Prince Consort,* you have no need to worry. This much I can tell you now: the *Prince Consort* is not to proceed in company, but alone." At that moment a seaman messenger knocked and entered with word that the admiral was ready to see Lieutenant Halfhyde.

Preceded by the flag lieutenant, Halfhyde made his way to the commander-in-chief's room, feeling oddly excited yet at the same time most anxious: commanders-in-chief of the port divisions did not normally receive junior officers upon appointment, and this appointment had all the trappings of a special mission. Halfhyde, who was first and foremost a seaman, had no wish to become tagged in Admiralty records as an officer with too much special mission experience—and already he had carried out two such assignments. This was how naval officers became, almost willy-nilly, sidetracked and detached from the main stream of sea appointments and eventual command of ships and squadrons and battlefleets. General service was important, even in an age that was becoming increasingly slanted to the advantage of the specialist, which Halfhyde, as a salt horse, was not. Going along the passage to the admiral's room, he glanced at a succession of paintings depicting former Commanders-in-Chief Plymouth and great ships that under sail and steam had carried the flags of admirals dead and gone—a veritable gallery of naval power and pride, a pictorial storehouse of war and empire that had begun with Raleigh and Drake and continued through Collingwood, Blake, Rodney, Benbow, and the great Lord Nelson to the present day with its Fishers, its Lord Charles Beresfords, and its Clanwilliams. Halfhyde passed beneath the portrait of Admiral Lord Nelson with a special feeling of affinity: under the great, little, one-armed, one-eyed seaman with all his human failings Halfhyde's own sole naval connection had sailed—Daniel Halfhyde, gunner's mate in the fighting *Temeraire,* a simple and uneducated man who now perhaps looked down from aloft with pride in a descendant who had achieved ward-room rank . . .

"Lieutenant Halfhyde, sir, reporting in accordance with his orders."

"Let him come in," a resonant voice said from the end of the long room. The room was furnished with old dark leather chairs, a deep pile carpet from India, and more seafaring paintings of admirals and ships of the line: over the fireplace hung a reminder of the ultimate power of the landbound, a splendid portrait of Queen Victoria, with the blue ribbon of the Garter wide across her ample bosom and her expression disdainful beneath the white hair and lace cap, as though she resented being placed in close proximity to seamen: it was well known throughout the fleet that Her Majesty had more regard for her soldiers than for her sailors.

Halfhyde, rigid at attention with his cap beneath his arm, waited for the commander-in-chief to speak. The face, heavy and formidable and with a bleak look in the eyes, broke into some semblance of a welcoming smile; an arm, the uniform cuff rich with the broad gold band and the three thinner ones of no less a personage than a full admiral, waved towards an armchair.

"Be easy, Mr Halfhyde, and sit you down."

"Thank you, sir."

Halfhyde sat as bid; the admiral nodded to the flag lieutenant, who left the room. The admiral remained standing,
hands clasped behind his frock-coat, a tall, dominant figure: for
some moments he stared at Halfhyde, as if summing him up.
The admiral's eyes were shrewd and searching in a hard, deeply
lined face. He had no beard, but heavy side-whiskers, grey
turning to white, met beneath the chin. Above the thick eyebrows that completed the frame the head was as bald as any
cannon-ball; and inside the frame the expression held all the
power and promise of a battleship's broadside.

"You are a Yorkshireman, Mr Halfhyde, a northerner." The
voice, to Halfhyde, was tinged with contempt.

"But not a foreigner, sir, as your tone suggests."

The face glowered. "Kindly do not answer me back. I have
noted truculence in men from the north before now, and I do
not like it, Mr Halfhyde, I do not like it at all."

"For that I'm sorry, sir. But I make no apology for the county
of my birth. Indeed, I'm proud of it."

"Very well, Mr Halfhyde, you may continue so to be."

"I shall, sir. I'm most grateful for your permission."

Their eyes met and held: the admiral's look was murderous,
but neither broke the other's gaze. Still staring, the admiral said,
"We have not met before, Mr Halfhyde, yet your reputation goes
before you, as in the case of any officer or man who steps out
of the line. I have no need to remind you that in the past your
captains have had occasion to report you as insubordinate and
arrogant—"

"In the *past,* sir."

"And you now add blatant rudeness to the list," the admiral
said angrily, "and since I am unaccustomed to being interrupted

by officers of lieutenant's rank, you will be good enough to hold your tongue until I tell you to loosen it. Bear in mind that the good of the Service is paramount, Mr Halfhyde, and its best interests are served only by strict discipline and the exercise of unquestioned authority. Now then—to your orders. These are of the utmost importance to the government. You will listen carefully, for there will be nothing in writing."

As the admiral turned away towards a door leading from an ante-room the gaze was at last broken. Halfhyde found himself, somewhat to his own surprise, sweating badly: the commander-in-chief was a tough character and he felt he could congratulate himself upon sustaining the glare. But he was unprepared for what happened next: the admiral, opening the door, said, "Sir John, if you please, we are ready."

Halfhyde started. Through the door came a short, stocky figure in plain clothes, red-faced, blue-eyed, pugnacious. Halfhyde recognized him instantly: Rear-Admiral Sir John Fisher, since 1892 Third Sea Lord and Comptroller of the Navy, a man of terrible temper and immense ambition whose aim in life was the modernization of the fleet. He was a force to be reckoned with, and one that had split both the Admiralty and the fleet itself into pro- and anti-Fisher camps. If he was to be concerned in orders given to a mere lieutenant, then something big must be astir for a certainty.

The commander-in-chief introduced Halfhyde: Fisher shook his hand, seeming friendly, almost informal, though the set of the mouth was firm and arrogant. Jacky Fisher . . . a legend in the fleet already! They were bidden by the commander-in-chief to sit, and Fisher lost no time in expounding his orders. Halfhyde listened to his utterances in growing chagrin, his worst fears confirmed now: the Home Office had asked for, and had obtained, Admiralty assistance in what sounded like a mere manhunt, though in all truth the word "mere" could scarcely be applied to anything in which Fisher was concerned! The facts were bald: Sir Russell Savory, a permanent official of high standing in the Directorate of Naval Construction at the Admiralty, had vanished some weeks earlier while on an official visit to Brazil. All trace of him had been lost. Lost, that was, until word had reached London that he had been seen in Santiago, Chile. Simultaneously another fact had come to light— he had made copies of the blueprints of every battleship and cruiser currently under construction and projected for the British Fleet.

"My fleet," Fisher stated furiously and uncompromisingly. "My construction programme—all my hopes for our naval supremacy for the future! All set at stake by the actions of a damn *traitor* who should be flogged round the fleet at Spithead before swinging from a scaffold in the Tower!"

Halfhyde asked, "How is it known, sir, that he has made these copies?"

"Because the bugger told us so himself!" Fisher stormed, rising from his chair to stamp up and down the room, hands clasped beneath the tails of his morning coat. "He's holding his country to ransom, Mr Halfhyde! Holding it to ransom! If the British government does not pay him a million pounds in sterling in Chile, then he will pass all his blueprints and his own knowledge, gained over many years, to the Kaiser. He has telegraphed the First Lord to this effect—and has had the damned impertinence, the sheer damned *effrontery,* to use an Admiralty cypher for his purpose!"

Halfhyde dutifully concealed a degree of amusement: shocking as the revelation might be, he felt some affinity with any person, however nefarious, who cocked such snooks at Their Lordships. He asked, "So there are secret cypher tables missing also, sir?"

Fisher waved a hand. "Yes, but that is of minor importance. Cyphers can be, and are, of course, changed at intervals—you know that. But the construction programme—this is the vital thing—its security from foreign powers is vital to the country, Mr Halfhyde, and to the very existence of the empire! The whole of my naval strategy is dependent upon my shipbuilding programme! The foreign policy of Her Majesty's Government is dependent upon it—the country has been crying out for modernization of the fleet and at last public opinion is being met. It would be a tragedy if one wretched man's personal greed for money should set it all at naught!"

"Yes indeed, sir—"

"I find it hard to believe that any man can do such a thing! But Savory . . . trusted, honoured by Her Majesty with a knighthood! Bah!" Fisher almost spat: he was shaking with fury. "Such a thing has never happened before. The disgrace! The damn traitor! Words fail me!"

"Yes indeed, sir," Halfhyde said again. "And the German emperor—"

"We all know the vainglorious aspirations of Kaiser Wilhelm to build a German Navy comparable with our own. If he has access to our secrets, we are done for! I understand His Royal Highness the Prince of Wales has been confided in by Lord Salisbury—and is beside himself with anger!"

"The Prince of Wales has little love for his nephew, so it's said," Halfhyde murmured. "And my part in this, sir?"

"You're going to get Savory back!" Fisher shouted. "The prime minister will not even consider meeting his ridiculous and impertinent demand!" Forcing himself to calm down, he continued with his exposition. Sir Russell Savory, it appeared, had moved on after the prime minister's refusal to pay up had been intimated to him. Though the British government had found itself powerless to touch him in Chile, and though it might have been possible for him to pass his blueprints to the German embassy in Santiago, he was known to have left Chile in disguise after sending his telegraphed demands and making arrangements for the reception of the "ransom" money by a Chilean bank.

"But why, sir?" Halfhyde asked. "Why not hand the blueprints to the German embassy?"

"We believe," Fisher said, "he feared he might be double-crossed. He prefers to part with his stock-in-trade only in Berlin. Besides, he knows the importance of his own brain—he himself is a vital part of this saleable information. He's been very much on the inside, of course, and close to the top."

"But not at the very top, sir?"

Fisher shook his head. "That was denied him. It's true Her Majesty gave him a knighthood, but he upset her during a subsequent audience. She let it be known that she detested the sight of him and regretted the knighthood. Her Majesty is an old lady of strong views and utterances. In short, Sir Russell would have gone no further, Mr Halfhyde."

"But has gone a good deal further now, sir."

Fisher, about to say more, stopped with his mouth open. "Was that a joke, a witticism?" he snapped.

"I'm sorry, sir."

"I should damn well think so!" Fisher's face reddened dangerously beneath the untidy shock of grey hair. "You shall not laugh at traitors, Mr Halfhyde! They are despicable! We shall never live down the disgrace!"

"No, sir."

Fisher continued. Savory was believed to have taken ship across the South Atlantic aboard a Portuguese merchantman bound for São Paolo de Loanda. From there, the reports suggested, he had moved easterly: there had been indications from possibly doubtful sources that he had been seen at Malanje, Vila Henrique de Carvalho, and Sandoa in the Belgian Congo.

"A long way from Berlin, sir."

"Agreed. But if the reports are correct, he appears to be going in the right direction. It's thought likely his first destination is German East Africa, where he can take ship to Europe."

"And if the reports are not correct, sir?"

"You mean if we lose him altogether! If that happens, Mr Halfhyde, the world ends! The government could fall. The fleet will be in jeopardy for years to come. My programme will lie in ruins. Germany and its damned popinjay of a Kaiser will crow like fighting cocks, and will prepare for a war that they're likely enough to win!" Fisher seethed, and smashed a fist into his palm in front of Halfhyde's face. "We are not to lose him! He is to be stopped before he reaches German territory! Any German territory, anywhere on the map!"

"Stopped by a battleship, sir?"

"By some of a battleship's company." Fisher went on to indicate that Halfhyde's personal career had given him considerable experience of Africa and its peoples, its coasts and its rivers: also that Halfhyde was ambitious for a command of his own. He might well be about to achieve this ambition, for the *Prince Consort* carried upon her after superstructure two 60-foot torpedo-boats which would prove capable of navigating shallow rivers. "Captain Bassinghorn's orders are for Simon's Town, Mr Halfhyde, and thence, after reporting to the local command for detailed orders, for the mouth of the Zambezi River. You will find the Zambezi navigable as far as the Kebrabasa Falls in Portuguese East Africa. From there you will find yourself handily placed to cut off Savory, either by a land march or by means of native canoes which you shall purloin, if necessary, after outflanking the falls."

"Your pardon, sir. Why cannot the apprehension of Sir Russell Savory be left to our forces on the South African station?"

Fisher snorted and said, "The Metropolitan Police!"

"Sir?"

"Certain highly-placed personages," Fisher answered irritably and with a rising colour, "have decided for reasons of state that the arrest is to be made by a man from the Metropolitan Police."

"Good God!"

Fisher scowled. "Pray do not invoke the deity to me, Mr Halfhyde. I've done so myself to the damn Board of Admiralty, and the Home Secretary, and the Foreign Secretary—all to no damn avail. Indeed I may have said too much—they're a set of blasted old women who react against sailors' talk—straight talk."

Halfhyde reflected that Sir John Fisher might well have antag-onized the whole of Whitehall: he had a reputation for hot temper and intolerance. So often—though by no means invari-ably—senior naval officers harried civil servants into ill-considered judgments and hasty actions by a firework display of bombast, pompousness, screaming, and other indications of temperament; and Fisher, the Navy's most difficult admiral, was a man who aroused violent emotions whatever he did. But this was alarming. Fisher continued: "This person, a detective inspec-tor, has already reported aboard the *Prince Consort*."

"I see, sir. Certainly I can understand a degree of circum-spection being required. The Belgian Congo, Portuguese posses-sions in Africa, the Germans . . . yes, the diplomatic involvements are legion. But a policeman, in Africa!"

"It was no wish of mine," Fisher stated. "As to the delay, it need not be of great moment. We have agents in Africa, I'm told, who will be watching the situation and so far as possible keeping Savory under distant surveillance. But you spoke of diplomacy: Portugal is our very good friend and ally, but at this particular time neither she nor the Belgians have any wish to upset their relations with the Kaiser—and a lot has had to hinge upon that." Fisher drew a gold half-hunter from a pocket and studied it. "And now, time presses towards your sailing, Mr Halfhyde."

"Yes, sir. But your pardon once again. Pray forgive me, but I find this appointment much to my distaste—"

Fisher stared, eyes wide. "What damned impertinence!"

"An old and slow ship—she'll take all of twenty days to reach the Cape alone—and the doubtful company of a London flatfoot upon the Zambezi River, a man who knows nothing of ships or boats and acts only upon the advice given in some obscure police manual!" Halfhyde's voice rose. "I am a seaman, sir, a naval officer—not a mud pilot!"

Fisher exploded. "Get out! Your ship sails in one hour precisely—unless you prefer to travel in irons to the barrack hulks, to face court martial!"

Halfhyde hesitated, then shrugged: protest was, as ever, useless. He gave a formal bow, and turned towards the door. Fisher's voice pursued him. "Come back here!" Halfhyde turned politely, and Fisher said, "One thing more: during the voyage you'll speak of our conversation to no one but your captain and commander, and when necessary to the detective inspector, who will let it be known to all other personnel that he is proceeding to investigate a case of simple fraud—and who will make no mention of the Cape until permitted to do so by the captain."

Leaving Sir John Fisher's irascible presence, Halfhyde was driven, in a mutinous frame of mind, to the *Prince Consort's* berth, bumping up and down on the springs as the cab bounced over cobbles. He was livid: mud pilot, prison warder, bloodhound, detective's aide—this was a fine appointment to interrupt his leave! He was no lover of the Metropolitan Police; he had seen too much of them and their activities while he was unemployed in Camden Town. The truncheons had been used too often and too freely on the unfortunates, the unemployed like himself but without the benefit of even half-pay; and the prostitutes had too often been hounded in the pursuit of a necessary if unpleasant trade. To the Metropolitan Police poverty itself was a crime,

and the poor had never been allowed to get away with anything while the gentry—short of committing a crime of the
magnitude of Sir Russell Savory's—were virtually immune. The
police forces were there for the protection of gentlemen against
the common herd. Halfhyde, though a law-abiding citizen himself, felt degraded and diminished by the blatant injustice.

Yet there were current blessings to be counted: within the
hour he would be back at sea, swallowed and digested by the
changeless routine of one of Her Majesty's ships of war where
every man aboard knew his place and his duty and where the
clock was replaced by the bell and the bugle. That was pleasant; so was his first sight of the *Prince Consort,* immaculate with
buff funnels, white upperworks, and black hull alongside the
dockyard wall, splendid beneath the declining sun. Slow she
might be, and difficult to handle, but she was fair to look at,
heavily gunned with her four sixteen-inch muzzle-loaders, each
weighing 81 tons and set in turrets placed *en echelon* amidships.
It was these guns and her extraordinarily heavy 24-inch armour
belt that slowed her down and made her unwieldy. There were
several imponderables in Halfhyde's mission, many things yet
to be explained, and one of them was: why send the old *Prince
Consort* when a faster and less heavily armed second-class cruiser
could reach Simon's Town with days to spare? One did not,
surely, hunt down an absconder with sixteen-inch main armament!

Chapter 2

"I DID NOT NEED to ask for your appointment, Mr Halfhyde. Your particular qualifications commended themselves to Their Lordships. As it is, I'm delighted to sail with you again. I appreciated your loyal support in the *Viceroy*."

"Thank you, sir." Halfhyde, reporting formally to the cuddy, felt gratified: Henry Bassinghorn had spoken with his usual gruffness but with the sincerity that Halfhyde had learned to expect of him. The captain was not a man of many words, and he now appeared embarrassed, tapping a vast hand, the hand of a prizefighter, on the flap of his roll-top desk.

There was a moment's silence in which Halfhyde heard the lap of water against the *Prince Consort*'s hull, the wash from the duty steam picket-boat going busily about her business across the harbour from the guardship. There was a shrill of boatswain's pipes as a torpedo-boat destroyer swept past towards Devil's Point out of the Hamoaze and saluted Captain Bassinghorn's commissioning pennant drooping idly from the main truck. Bassinghorn heaved himself to his feet, strode across to a port, and looked out, hands clasped behind a broad, long back, starched cuffs reaching a full two inches below the four gold rings of a post captain. As the torpedo-boat destroyer vanished outwards, Bassinghorn turned again and swung round on Halfhyde, his face now troubled.

"You will have been made aware of our orders already. They are not pleasant. It appals me to think of any man being prepared to sell his country's secrets. I find it hard to express my feelings adequately. Really I do not know what things are coming to—a man in Savory's position, a position of high trust—it makes it so much the worse!"

"Indeed it does, sir."

"However, it has happened and we must carry out our orders. Time is short to sailing, Mr Halfhyde, but if you have anything to ask me, pray do so."

"Thank you, sir." Halfhyde's question came directly: "Why the *Prince Consort,* sir? Why a slow, big-gun ship?"

"Heavy guns, Mr Halfhyde, are useful in action, are they not?"

Halfhyde looked back at him, eyes narrowed thoughtfully. "Action? The man Savory . . . he's somewhere in the middle of Africa according to the admiral. Pray, sir, how does our main armament cross the desert and the mountains?"

Bassinghorn frowned. "There is no occasion for levity, Mr Halfhyde. But to answer your question—" He broke off as a tap sounded on the polished mahogany of his day-cabin door. On the heels of the tap, the executive officer entered and stood at attention with his cap beneath his left arm. "Yes, Commander?"

"I'm about to pipe Special Sea Dutymen, sir. Do you wish further communication with the shore?"

"Thank you, no, Commander. You may lift the brows and ladders."

"Aye, aye, sir." A dark glance rested for a moment upon Halfhyde. "Lieutenant Halfhyde and I have had words together, sir, of course. I understand he is to be free of ship's duties, but perhaps he would care to familiarize himself with the ship?"

"You'll take him round, Commander?"

"Yes, sir. I shall be making my final sailing rounds presently."

"Thank you. Just one moment, and when I've finished with him I'll send him to join you. Is there anything else, Commander?"

"There is just one matter—the accommodation of the policeman. His rank being that of an inspector, the mess decks would scarcely, I suppose, be suitable. Nor perhaps the chief and petty officers' . . . I suggest, perhaps, the warrant officers' mess, rather than the ward-room, sir?"

Bassinghorn shrugged. "As you wish, Commander. It's something you should have raised earlier, I think. Do the best you can for him—possibly he'd not feel at home in the ward-room in any case."

"Very good, sir." The commander turned and left the cabin.

From the door as it closed behind him came the crash of boot-leather as the Royal Marine Light Infantry sentry came to attention. Bassinghorn caught Halfhyde's eye and set his lips.

"You must walk carefully with Commander Percy. He has made it plain that he resents an appointment for special duties that takes you, as it were, out from under his own orders. Since you are not a tactful man, Halfhyde, I would have wished a different executive officer—but that is between you and me alone."

"As, I understand, is any discussion of my mission—with the inclusion of the detective inspector and the commander."

"Just so. When we are cleared away to sea, we shall talk to the detective inspector. In the meantime, I stress again the need for tact. Commander Percy is not an easy man. Carry on for now, if you please, Mr Halfhyde."

"Aye, aye, sir." Halfhyde left the cuddy, past the salute of the captain's sentry, along an alleyway lined with rifles secured to racks by chains through their trigger guards. He went on through the ward-room officers' cabin flat and up the ladder to the hatch giving access to the quarterdeck. Already the boatswain's calls were piping the orders around the ship: "Special Sea Dutymen to your stations . . . cable and side party muster on the fo'c'sle . . . all men not in the rig of the day, clear the upper-deck . . . Divisions fall in for leaving harbour." Everywhere barefoot seamen were moving at the double, running to fall in under the orders of grizzled petty officers and leading seamen. The quarterdeck and gundeck were alive with blue and white. The declining sun struck golden fire from the polished brass of bollards and scuttles, and lit upon the White Ensign drooping from the ensign staff. Halfhyde found the commander standing by the great gun turrets amidships, beneath the barrels with their gleaming tampions in place against possible bad weather. The commander was speaking to the boatswain, but dismissed him as Halfhyde approached and saluted.

"Ah, Mr Halfhyde. It's my practice to make rounds personally before reporting the ship ready to proceed. I'm about to go below. You shall accompany me."

"Aye, aye, sir."

The commander walked forward on to the fo'c'sle past the funnels, from which smoke was already coming as the black gang below stoked the furnaces. Halfhyde followed him down a hatch into the battleship's mess decks where the scrubbed tables and benches, bread barges, and other mess traps had been neatly stowed away; then down again to the magazines and storeroom flats where the below-sea-level watertight doors were being clipped down hard by sections behind the commander as he stalked through, cold eyes watchful below heavy eyebrows that seemed almost to curl up to the gold oak leaves on his cap peak. Halfhyde formed the opinion that little would escape Commander Percy. As they went aft along the alleyways, down to the tiller flat and up again, the commander threw brief conversation over his shoulder, his head jerking in an oddly bird-like fashion as he did so.

"A Yorkshireman, Mr Halfhyde."

"Yes, sir."

"I'm from Northumberland. One of the Northumberland Percys, don't you know."

"I didn't know, sir."

"What?"

Halfhyde coughed into his hand. "A highly placed family, sir."

"Yes. Mainly *military* connections, of course."

"Then I have the advantage of you, sir. I'm a Yorkshire Halfhyde . . . with an ancestor at Trafalgar."

"Really?" Commander Percy looked right round, ran his eyes up and down Halfhyde. "What ship?"

"The *Temeraire,* sir. Daniel Halfhyde, gunner's mate."

"What was that?"

"Gunner's mate, sir."

"Really." The commander stalked on, head held back, disparagement in the very set of his shoulders. Nothing more was said about family. As they came back to the upper-deck the commander said, "You're going to be something of a passenger until your special orders come to fruition, Mr Halfhyde. The time will hang heavily for you."

"I'm prepared to take a watch, sir."

"No doubt. But if something should happen—"

"And I not appointed for watchkeeping duties? I am a salt horse, sir. I have not lost my touch! Nothing will happen that should not happen. I believe the captain will confirm my abilities."

"Perhaps—we shall see. I was going to suggest that you relieve our policeman's boredom as much as possible. He will find few kindred spirits aboard a battleship, I fancy!"

"And you think I am one?"

Commander Percy shrugged, with a touch of disdain in the movement. "You are to work together, I understand."

"Or do you relate a gunner's mate with a detective inspector, sir?"

"I think you're as touchy as any Yorkshireman, Mr Halfhyde." The commander gave a dismissive nod and made his way towards the navigating bridge with a springy step. Halfhyde glowered at the retreating back, and felt like adding to the spring with such force that Commander Percy would bounce to Plymouth Hoe and back again into the Sound. But fortunately he managed to retain his temper as he turned aft and looked along the quarterdeck. Here he had a surprise, and a pleasant one. Reporting to the lieutenant of the quarterdeck division was a familiar figure, small, eager-faced, youthful, his uniform bearing on the lapels the white patches of a midshipman. At the same instant the eye of the snotty was caught by the approach of Halfhyde, and his face reacted in equal pleasure, though, conscious of his lowly status, he at once looked away again. The lieutenant turned and Halfhyde walked towards him.

"Mr?—"

"Acland."

"And I'm Halfhyde. Mr Acland, your midshipman and I are old shipmates. Have I your permission to speak to him?"

"Why, of course."

Halfhyde gave a small bow. "Thank you indeed. Mr Runcorn, I am delighted to see you again."

"And me too, sir!"

"A familiar face in a new ship is always a most welcome sight, as you will find during your service."

"Yes, sir."

"And we're doubly fortunate in being back with Captain Bassinghorn."

"Yes, sir."

"You've had words with him?"

"No, sir, not yet, sir. I doubt if he knows I'm aboard, sir. The captain joined only the day before yesterday, sir."

"Ah. And your previous captain?"

"Dead, sir. Of an attack of malaria, sir, as we came into the Channel from Ushant, sir. The commander was temporarily appointed in command, sir, until Captain Bassinghorn—"

"*Mr Halfhyde!*" The voice was sharp, and came from the commander on his way from the bridge to go below and report to the captain. "Kindly do not delay the ship's sailing routine. Mr Runcorn, to your place at once."

"Yessir!" Mr Midshipman Runcorn saluted hastily, his face a deep red. Halfhyde gave him a wink behind the commander's back. The commander vanished down the hatch, and reappeared within a minute behind the large form of Captain Henry Bassinghorn, whom he followed deferentially to the navigating bridge. On the bridge the fleet engineer was waiting. He was a stumpy figure whose uniform cuffs bore purple distinction cloth between the three gold rings, in his case as a non-military officer unsurmounted by the gold curl of executive authority. He reported his engines ready and was dismissed to go below. The captain caught the eye of the chief yeoman of signals.

"Ask permission to proceed, Chief Yeoman."

"Aye, aye, sir." Without delay the formal signal was made to the commander-in-chief by way of the Queen's harbour master, and permission was given. The last orders were passed. The ropes and wires were let go fore and aft and their dripping ends were hauled inboard by the side party. The tugs for the passage around Devil's Point nosed up alongside. On the fo'c'sle a carpenter's mate stood by the center-line capstan, with other men handy at the catheads. From the starboard hawse-pipe the bower anchor was veered to the waterline in case the captain should need to knock away the slips and let it go to steady the great ship around Devil's Point. The main engines were rung astern on the telegraphs. Watched by a handful of dockyard mateys of the unberthing party, the *Prince Consort* slid away from the wall, while the band of the Royal Marine Artillery, positioned amidships by the guns they would fire in action, struck up "Rule, Britannia." Halfhyde, watching from the lee of one of the ship's cutters hoisted and griped-in to its goose-necked davits, heard the splendid music with the customary tug at his heartstrings. Indeed, Britons never would be slaves . . . and the guns, should they fire in action, would be well served by the *Prince Consort*'s company of seamen and marines. Halfhyde's mind went back to his mission: Bassinghorn had been speaking, when interrupted by the arrival of the commander, of possible action, and he had obviously meant action at sea. Within the context of what Savory had done and was hoping to do, action must presumably mean action against the German Navy: it was highly intriguing and lent itself to much speculation. The German naval command could well have ordered ships to sea to watch the coasts of both German East and German South-West Africa in case the British Navy should attempt any blockade designed to prevent Savory running for it—but time would tell.

Halfhyde, looking up at the bridge as the battleship started to turn towards Devil's Point, saw Bassinghorn staring aft from the port bridge-wing: and he found an affinity in the captain's large square face with old Reuben Rumbelow in Wensleydale. He recalled his thoughts of the day before on the Yorkshire fells: those two breeds of men, the seaman and the man of the soil, shared an inherent honesty and decency and integrity of purpose, attributes that in the mid-1890s Halfhyde found were beginning to recede from English life. A different type was coming along, he fancied, lesser men too much concerned with their own advancement. It could be an injustice to the scion of a noble house, but Halfhyde had a suspicion that Commander Percy would not prove to be a man such as Henry Bassinghorn. Though it was true enough that efficiency at sea was increasing, an unwelcome careerism was creeping into the British Navy, due in no small measure to the reforms and personal desires of the dynamic but despotic Rear-Admiral Sir John Fisher. To Fisher, men were inconsiderable except when they agreed with him; he climbed upon men's backs, using them as his ladder, though certainly in his case to the Navy's advantage and not his own. Halfhyde happened to know that Bassinghorn, whose training had been in sail, was no Fisher man, and that Fisher would have no regard at all for what he would consider a shellback. If Bassinghorn should ever cross swords with Fisher, the result would be a foregone conclusion.

From the after end of the bridge, as the battleship headed on her outward course, a bugle sounded the Still and then a salute to the flag of the commander-in-chief—all hands on deck came to attention until the salute had been returned and the Carry On had sounded out across the sunset-reddened waters. Round the sharp turn of Devil's Point from the Hamoaze, then out to the wide waters of the Sound, leaving Plymouth Hoe on their port quarter with its memories of Drake and the defeat of the Spanish Armada. On the port beam lay the Cattewater and the Barbican from where the Pilgrim Fathers had sailed in the *Mayflower* to the American colonies. With the tugs cast off, the battleship's great bulk came up past the transport *Malabar,* whose hawse-pipes streamed water as she weighed anchor to take her Highland battalion out for Bombay and a seven-year stretch of Indian service. Salutes were exchanged, and then spontaneous cheering broke out from the transport's decks. From the *Prince Consort's* bridge Bassinghorn authorized a disciplined response: to orders, and led by the divisional officers fore and aft, the ship's company lifted their caps in the air and gave three cheers that echoed across the Sound, striking off the great stone bastions of the military fortifications. The last of the evening sun reddening her masts and yards, her decks and guns, the *Prince Consort* moved on, slow and majestic, for the open water of the English Channel, to head for Ushant and the Bay of Biscay.

Halfhyde was about to go below when he was approached

by a man in a dark blue suit, shiny at knees and elbows; a high white collar, well starched; a pearl tie-pin thrust into a wide silk cravat; and a bowler hat anchored against the sea wind by a kind of cord toggle, the end of which was secured to a miniature ring-bolt set into the person's lapel. The pale face was cut in half by a jet-black walrus moustache. The feet were large and heavily booted: the man needed no introduction although he gave one.

"Detective Inspector Todhunter, sir, at your service. I understand you're Lieutenant St Vincent Halfhyde, of the Royal Navy? Is this correct, sir?"

"It is."

"A seamanlike name, sir, if I may make so bold."

"As appropriate to my circumstances as is your own to yours, I think."

"Eh?"

"A sleuth-like name, Mr Todhunter."

"Oh yes, sir, I take your point. Ha, ha." The laugh was self-satisfied. "The witticism has been made before now, if in plainer words than yours, sir." He paused, took a deep breath of sea air. "We are to work together later, sir, as you will know. My experience of boats is limited to days spent at Southend-on-Sea."

"And my experience of sleuthing is non-existent, Mr Todhunter."

"No matter, sir, no matter at all. Each man to his own last, I say." The detective inspector pointed towards the *Prince Consort's* after superstructure, where the two 60-foot torpedo-boats lay in their crutches. "There is your kingdom, mine is the world at large, or at any rate the African continent—until I have

Sir Russell Savory safely in handcuffs." Todhunter reached into a deep and capacious pocket and brought out a pair of handcuffs, sinister, heavy, linked with chain. He shook them in Halfhyde's face: the jingle was sadistically suggestive, as doom-laden as the closure of a cell door; the look in Todhunter's eye was dedicated and the mouth, hitherto loose-lipped and rosy red, had hardened and whitened. Though the policeman's aim could not be faulted, Halfhyde found in himself no more love for the Metropolitan Police *per se* than before. Pity, for the good warrant officers of the *Prince Consort,* came uppermost . . .

Chapter 3

THE ENGLISH CHANNEL was unpredictable but tonight, as the *Prince Consort* made her ponderous turn to starboard between Rame Head and the Great Mew Stone, and headed on a south-westerly course to stand clear of the Lizard after leaving the Eddystone light to port, the night seas were as flat as any pancake that might be made for the ward-room officers in the steamy heat of the galley. Halfhyde, pacing the quarterdeck in solitude, hands behind his back in the traditional attitude of a naval officer taking exercise, looked up at a starry sky. There was no cloud, and no wind beyond that made by the battleship's own passage through the water. On such a night, even soldiers should not be seasick, nor detective inspectors either. Halfhyde smiled to himself as he shifted his gaze aft: the turbulence of the wake, the tumbling water thrown up by the revolutions of the churning screws, streamed away eastward towards the North Sea—or, as the Germans would have it, the German Ocean. Halfhyde's smile was for the strange juxtaposition of the Metropolitan Police Force with the German High Seas Fleet, which Halfhyde's cogitations had led him to regard as a very probable manifestation for the not too distant future. Mr Todhunter had a predatory look, as though he would attempt to sink his teeth, his somewhat large and yellow teeth, into the flesh even of a German admiral, should that admiral come between him and his quarry.

Reaching the after end of the quarterdeck above the captain's stern-walk, Halfhyde turned forward again between the crutched torpedo-boats. Now he faced the thick black smoke trailing from the two great funnels, most of it fouling the air astern but some of it coming down in greasy whorls to choke men on deck and leave its traces on scrubbed woodwork and polished brass and the pipe-clayed turk's-heads that terminated the guardropes around the hatches. That smoke was anathema to men trained in the cleanliness of sail, men such as Henry Bassinghorn. But Halfhyde felt only gratitude that his own lot was not that of the engineers, men doomed to spend their working lives among the stench of oil and coal or in the cruel heat of the stokehold and its furnaces fed by the sweat-soaked, coal-stained, cursing members of the black gang who wielded their great steel shovels unceasingly for solid two-hour stretches in the ferocious surroundings of an earth-bound hell. Better—perhaps—even Todhunter's lot than theirs . . .

A figure came into sight, bowler-hatted and slightly unsteady, arms reaching for support from anything handy.

"Think of the devil," Halfhyde said.

"Beg pardon, sir?"

"My apologies, Mr Todhunter, my thoughts were below, partially at all events." He paused as the police officer ventured closer. "I see you have not your sea-legs yet."

"Some movement of the ship, sir—"

"I don't perceive it myself, but never mind. The passage of time will alter matters one way or the other, I assure you. You've heard tales of the Bay of Biscay, no doubt?"

"I have, sir."

"We have a surgeon, who will perhaps prescribe."

"I have scant belief in the medical profession, Mr Halfhyde. I've brought my own remedy." Mr Todhunter reached up, removed his bowler hat, and with a big handkerchief wiped sweat from his forehead. In the loom of light from the sky, his pale face looked paler already. "Doctor Datchet's Demulcent Drops."

"I beg your pardon, Mr Todhunter?"

"Two, sir, taken thrice daily upon a lump of sugar. They were recommended by my mother, now sadly deceased, who once took a steamer to Ryde from the Clarence Pier at Southsea."

"I see. Well, I trust they'll work as well in the Bay of Biscay! Are you comfortable aboard, Mr Todhunter?"

The detective inspector replaced his bowler hat and steadied himself against one of the torpedo-boat hulls. "I find it, shall I say, not so comfortable as my lodgings, Mr Halfhyde, but I must not complain."

"Your lodgings?"

"I have an excellent landlady, most kind and thoughtful. Since my mother passed away—"

"I gather you are not a married man then, Mr Todhunter?"

"No, I am not. There is no time for marriage in a policeman's life, that is if he is a dedicated policeman, Mr Halfhyde."

"Such as you are."

"Indeed yes." The detective inspector lowered his voice, and cast looks over his shoulder. "We are alone, sir, I fancy, quite alone." As the policeman moved closer, Halfhyde detected from his breath that he had already fortified himself against seasickness with some of the warrant officers' whisky. "There are matters that should be discussed—"

Halfhyde held up a hand and spoke sharply. "There is plenty

of time. In any case, I have not yet fully consulted my captain, and until I have done so I am not free to have any discussion with you, Mr Todhunter."

"As you wish, of course," the detective inspector said with a touch of coldness. "I only thought you might be wondering why our friend appears to be making for German East Africa rather than German South-West Africa, which would be nearer—"

"Please!" Halfhyde smiled, but held up a warning hand as he interrupted. "I am consumed with curiosity indeed, Mr Todhunter, but that is no excuse for my going behind my captain's back. Good night to you, Mr Todhunter, and sleep well. By tomorrow morning, I fancy you will find a difference in the weather."

Halfhyde strode forward; as he started down the ladder to the gundeck amidships, he glanced back. Mr Todhunter was still *in situ,* and was once again mopping his brow. The night was cool. Sweat in such conditions meant but one thing: neither the whisky of the warrant officers' mess nor Doctor Datchet's Demulcent Drops were having their proper effect. Halfhyde grinned to himself, wickedly. He had come across many people in his life who mistrusted the medical profession and they all had one thing in common: provided they chose their own panacea, the word "Doctor" on the bottle drew them like a magnet. Like so much else, it was a curious contradiction. Once, Halfhyde had joined a crowd gathered in strength upon Tower Hill in London. A self-styled doctor had been selling a potion beneath a banner that read: CURES COUGHS, COLDS, SORE HOLES, AND PIMPLES ON THE BOTTOM. The purveyor, dressed in tall hat and morning coat like any medical man from Harley Street, had been doing excellent trade at a florin a time.

. . .

England slipped away: the troglodytes, shiny red in the glow from the furnace-mouths, urged on by the stoker petty officers and leading hands, gave steam for ten knots. The Lizard was passed and left away to starboard early in the middle watch; only then did Captain Bassinghorn and his navigating officer leave the bridge in the charge of the officer of the watch. The *Prince Consort,* starting to wallow a little as she came out of the lee of England's toe, steamed on along her set course for Finisterre and the passage of Biscay. Spray came up from the thrust of her great ram, flew back in spindrift over the fo'c'sle head to dapple the cables clenched down hard by the compressors, over the center-line capstan and on towards the twin gun turrets pointing their great shards to either bow. Halfhyde, on deck again at six bells in the morning watch, breathed deeply the good, clean air free from the taint of the land, and exultantly faced a rising wind from the south-west quadrant. Again he paced the decks, bracing his steps against the pitch that at one moment threatened to send him headlong down hill and the next brought him almost to a halt as the hill formed in front of him the other way, as though Sutton Bank on the fringe of the North Yorkshire moors were performing some weird dance. In due time the battleship came alive: a bugler of the Royal Marine Light Infantry, accompanied by boatswain's mates and ship's police, made the rounds of the mess decks and flats, rousing out the hands to show a leg from the hammocks.

Halfhyde heard the distant, muted shouts as they floated up the hatchways: "Rise an' shine, rise an' shine, the sun's a-burning your eyes out! Show a leg, show a leg there . . . lash up an' stow, lash up an' stow . . ." The voices became more raucous, more demanding as they met sleepy-eyed resistance. In his mind's eye Halfhyde saw the stonachies come out, and the rattan canes of the ship's police, modern replacements for the ropes'-ends used by the boatswains and masters-at-arms of old to hasten obedience from slow-moving seamen. Soon more bugles blew, and the hands fell in amidships, daymen of the divisions, dressed in a motley assortment of white duck uniforms and night clothing, mustering for early work under the chief boatswain's mate. Not yet having breakfasted, they were not in the rig of the day. Halfhyde watched as the various working parties were detailed by the chief boatswain's mate, then fallen out and doubled away by the leading hands. The decks drummed to the vibrations of barefoot men and echoed to many orders.

Halfhyde went below to breakfast in the ward-room. The meal never changed from ship to ship—porridge, fried eggs and bacon or kedgeree or kipper, toast and marmalade, coffee. It was like a homecoming. As in his father's house in distant Wensleydale, breakfast aboard one of the Queen's ships was a time for silence. In Devonport the day before, the newspapers had come aboard, and now they formed blatant screens of taciturnity for officers who had already perused them from cover to cover. The commander was in isolation behind *The Times;* the fleet surgeon and some off-watch lieutenants were similarly protected by *The Morning Post;* the fleet paymaster and the senior engineer displayed their lesser social status by munching behind the privacy of *The Daily Mail.* Only the chaplain was newspaperless, heavy bluish jaws moving solemnly above the clerical collar while a steward hovered with milk and coffee jugs poised.

Halfhyde sat down, said cheerfully, "Good morning, padre."
"Good morning, good morning. I don't believe we've met?"
Halfhyde identified himself.
"A curious name—Halfhyde."
"I'm sorry."
Pale blue eyes stared. "What was that, my dear fellow?"
"I said, I'm sorry. Oh—never mind, padre, never mind. It was the will of God that decided I should be Halfhyde." He turned to the waiting steward and gave his order. The chaplain, he noticed, was looking flummoxed; at the head of the table Commander Percy got to his feet with a jerk, threw down his napkin, glared at the chaplain and Halfhyde, and stalked out of the ward-room.

In the warrant officers' mess Mr Todhunter was faced with a similar meal but with a more restricted choice: kedgeree was for the gentlemen only. This was unimportant. Mr Todhunter had closed his eyes and appeared to be praying, a fact that was not lost upon Samuel Strawbridge, boatswain and president of the mess, who buttonholed the steward.

"The policeman," he said in a hoarse whisper. "Get 'im out for Gawd's perishin' sake!"

"Yessir." Discreetly, the steward bent his head. "How, sir?"

"Don't you ask me how!" the boatswain answered crushingly. "Just do as I say before he throws up on the table."

Rolling his eyes to heaven, the steward advanced upon Mr Todhunter. Bending again, he gave a gentle cough. "Sir, if you'd care to take my arm . . ."

The Dectective Inspector made an indistinct sound but gave no sign of motion. The steward glanced at the boatswain. Sam

Strawbridge was generously built and much beer and gin over the years had added extra girth: he looked formidable, for the size of his face matched that of his body. His mouth opened, but the steward was saved by a tap on the door of the mess, which stood open, and the entry of Mr Midshipman Runcorn, cap under his arm.

"Good morning, Mr Strawbridge. May I come in, please, and speak to Mr Todhunter?"

"You're welcome, Mr Runcorn, sir, very welcome."

"Thank you." Runcorn approached the detective inspector. "The captain's compliments, sir, and he wishes to see you at once in his sea cabin."

Todhunter looked up, his face haunted. "Tell him I'm sorry. I can't."

"Can't, Mr Todhunter?" Sam Strawbridge was on his feet, looming ponderous and horror-struck. "No one says 'can't' to the captain, not in my hearing, Mr Todhunter. You 'eard what the young gentleman said—the captain wants you! The captain's wish is 'is command. You are *ordered* to attend. Steward, Mr Todhunter's left arm. Mr Runcorn, if you'd be so good, sir?"

Runcorn grinned his understanding, and went to the right side of Mr Todhunter. The detective inspector, hoisted like a sea-boat on the falls, was propelled willy-nilly to the door. Once in the fresh air of the upper-deck, he was led hastily to the ship's side.

Mr Todhunter made his points more slowly than he would have done in a London magistrate's court or at the Old Bailey: there were long pauses while he fought his inner battle. At one stage he begged a lump of sugar, for which Bassinghorn's servant was despatched speedily. When the lump came, Mr Todhunter brought out his bottle of Doctor Datchet's Demulcent Drops, and shook it. The sugar lump went slightly pink and was consumed. Captain Bassinghorn stared in some astonishment. "They're effective, Mr Todhunter?" he asked.

"So I am informed, sir."

"I shall recommend them to my fleet surgeon," Bassinghorn said gravely. "Now, Mr Todhunter, if you're well enough to proceed. Yes, Mr Halfhyde?"

Halfhyde said, "It may be of help, sir, if we were told more about Sir Russell Savory himself—Savory the man. As an instance—is he known to be acquainted with Africa? If not, he's facing a hard task! Can you tell us anything of that nature, Mr Todhunter?"

"Oh, I can indeed. I've made a study of him, as was my duty. I can tell you that his history shows no indication of African knowledge, indeed I can be positive that he's never set foot upon the Dark Continent." Todhunter shuddered a little and cleared his throat. Halfhyde drew involuntarily away from him: the sea cabin, situated abaft the navigating bridge and alongside the chartroom, was small; Halfhyde felt dangerously exposed to Mr Todhunter should the latter be overcome. Outside, the freshening wind buffeted the bulkheads and blew strongly through the open port. Beyond the guardrails of the bridge wing the sea was dappled with foam beneath a bright sun. It was a splendid morning. Todhunter proceeded with his exposition. "Savory is a single man with no close family. He is dedicated—to his work, if not to Great Britain. He is a man of ambition, much desirous of prestige, and frustrated, it appears, by having fallen foul of Her Majesty. He is not a man of means, but he is a man of expensive tastes. He has remarked to his colleagues on more than one occasion that he suffered the difficulties, in a financial sense, of having champagne tastes but only a gin income. He—"

"He drinks?" Bassinghorn interrupted.

"Upon festive occasions only, sir. He is not addicted—I intended a figure of speech only—"

"Yes, yes, I understand. Which comes first to him, the money or the prestige?"

Todhunter seemed in no doubt: his answer was prompt. "The prestige, Captain, for he has set his financial demand so high that he cannot expect it to be paid. Yes, prestige comes first—"

"But to turn traitor! That brings no prestige, Mr Todhunter!"

"No, indeed not, sir, indeed not. Not in Britain, nor even perhaps in Germany, for traitors are not held in esteem even by those they benefit. But my studies lead me to suppose—to believe—that he is acting in a perverse sense. Denied the ultimate plum, he is taking his revenge—denied the highest prestige, he is hoping to acquire a prestige of a different sort: notoriety, intense interest in his activities from Her Majesty downwards. Also, he is said to be much aware of his intellect and capabilities, of his immense personal value. He is now drawing attention to this." Todhunter paused. "The psychology of the criminal mind, sir—"

"Psychology!" Bassinghorn said with a snort of derision. "Thank you, Mr Todhunter, but I prefer facts!"

"As you wish, sir. Then perhaps we should consider the suspect's destination—"

"You refer to him as the suspect?" Bassinghorn sounded irritable. "Is it not certain that he is in fact guilty, Mr Todhunter?"

"No one is guilty under English law, sir, until he is proven guilty."

"Quite. But he is known to be about to sell purloined secrets, is he not?"

"Indeed he is, sir. That's beyond dispute."

"But he's not guilty?"

"No, sir."

Bassinghorn met Halfhyde's eye, then looked back at the policeman. "Sailors are simple people, Mr Todhunter, unaccustomed to police affairs. Nevertheless, to call Sir Russell Savory the *suspect* sounds a note of woolly thinking in my view. However, we shall not argue the point. Now—you were about to comment upon his destination, were you not?"

"I was. I have views upon it, sir, that do not check with those of high officials in Whitehall. I believe that the . . . that Savory is not in fact proceeding towards German East Africa at all!" Todhunter scanned the faces of his audience, seeking a reaction. "I believe he is using a subterfuge. Because German South-West Africa is a more obvious choice of destination, he is putting it about that he is making for German East Africa."

"Putting it about?" Halfhyde lifted an eyebrow. "Does not this suggest accomplices?"

Todhunter nodded. "Indeed it does, and I might add that he couldn't do what he's doing without assistance. Yes, there are undoubtedly persons blazing a false trail."

"But where is he *actually*," Bassinghorn asked, "where is he at this moment?"

"That, sir," Todhunter replied smugly, "is what we have to find out."

Bassinghorn shifted impatiently in his chair. "I'm aware of that, Mr Todhunter, even though I'm unaccustomed to police work and have an intense dislike of seeing my ship used in this way. What I wish to have is your assessment. If you like, your guess."

"I think the matter is very open, Captain." Todhunter shrugged. "The man could be anywhere! Upon the African continent—any part of it—or even still upon the sea for that matter, not really having landed as he would have us believe."

"Waiting to enter a port in German South-West Africa—yet in the meantime, the official pursuit is being directed north and east?"

Bassinghorn stared out through the port, frowning, drumming his fingers on the arms of his chair. "Mr Halfhyde, have you any thoughts to offer?"

"None of much worth at this moment, sir. But if I may ask a question?—"

"Of course."

"Then will you tell me what your precise orders are, sir?"

"I presume you mean my own orders from the Admiralty." The captain paused, glancing at the detective inspector. "Very well, you shall know them, as indeed Mr Todhunter already does. I am ordered in the first instance to enter Gibraltar to coal ship to capacity. This is common knowledge to the ship's company. From that point onward, common knowledge ends. Word has been allowed to spread that the ship is to proceed through the Strait to Malta and join the Mediterranean Fleet in the Grand Harbour."

"Allowed to spread, sir—by order of the Home Office, I take it?"

Bassinghorn nodded. "Via the Admiralty, yes."

"If I may put a point, sir," Todhunter said deferentially. Bassinghorn nodded, and the detective inspector addressed Halfhyde. "This impinges upon the reason why I am being sent to Africa. It is not desired that Sir Russell Savory's defection be known—for one thing, the public would be most scandalized, though I confess I feel that it is bound to come out in the end— a personal view, is that. Secondly, and more important, Mr Halfhyde, the fact that a London police officer is entering their territory to make a simple arrest for fraud is more acceptable to our friends the Portuguese than if the military were to be employed on a large scale to apprehend a man whom some might see as a political refugee."

"Political refugee, fiddlesticks!" Halfhyde said with a harsh laugh. "However—your orders, sir," he added, turning to the captain. "What are they in reality, after Gibraltar?"

"In reality I am under orders for Simon's Town—so much you know."

"Yes, sir. But my query had another point. Are you ordered, if necessary, to use your guns *en route?* Is this in fact why a heavy gun ship such as ours was chosen?"

Bassinghorn pulled at his beard. "My interpretation of my orders runs along those lines, Mr Halfhyde. Such, in my view, is the real nub of my orders, though it is quite certain the Admiralty would not welcome the actual use of the guns. But a threat—that would be acceptable, I fancy—"

"You fancy, sir?"

"Mr Halfhyde, we've faced this kind of situation before, you and I! It's what has *not* been said in my orders that is important.

Omissions are frequently of more consequence . . . and upon this occasion the omission appears to connect with what Mr Todhunter has just said—that Savory may yet be at sea."

"You mean, sir—"

"I mean that we must expect trouble once we pass 15° south latitude, and drop down towards German South-West Africa." Bassinghorn glanced at Todhunter. "I think Mr Todhunter is not wholly alone in regarding German South-West Africa as a likely destination."

"A needle in a haystack, sir. If Savory is still at sea—"

"We shall be most unlikely to fall in with him—I agree. But that was not my point. If a number of German warships should be in the vicinity it may prove a different story. I have spoken already of possible action, of the use of my main armament." Bassinghorn's face was grave: trouble and anxiety showed, and an unusual uncertainty. "The ways of the Board of Admiralty are difficult to understand. Often, orders are imprecise." Halfhyde was aware that, had Todhunter not been present, Bassinghorn would have used the word "devious." "I must bear it in mind constantly that the empire is at peace with Germany and that a war against Her Majesty's grandson must not be lightly provoked—"

"Provoked, sir? Is not the man Savory the provoker, if it should come to that?"

Bassinghorn gave a short, rueful laugh. "Of course, and he must be apprehended before he does damage. But post captains in Her Majesty's Fleet, my dear Halfhyde, are uniquely placed for the apportionment of blame when matters go too far . . . and the government wishes to have clean hands!" Abruptly, he stood up, a heavy, towering figure whose grey hair almost touched the deckhead above. "That is all for now, gentlemen. It is possible that further information will be available to us from the rear-admiral when we reach Gibraltar."

The *Prince Consort,* leaving Finisterre on the port beam, entered the Bay of Biscay and a world of heaving water enclosed by mist that made the horizon close yet indeterminate. The air felt heavy; the wind had fallen away but the sea lifted to a long swell left behind by an earlier gale blowing up from the South Atlantic. The battleship, slow and solid, clove her forefoot through the heave of the sea, sending tons of water cascading back along her fo'c'sle, washing over cables and capstan to surge amidships and spurt from the wash-ports. She resembled a wallowing, seaborne water-cart like those that kept down the dust and grime of Britain's towns with cocks and hoses busy behind the patient horse. Every now and again an extra heavy swell slid below the flat bottom-plating and lifted the great ship's 11,000 tons as easily as a dinghy, so that she appeared to slide bodily down a hillside. It was a stomach-sinking sensation and the detective inspector had long since vanished from sight. After clinging, a forlorn wreck, to the guardrails of the after deck and committing the previous night's dinner to the deep, he had lurched and staggered down to his allotted cabin in the warrant officers' flat, his bowler hat waterlogged, and cast himself upon the bunk, moaning and praying for merciful death. Sam Strawbridge, who earlier had personally advised that seasickness was best pandered to on the leeward, rather than the windward, side of a ship even in the slightest breeze, went at length to Mr Todhunter's cabin to commiserate.

"It'll not last, Mr Todhunter. You'll get your sea-legs, and the quicker the better, as no doubt you'll agree. When I went first to sea, I got it over very quick indeed." He sucked his teeth loudly. "I went to sea the real way, the hard way—in sail. A ship of the line, a three-decker mounting one hundred guns. Are you listening, Mr Todhunter?"

"Please go away . . ."

"In a moment. I was lying sick as a dog in the scuppers, down channel out of Pompey." Once more Sam Strawbridge sucked at his tooth, a wickedly gleeful sound. "Along comes the chief buffer . . . chief boatswain's mate . . . with a piece of fat pork in 'is hand, on a length o' spunyarn. He pulls open my jaws and thrusts down the fat pork on the spunyarn, then pulls it back up . . . Bless my soul, Mr Todhunter, now what's the matter?"

Post captains, as Bassinghorn had said, were vulnerable. Men of immense power within their commands, it was that very power that gave them their vulnerability. Much responsibility went hand-in-hand with the control of heavy guns and many men, and much could, when it suited the Board of Admiralty, be thrown back in their faces. Staring out from the navigating bridge, Halfhyde's thoughts were bitter: he as well as Bassinghorn knew the ways of Admiralty. Their last mission together, though it had ended successfully, had been carried out on a tightrope held at the one end by the Russian Admiral Prince Gorsinski, and at the other by the Board of Admiralty. Ships and men were dispensable, the Lords of the Admiralty were not, at any rate in their own estimation, and they held the ultimate power. Hence, more often than otherwise, Admiralty orders were oblique and capable of more than one interpretation. The loophole was always there, and every officer commanding a ship at sea knew it well and it behove him to remember the fact at peril of his appointment. *Uneasy lies the head . . .* Halfhyde's thoughts took a different tone as the gold oak leaves edging Commander Percy's cap mounted the after bridge ladder.

"Mr Halfhyde?" The voice was sharp. "You're aware, I take it, that unless you have duties upon the bridge, you're liable to be in the way?"

"I am a competent officer, sir, and scarcely likely to be in anybody's way."

"An argumentative officer, I think." The commander stared at Halfhyde, cold eyes raking him from head to foot. "Like many other senior officers of your reputed acquaintance I prefer not to be answered back."

"You prefer, sir, to be allowed your rudeness without retort?"

Commander Percy gave a visible start, and glared harder: there was murder in the cold eyes. "Mr Halfhyde, you are asking to be placed in arrest. For your own good, I advise you to leave the bridge at once. I—" He broke off suddenly, sharply, clutching for support at a stanchion, feet sliding on the deck. Halfhyde also grabbed for a stanchion, missed, slid and ended up in a staggering rush against the starboard guardrail with the yeoman of the watch in his arms. An enormous swell, a mountain of water that had reared up on the ship's broadside, had passed beneath her, lifting her as it seemed to the skies so that she was held poised on a summit of the sea, with deep valleys of grey-green water on either side. There was a sharp shout from the commander: *"Take her down, Mr Portaby, before she breaks her back!"*

Lieutenant Portaby, officer of the watch, was as white as a

sheet. It was Halfhyde who answered: "There's nothing Mr Portaby can do now, sir. It's in the hands of God. We can only wait."

In a silence broken only by the eerie sigh of a light breeze in the rigging and the slap of water on the battleship's plates, they waited: the wait seemed endless as they hung poised as if for a dive down a ski-slope. Urgent heavy footfalls on the ladder heralded Bassinghorn, his face working. With appalling slowness the mountain began to flatten out, and they sank down into the valley, closed in by further swells. Then, just as Bassinghorn wiped the sweat from his forehead in relief, there was a curious and alarming noise from aft, a sound of tearing metal followed by great clangs as though a drum had been beaten by a gigantic drumstick, and then a tremor ran through the ship. A moment later her stern appeared to lift a little, and her head to go down into the swell correspondingly.

Bassinghorn ran for the standard compass in its binnacle. "Mr Portaby, she's paying off to loo'ard! Bring her round, man, bring her round!"

Portaby was bent to the voice-pipe from the wheelhouse, his ear flattened to the brass mouth in close concentration. He straightened. "Sir, the steering's gone and she won't answer the helm. I believe we've lost the rudder!"

Chapter 4

THE COMMANDER led the way aft, going fast down the ladders, sliding on his palms along the rails, no sluggard in an emergency. Halfhyde was behind him: his virtually passenger status could scarcely hold in such a crisis. Although there were no storm-lashed waves to drop their tons of water aboard and send the *Prince Consort* to the bottom, considerable damage could yet be done. The lives of all men on the upper-deck were in jeopardy as the great battleship lifted and slid cork-like down into the tremendous valleys of water, broadside now to the sea's send.

They reached the stern, held fast to the guardrail, and peered downwards, eyes searching as the ship's counter rose and fell again. At one moment the water of the bay boiled up in foam that spilled over on to the captain's stern-walk, washing deep against the battened-down entry port to the cuddy. The next moment it dropped away, and the black-painted plates rose, showing the boot-topping, almost showing the twin screws that until lately had been churning below at the ends of the port and starboard main shafts, but were now stopped on the captain's order.

Halfhyde, taller than Commander Percy, leaned far out from the ship's side, legs braced hard against the guardrail. He called back, "I believe Mr Portaby was right, sir: I see no rudder."

"Tell me what you do see, Mr Halfhyde."

"I repeat, sir, I see no rudder. The blade's gone and I suspect the stock has sheared from the gudgeons."

Commander Percy's face was white. "Impossible!" he said.
"There was work done on the rudder only recently, by the dockyard—"

"What work? You've had trouble before?"

"There was some damage from a heavy sea while returning
from Bermuda. That was made good at Devonport."

"Made good, I think, is scarcely the word, sir. You say it is
impossible for the stock to shear. In theory perhaps it is. Yet it
has happened, I assure you." Halfhyde pulled his body back
inboard of the guardrail, saw a thick-set warrant officer coming aft at the double with a party of seamen wearing oilskins.
"Who's this, sir?"

"The boatswain—Mr Strawbridge—"

Halfhyde nodded at the boatswain. "Well met in a tight spot,
Mr Strawbridge. We have trouble on our hands!"

Sam Strawbridge steadied himself against a stanchion. "The
rudder, sir?"

"Yes, the rudder as was—it's gone. I fancy the locking pintle
has sheared, and the stock has jumped out of the gudgeons and
has cracked away below the tiller flat. I suggest—"

"Mr Halfhyde, if you please, you will suggest nothing at this
stage." Commander Percy, interrupting, looked frigid. "I shall
report to the captain. Mr Strawbridge, kindly come to the bridge
with me. Mr Halfhyde, you will—"

"I shall come as well, sir."

Percy glared. "You will not, sir. You will do as you are told—"

"With great respect, sir, the ship is in some danger and I
have met, and dealt with, similar trouble before. Also, I am eye

witness to the damage, which you are not. Therefore I shall make my own report to the captain." Halfhyde, his eyes glittering, gave a small, formal bow and with one hand indicated the bridge. "After you, sir."

The commander's mouth opened, then shut again in a thin, angry line. Without further words, he swung about and made for the bridge ladder, body angled against the rise and fall of the deck. Halfhyde and the boatswain followed, the party of seamen remaining by the after guardrail in obedience to a word from Mr Strawbridge. At the head of the ladder stood Captain Bassinghorn, the big figure braced with vast hands on the head of the rails, face staring down anxiously.

"Well, Commander?"

"We've lost steerage, sir. The rudder's sheared away—according to Mr Halfhyde."

"And according to you, Commander?"

"I did not myself see the damage, sir."

"And Mr Halfhyde did? If it's the rudder, then Devonport dockyard will feel a weight of Admiralty censure. Mr Halfhyde, your estimate quickly, if you please."

Halfhyde explained. "The bangs we heard and felt earlier, sir, were due to the rudder plate swinging from side to side after parting the locking pintle. The swinging would have caused the stock to fracture and break away at the head." He paused. "I take it we have a spare rudder? If not, a jury—"

"There's the problem of the time factor, Mr Halfhyde." Bassinghorn's face was pinched with anxiety: delay could well be fatal, and much displeasure would be duly passed down from Their Lordships in their comfortable Whitehall offices. "It's possible to steer by engines as far as Gibraltar, and then make use of the dockyard's repair facilities. Commander, your views, if you please?"

"In full agreement with your own, sir. I think we should make Gibraltar."

Bassinghorn breathed hard down his nose. "I have not said those are my views. Mr Strawbridge?"

Sam Strawbridge shook his head dubiously. "I'd not be happy to make the rest o' the passage o' the bay without proper steering, sir. It can be tricky to enter Gibraltar too, sir, if we get a blow in the Strait on to a lee shore. We may need full power ahead or astern on both engines at once, sir, and then what becomes of the steering, sir?"

Bassinghorn nodded and looked out across the heaving swell, feeling the sick lurch of the battleship beneath his feet, a helpless and unnerving feeling. "Then you suggest rigging the spare rudder, Mr Strawbridge?"

"I do, sir, yes."

"Mr Halfhyde?"

"So do I, sir. We know it can be done—not easily, not safely, but it can be done. And there is another point: dockyard mateys, and especially Spanish ones, are not fast workers. The delay will be less if we use our own ship's company, sir. I believe the job can be finished within 24 hours."

"Twenty-four hours, Mr Halfhyde? I doubt if we can spare that much."

Halfhyde shrugged. "There is a degree of inevitability, sir. I shall do my best to shorten the time . . . that is, if I may take charge myself?"

Bassinghorn lifted an eyebrow at Percy. "Commander?"

"As Executive Officer, sir, *I* shall naturally take charge. By all means Mr Halfhyde may assist, as I understand he has lost rudders before."

The commander's eye was bleak as it rested upon Halfhyde, and his face was stiff, arrogant, sneering. Bassinghorn gave an involuntary sigh, but having no alternative nodded his acquiescence. "Very well, Commander, you will make preparations to rig the spare rudder as soon as may be. I wish you to take all possible precautions for the safety of the hands throughout. No unnecessary risks are to be taken, do you understand?"

"I understand, sir—"

"I shall use my engines from time to time, if not for giving the ship headway, then for keeping her head in the proper direction of the compass. When you have men working below the counter, I shall warn you by megaphone before passing orders to the starting platform. I shall be upon the bridge until the operation is complete."

"Yes, sir."

"You must have the stern lifted to make the work easier and safer, Commander, but not so far as to render the screws useless. I suggest you shift enough weight of stores, ammunition, and other movables from aft to for'ard, and as many men to go for'ard as can be spared."

"Yes, sir."

"Carry on, if you please, Commander."

"Aye, aye, sir." Commander Percy saluted smartly, beckoned to Sam Strawbridge, and went with the boatswain down the ladder.

Bassinghorn watched him go, then turned to Halfhyde. "A word in your ear," he said, and led the way to the starboard wing out of earshot of the officer of the watch and the rest of the bridge personnel. "I'm sorry, Halfhyde," he said. "I must naturally allow the commander his proper function."

"I understand that, sir, of course."

"I've warned you already—treat Commander Percy tactfully. That is," he went on, a different note audible in his voice now, "so far as is consistent with the safety of the ship and the men and with the speedy execution of our particular orders. Do you follow me, Halfhyde?"

Halfhyde nodded, his eyes gleaming with a hint of amusement. "I think I do, sir. I may put my point of view to the commander, and should there be disagreement—"

"Precisely! I have learned to trust your seamanship and judgement. Commander Percy is an unknown quantity, and my feeling is that he is more at home upon the parade ground at Whale Island than when involved with matters of pure seamanship. I promise you my backing, but you must be tactful."

"Tact and I, sir, are not totally at loggerheads when the prize is great."

Bassinghorn smiled. "Well said, Mr Halfhyde, and I shall trust you to make it so. Carry on, if you please."

"Aye, aye, sir." Saluting, Halfhyde left the bridge and went aft. Already the boatswain's calls were shrilling throughout the ship, piping all off-watch personnel not required aft or to shift stores to remain in the fore part of the ship. The commander was conferring with the lieutenants and sub-lieutenants while the hands needed to ship the spare rudder began to fall in under the midshipmen and petty officers, and the necessary tackles and other gear were brought aft, heavy blocks bumping along the decks with rope trailing from the sheaves. Up from one of the after hatches came the blacksmith, carrying an immense hammer. Halfhyde studied the brisk, authoritative demeanour of Commander Percy: authoritative on the surface, yet Halfhyde suspected a basic lack of assurance in an unfamiliar situation. It could prove to be the case that the commander, finding himself out of his depth, would be only too pleased to leave matters in the hands of another officer . . . but time would tell, and in the meantime discretion was needed. Halfhyde approached the commander, saluted, and said, "If I may suggest it, sir, a sheer-legs rigged right aft would be—"

"That is already in hand, thank you, Mr Halfhyde."

"Of course, sir. I imagined it would be."

"Then why waste your breath?" Percy snapped.

"Because I would like to supervise the rigging of it myself, sir. I have known a sheer-legs to shift upon an unsteady deck, and I have devised a means of my own to hold it fast."

"What means, Mr Halfhyde?"

"Means, sir, that are better demonstrated than described. I shall take full responsibility for its safety."

The commander glowered, but nodded. "Oh, very well then, you may see to it yourself."

Halfhyde saluted again, and turned about, calling to Mr Runcorn. He sensed the start of victory: the commander would not be averse to having a scapegoat if anything did go wrong, while at the same time claiming all credit for eventual success. Halfhyde grinned inwardly: there was a use for tact after all.

From his swinging, lurching cabin where the curtains over door and portholes executed strange and queasy antics, standing out stiff and straight into the cabin as the vessel negotiated oceanic hills and valleys, Detective Inspector Todhunter heard the thumps and bangs from the deck above, and the sound of sea-men running barefoot. He was also aware of a curious and unexpected silence, of no engine noise except at intervals, and no resultant vibration of the ship's plates. Stopping at sea, he fancied, was unusual; it could spell danger and it certainly spelled delay. Todhunter, sick and giddy as he was, recalled the very high official of the Admiralty who had come in person to Scotland Yard to warn him, in the presence of the commis-sioner, against delay. The person, a man with the air of a duke or marquis, a man who spoke in harsh monosyllables as to one of his peasants, had not precisely indicated the extent to which Mr Todhunter's career and pension and honour depended upon success, but had dwelt much on the great necessity for speed in the pursuit of the absconded Sir Russell Savory. Mr Todhunter's sickened, reeling brain gave him no peace as time passed, and the engines continued to move only in spurts, and the thumps and bangs increased alarmingly. After a while he became aware of activity in the flat outside his cabin, and in desperation for news, he shouted out:

"I say, I say! Will somebody please come in? *I say!*"

There was no response. Manfully, Mr Todhunter sat up in his bunk, swung giddily, put a foot on the deck, and, with arms outstretched against the horrid motion, managed to climb uphill to the door and jerk the curtain aside. His green face peered out like a rat from a ball of oakum and met that of Sam Strawbridge.

The boatswain paused in his work. "Feeling better, Mr Todhunter?"

"No, I'm not . . . not at all. Can you tell me what's hap-pened, Mr Strawbridge?"

"Lost the rudder, that's what's happened."

"My God." Todhunter swayed, eyes wide. "That's dangerous, isn't it?"

"Very dangerous, but—"

"How long shall we be delayed?"

"Can't say. A day or two maybe. Now if you'll excuse me, Mr Todhunter—"

"A day or two! Oh, my God." Todhunter flapped his arms. "I wonder if the captain could spare a moment to come down? I must impress upon him how urgent it is to reach land."

"It looks it an' all," the boatswain said shortly, staring at the policeman's face. "If you want to talk to the captain, up you go to the bridge, Mr Todhunter, not that you won't be kicked right off it the moment you show yourself." He turned away, rejoining the working-party manhandling some heavy gear down to the tiller flat and the head of the rudder stock. As the seamen went past, there was a strongly pervasive stench of sweat, tarred rope, and machine oil. Its effect was magical—Mr Todhunter's face vanished like a genie from a lamp, his passage marked only by the slow and rigid swing of the door-curtain as it chased him back to bed.

The cuddy was being used by the repair party: with the sheerlegs rigged on the deck above ready to take the strain of the spare rudder when it was moved from its quarterdeck stowage, the captain's stern-walk would prove a handy platform from which to send men down for the tricky, dangerous business of securing the new rudder to the gudgeons in the battleship's stern post. The commander being safely on deck, Halfhyde was patiently detailing the method of operation.

"My examination from the quarterdeck and the stern-walk," he said, "tells me that the gudgeons are probably themselves undamaged, although the bolts will have been stripped when the rudder sheared the locking pintle and jumped off the gudgeons. This we must accept—Able Seaman Bates, if I may have your full attention?"

A stout, oilskinned seaman lifted a hand to his forehead. "Yessir. Beg pardon, sir."

"You've not been in the captain's cabin before?"

"No sir, not me, sir." An eye roved. "The carpet, sir, and the woodwork, and the brass—"

"Dwell not upon luxury, Bates, for we're in for a hard spell of work. Yes, Mr Runcorn, what is it?"

Mr Midshipman Runcorn, his voice high with anxiety, said, "Sir, if the locking pintle parted, is it not likely that the—"

"That the corresponding gudgeon is damaged, Mr Runcorn?"

"Why, yes, sir—"

"Why, no, sir, not necessarily."

"But if it is, sir—and if the threads are stripped, sir, how do we—"

"Secure the new rudder, Mr Runcorn? Lock it down?" Halfhyde smiled. "The answer is, we don't."

"Then, sir—"

"Then we pray, Mr Runcorn, but we back up our prayers with a chain lashing passed around the stock and at least one of the intact gudgeons. I think that should last as far as Gibraltar, where dockyard assistance can speedily restore the locking pintle's gudgeon and renew the threads while the rest of us are coaling ship." Halfhyde went on to describe what was out of sight below the counter and what would have to be done. When the new rudder had been brought aft and lifted out by the sheer-legs, it would be swung below the stern-walk, with two 3-fold purchases, one on either side, suspended from the after bitts and made fast to the spindle with a chain lashing below the coupling flanges. Each would be secured to ring-bolts to be riveted to the top and bottom of the rudder blade by the black-smith; this would prevent the side-to-side swing. While this was being done, another party in the tiller flat would be clear-ing the way for the rudder head by taking off and examining the crosshead and quadrant, and clearing out the stuffing box. When all this was ready, the difficult and time-consuming part of the operation would begin: the accurate manual positioning of the rudder so that its pintles would drop neatly over the gud-geons in the vessel's stern post while the detached head of the stock was slotted firm and true to the crosshead through the stuffing box, before being screwed down to the main part of the stock.

"The ship will not keep still for us," Halfhyde reminded the men meaningfully. "That is where immense patience will be needed, and that will be the dangerous part for us all. Every man working over the side will wear a lashing, to be tended from the stern-walk. Mr Runcorn?"

"Sir?"

"Remain in charge upon the stern-walk, if you please. I'm going over the side myself on a line, to take a closer look before we start."

"You're going now, sir?"

"I am, Mr Runcorn. Kindly inform the bridge. Bates, I see you have a line handy—"

"Yes, sir."

Halfhyde took the thin rope, formed a bight around his body, hove it close up beneath his armpits, and secured it with a bow line while Mr Runcorn spoke through the voice-pipe to the captain. His sou'wester tied firmly beneath his long chin, Halfhyde moved out of the cabin on to the stern-walk, followed by Bates and Runcorn. Outside, the air was damp and cold, the stern-walk wet with spray and occasional solid water that welled up through the basket-work as the stern went down. The hills and valleys were there still, immense and frightening from so low down in the ship. From overhead came the creak of wood blocks as ropes ran around the sheaves. Halfhyde glanced up and saw the stout purchase dangling from the head of the sheer-legs: when the rudder was bent on and lowered sorry damage could well be done to Bassinghorn's stern-walk, but that was of minor importance now. He got himself astride the guardrail, letting the life-line run through his fingers, and launched himself out and down, inching towards the heaving sea, his outstretched legs fending him off from the after plating. Filthy choking fumes swept aft from the funnels. With caution he let himself down and down, coming between, but still as yet above, the twin screws that were now held motionless on the order from the bridge to the engine-room. If something should go wrong and those screws should turn, his body would be minced to bloody fragments: it was a nasty thought and one that Halfhyde put firmly from his mind. A sea rose beneath, sweeping over him, submerging him for several feet until it fell away to leave him gasping like a rat in a pond. He got a handgrip on one of the gudgeons in the stern post, and pulled himself closer inwards, feeling for the bolt. He found that the thread had indeed been stripped by the shearing of the nut. Reaching lower, he took a

deep breath and pulled himself down the line of gudgeons.
Now he was working totally submerged—as yet, not enough
stores and other movables had been shifted to take effect. His
lungs bursting, he felt for the bottom gudgeon that would in
due course take the bearing pintle and the main weight of the
rudder. Like the others, it was intact but for its thread. Knowing
for certain now that success was at least possible, Halfhyde let
go his hold of the gudgeon and kicked out for the surface. He
broke thankfully into the fresh air, flinging the seawater from
his eyes, and as he did so the *Prince Consort's* great bulk lurched
to an immense shift of water that swelled in from the North
Atlantic to pass below the bottom. Halfhyde was lifted high into
the air at what seemed a tremendous speed, was conscious as
he was flung above the stern-walk of the urgent whistle from
the voice-pipe in the cuddy. Coming down again as the wave
dropped him, he felt slackness in his life-line, saw that the
inboard end had been snatched from Bates's grasp, saw the hor-
rified white faces lining the stern-walk's guardrail, and saw,
some distance off, another oilskinned figure floundering with
upflung arms. Then he was once again beneath the surging
water, blinded, bewildered, his body flung like a helpless, inan-
imate toy.

Chapter 5

HANDS GRIPPED on the guardrail till his knuckles showed white, Commander Percy stared down into the sea, then swung round on a leading seaman.

"Report to the bridge. And pipe the sea-boat's crew and lowerers of the watch—"

"No, sir." Sam Strawbridge, standing by with his face streaming sweat and seawater, shouted the negative. "No sea-boat would last in the swell that's running, nor would we be able to hook her to the falls afterwards without a proper lee. We can't risk it, sir, not for two men. I suggest a grass line, sir, and at once, without waiting for the captain."

"But look here—" The commander broke off, ashen-faced, biting his lip. Already Sam Strawbridge was on the move, fast and nimble for a bulky man. Shouting at the hands on deck, he got a heavy grass line over the side to trail down, floating in the manner of grass lines, streaming out astern towards the struggling bodies. Then, tearing off his oilskin and monkey jacket, kicking off his boots, he climbed the port rail where there was at least something of a lee, and dived clean and true towards the floating rope.

At the same moment that Mr Midshipman Runcorn's message had reached the bridge to report that Lieutenant Halfhyde was about to climb over the stern, the chief yeoman of signals, telescope to his eye, had also made a report to the captain:

"Ships astern, sir, closing, on our course."

Bassinghorn swung aft. "How many, Chief Yeoman?"

"Four smoke trails, sir, in line abreast. They're hull down as yet, sir."

Bassinghorn's telescope came up: he took a long look, then closed his glass with a snap. "Four in company—they'll not be merchant ships. I have no indication of a squadron steaming south from any of the home ports. Keep an eye on them, Chief Yeoman."

"Aye, aye, sir."

"Stand by to make our pennant numbers by flag hoist, but await my order."

"Aye, aye, sir." Orders were passed to the leading signalman and the dovetail numeral pennants were brought from their slots in the flag locker and bent ready to the halliard. Bassinghorn paced the bridge in anxious thought, sending up a prayer that the overtaking ships might not be German. Gradually the fighting-tops and funnels, the latter belching smoke for what looked like maximum speed, began to show in Bassinghorn's telescope, but not as yet closely enough for identification. Then the next report broke shatteringly into his other anxieties, a report from the quarterdeck that Mr Halfhyde and an able seaman had gone overboard aft and were floating astern of the battleship; and that Mr Strawbridge had gone in after them with a grass line.

Bassinghorn's voice was sharp. "Great God! How far astern are they?"

"Two cables' lengths, sir, and increasing."

"Very well, Mr Portaby. I shall drop astern and try to give them such lee as I can. Inform the stern-walk first, then ring down to the engine-room for half speed astern on both engines."

"Aye, aye, sir." Lieutenant Portaby hesitated. "The sea-boat, sir—"

"No. It seems Mr Strawbridge may have thought the swell too great, and if that is the case I agree with him."

"Yes, sir." Portaby bent to the voice-pipe and passed the orders down. Bassinghorn, craning out dangerously from the port wing of the bridge, looked astern. Now and again he could see a figure in the water: just one, dipping, plunging, rising again. He called to Portaby. "I may lose sight of them. I shall want continuous reports of their whereabouts."

"Aye, aye, sir."

Bassinghorn, lifting his head, sniffed at the air: he smelt wind in the offing—a good weight of wind, he believed—and this belief was confirmed by the cloud formation overhead. The general overcast was clearing, and clearing fast; and already the White Ensign was standing out more stiffly from its staff and his thin commissioning pennant was pointing like a finger to the north-east. The job must be done before the blow came . . . but now he was faced with a blow of a different kind. Hating to lose any man, he would be doubly grieved by the loss of Halfhyde, a good seaman, and a good friend. As his eyes stared aft from a troubled face, the captain's lips moved in heartfelt prayer. The appalling slide of the semi-helpless battleship down the looming walls of moving water made the rescue attempt most doubtful of success, though now Bassinghorn could see two bodies, one of them clinging to the grass line: that would be the boatswain. Tending his engines astern as the distance reports came in from the commander in person on the quarterdeck, Bassinghorn saw Strawbridge swoop down willy-nilly upon the other visible figure, by a sheer stroke of luck as it seemed making contact and grabbing with one hand for the oilskin collar, the other hand still holding fast to the grass line. A swing of the *Prince Consort's* stern brought the two figures on to the port beam until, as another huge swell passed beneath, they vanished into a valley on the farther side of the watery mountain.

Bassinghorn turned his head. "Stop engines, Mr Portaby!"

"Stop engines, sir." A moment later, as the repeater bells rang in the wheelhouse, Portaby called out, "Engines repeated stopped, sir."

Bassinghorn nodded and waited, hands gripping the rail hard. Slowly the water subsided, and the two men came into view again, closer now to the ship's side, drawn by many willing hands backing up the grass line. Two only, where there had been three: sadness was mixed with Bassinghorn's relief when Commander Percy reported that Halfhyde and Strawbridge looked like being safe. The urgent voice of the chief yeoman of signals broke into his relief.

"Captain, sir. Four ships of the German Navy. They're not making their pennant numbers yet, sir, but I recognize them all."

"And they are?"

"The flagship's the second-class battleship *Friedrich der Grösse,* sir, and in company, the *Kaiser Wilhelm, Nürnberg,* and *Königsberg,* all first-class cruisers, sir."

"And the flag—do you know that too, Chief Yeoman?" Bassinghorn demanded, his voice sounding ominous.

"No, sir, I'm sorry, sir."

"Then I shall tell you: it's the flag of Vice-Admiral Paulus von Merkatz, commanding the German Special Service Squadron. He has a reputation for fine seamanship and a taut command, in addition to a high degree of arrogance and a strong dislike of Her Majesty's Fleet." Bassinghorn turned his attention aft again. Halfhyde and Strawbridge were coming close, and the collision mat had been hung over the side in case they should be flung against the armoured belt. Hands reached down to grapple them aboard as they came up on the grass line. Commander Percy ran for the bridge to report, and Bassinghorn met him at the head of the ladder.

"Well, Commander?"

"Halfhyde and Strawbridge are safe, sir, and none the worse."

"And the third man?"

"Bates, sir, able seaman. Gone, I'm sorry to say. He had no chance. He couldn't swim."

Bassinghorn gave a sigh: one day, perhaps, an enlightened naval administration would make it obligatory for swimming to be learned by all those who went down to the sea in ships. To date many of the older seamen, and some of the younger ones also, resolutely refused to learn to swim in case they should thus take longer to drown. In the meantime, Bassinghorn's reflections upon his mission and upon Detective Inspector Todhunter were bitter. So early in the manhunt, one man had died, and Bassinghorn grieved for a seaman left behind to make his surging way down to the deeps where the pressure of the sea would in due time flatten his body to the thickness of a sheet of paper.

·   ·   ·

"It was no one's fault, Mr Halfhyde, least of all your own. An act of God."

"Or of Todhunter."

Bassinghorn, standing on the bridge in an increasing wind, shook his head. "No, Halfhyde, no. I understand such thoughts, but we must not blame Todhunter, who is doing no more than his duty, as we are ourselves."

"I see him as a Jonah, sir."

"Then do your best not to!"

"He's brought bad luck, sir. A rudder, a seaman. Who or what's to be next?" Halfhyde gave a short, dry laugh. "It's against the nature of sailors to be manhunters, sir!"

"They must nevertheless obey orders." Bassinghorn's tone was crisp, putting an end to argument. "The new rudder, Mr Halfhyde. Can it be done?"

"It can be done, sir—"

"Then as quickly as possible, if you please. There's wind in the offing, more than we have at present."

"And Germans in the offing, too!"

"Precisely. As to that, I must speak to Todhunter. Carry on, if you please, Mr Halfhyde. How do you estimate the delay now?"

"I can't be exact, sir. It's a straightforward enough job, but it's a question of balance—that, and a heaving stern post. We may ship the stock on to the gudgeons at the first go, or we may take all night and more." Halfhyde added somberly, "And we may lose more men into the bargain, sir."

"I'm aware of that." Bassinghorn gave a dismissive nod and turned away. As he turned, he was met by the chief yeoman. Away beyond the chief yeoman he saw the four German ships coming up hard on the starboard quarter, their decks awash and heaving, with water pouring from the hawse-pipes. The German naval ensigns stood stiff but overshadowed by their admiral's flag on the left of the line, as the *Prince Consort's* bugler sounded a salute. "Has the admiral made his pennants, Chief Yeoman?"

"No, sir."

Bassinghorn's mouth closed with a snap, his jaw jutting. "Then, until he does, we do not make ours. I shall not tolerate insults to Her Majesty."

The German squadron steamed on, proud, arrogant, heavily gunned, remaining totally silent as to flag hoists or any polite exchange of signals or salutes. The *Prince Consort* wallowed on behind, again under power and steerage of her engines until such time as Halfhyde from aft requested them to be stopped once more. Furious and apprehensive, Bassinghorn watched the German ships grow smaller ahead, clearly on passage south unless in due course they turned into the Mediterranean off Cape St Vincent, if only to request bunkers at Gibraltar before resuming a southerly track. The flag of Admiral Paulus von Merkatz whipped in the wind like a cocked snook to add point to his insulting manners.

"Mr Portaby, it is half an hour since I sent for Mr Todhunter."

"Yes, sir. I'm sorry, sir."

"It's not your fault, Mr Portaby. But I think a charge of dynamite applied to his backside—" Bassinghorn broke off, staring aft. "In God's name, Mr Portaby, what's this coming along the deck?"

Portaby followed the captain's amazed stare, and his jaw dropped. A procession, such as had perhaps never before been seen upon the deck of any of the Queen's ships of war, was advancing upon the foot of the bridge ladder. It consisted of two seamen bearing a filled hammock, one at the head, the other at the foot. Beside this hammock, which contained Detective Inspector Todhunter, strode the battleship's gunner, Mr Mainprice. Bassinghorn, hands behind his back, called down. "Mr Mainprice, may I believe my eyes? What's all this, for God's sake?"

The gunner halted the hammock party and saluted. "Sir, if Mr Todhunter stands up, 'e spews vomit, sir. I therefore hit upon a stratagem. I had him brought, sir, on the flat of 'is back. That way, sir, 'e *don't* spew. Right, Mr Todhunter?"

A protest floated up to the bridge: "Quite right, Mr Mainprice, but if I'm carried up that ladder I shall fall out on the way—"

"Oh, no, you bloody won't!" came the angry hiss from the gunner. "Not with men at your head and feet like a burial party you won't. Now then—"

"Can't the captain come down here?"

The gunner raised his voice. "No 'e can't, Mr Todhunter. The captain sent for you to come to the bridge, and to the bridge you goes." Mr Mainprice turned to the bearer party. "Now then! One, two, three . . . *hup* she goes!"

Once more Bassinghorn called down. "Mr Mainprice."

"Sir?"

"I shall come down. I fear the progress might prove a difficult one that could send more bile to Mr Todhunter's throat."

"'E can go up head first, sir, if—"

"No, no. The ship can do without me on the bridge for a few minutes." Bassinghorn went down the ladder, big feet clumping heavily on the treads. He stared down at the hapless figure wrapped in blanket and canvas, then turned to the gunner. "Thank you, Mr Mainprice. I congratulate you on your—er—

stratagem. Carry on now, if you please—and your bearers too."

"Aye, aye, sir." The gunner saluted and fell his party out. Todhunter's hammock was secured by its lashings to the rail of the bridge ladder at one end and to the shank of the sea-boat's forward davit at the other, so that the policeman lay slightly askew across the fore-and-aft line, feet foremost. The captain, as the bearer party shifted out of sight and earshot, moved towards Todhunter's head, and bent.

"I hope you're comfortable, Mr Todhunter."

"Not very, Captain. I am being jerked about."

"Yes. However, I shall not keep you long." Bassinghorn lowered his voice. "We have been overhauled by four ships of the German fleet, steaming to the south. I would appreciate your views, bearing in mind your mission."

Todhunter stared back at the captain. "This is bad news, sir. Or could be. At this of all times . . . on the other hand, I suppose, their purpose could be purely—er—"

"Manoeuvres, exercises. That's possible, Mr Todhunter, and such would be entirely their concern in normal circumstances— that is to say, and I would not be told in advance. On the other hand, in the particular circumstances, I would have expected the Admiralty to have warned me of the movement of German ships."

"If the Admiralty itself had known, sir."

Bassinghorn nodded. "Of course, but peaceful exercises are not usually kept secret, and I am confident they would have known—had there not been some nefarious intent. When we reach Gibraltar, I shall seek clarification from the flag officer. In the meantime, what interpretation do you put, as a police officer, upon the presence of German ships that are now most likely to reach an African port before ourselves?"

Sweat shone on Todhunter's forehead. "I trust they will not, sir! You must steam faster than they!"

"That is my concern," Bassinghorn said abruptly. "Your interpretation, if you please."

A white-fingered hand came out from the enshrouding blanket to wag in Bassinghorn's face. Todhunter's expression was anxious, the look of sickness becoming overlaid by the dedicated look of the detective in charge of the case. "German South-West Africa is what I see, sir. The ships will go there, and pick our man up, before—"

"My own views tend that way also, Mr Todhunter. Of course, the squadron could turn into the Mediterranean and approach German East Africa by way of the Suez Canal, and still have an excellent chance of making their arrival before ourselves. But I believe they will not. German South-West Africa offers less delay—and delay is as inimical to them as it is to us!"

"Very inimical to us indeed, sir. I think neither of us can afford to lose Sir Russell Savory. But I feel *I* can scarcely be blamed if I am not placed in a position to execute my warrant of arrest in time." The deck tilted suddenly to starboard, and Mr Todhunter's hammock twisted violently on its half-athwartships line. His face went very white. "I beg to be excused, Captain. I am being most dreadfully jerked about."

Bassinghorn, his face formidable with suppressed anger, called for the gunner and ordered Todhunter to be taken below again. Turning on his heel, he climbed back to the bridge, and from there watched the procession making its difficult way aft.

Striding the bridge, his thoughts were unhappy ones: the policeman's words were disturbing, the more so because they happened to be true. The responsibility, at least until Todhunter was landed ashore, was his, Bassinghorn's, alone. His was the motive power, his was the head upon the block of failure. And one thing was a dead certainty: unless a speedy restoration of her steering was effected, the *Prince Consort* had not a hope in hell of reaching Africa before von Merkatz.

"How long will you be now, Mr Halfhyde?"

Halfhyde shrugged, then looked around at the darkening sky and sea. The swell of Biscay was with them still; though a shade less heavy. But the wind had increased and was still increasing. The tops of the swell were being blown in spindrift and waves were forming to disperse the flat oiliness of the shifting water-mountains. The whole area of sea was covered with a carpet of foam and spray. Answering the captain's question Halfhyde said, "It's in the hands of God, sir. And, of course, of the commander."

Bassinghorn's eyes narrowed. "Why do you specify the commander, Mr Halfhyde?"

"A timid man, sir, when it comes to handling heavy gear that can take charge in a twinkling and crush men as flat as pancakes on Shrove Tuesday." Halfhyde paused. "How far, sir, do you wish to risk the ship's company?"

Bassinghorn faced the leading question squarely. "I wish no risk to them of any kind, Mr Halfhyde, as well you know. But the risk to the country is so great as to override all other considerations now. What do you propose?"

Halfhyde smiled, a grim twist of his wide mouth. "There is

a proverb, sir, regarding the stinging power of the common net-tle: 'Grasp it like a man of mettle, it will hurt you not at all.'"
He appeared to go off at a tangent. "The commander, sir, is in a bath of sweat, as bad as any pig I ever saw on my father's farm. Perhaps the fleet surgeon should look at him and take his temperature?" He lifted an eyebrow, grinning.

Bassinghorn met his sardonic eye. "Doctors do not succumb to subterfuges, Mr Halfhyde!"

"Indeed not, sir, indeed not. Or at any rate, they do not tell lies. Except, that is, by proxy?"

"What the devil d'you mean?" Bassinghorn snapped.

"A hot-water jug, sir, has a very positive effect upon a ther-mometer."

Bassinghorn exploded in a sudden laugh. "By God, Mr Halfhyde, you have criminal instincts to a high degree! But I confess I would rather bring the commander to bed than the German Fleet to action upon their return voyage with Savory, with all that would be at stake the moment my guns opened! My compliments, if you please, to the fleet surgeon. I would appreciate his presence in my sea cabin."

With Commander Percy, still protesting that he felt in perfect health, lying in his bunk under doctor's orders backed by those of the captain, Halfhyde took full charge aft. For some hours now the spare rudder, hoisted out on the sheer-legs and stead-ied on either side by the three-fold purchases, had been hang-ing below the counter, thickly wrapped in hammock mattresses sacrificed by the ship's company in the interests of preventing damage to the stern post and gudgeons. Abortive attempts had been made from the quarterdeck, by manipulation of sheer-legs and purchases, to drop the pintles over the gudgeons. The commander would send no men down until this, at least, had been done. After that, men would be needed to pass the temporary chain lashings and to clamp down the nuts and bolts that would secure the head of the stock to the main part. In Halfhyde's view, the rudder would never be shipped until there were men in place below, clinging, however dangerously, to life lines passed from the stern-walk and around their bodies from the bitts on either side. In a position now to give the order, he did so. His misgivings were many, but his duty was clear.

"Mr Strawbridge," he said, "I want six good seamen over the side from the stern-walk. I shall accompany them myself."

"Aye aye, sir. I'll be coming with you, Mr Halfhyde."

"You will not. You've done your part—you saved my life today. For more than that, my good Mr Strawbridge, you're too old and fat." Smiling, he put a hand on the boatswain's shoulder. "Besides, I want you to save my life again, and that of the men, by remaining in charge upon the upper-deck—you're worth all the lieutenants put together!"

The boatswain, his face showing a curious mixture of anger, disappointment, and pleasure in a compliment that had sounded more than flattery, gave the necessary orders. As soon as the life-lines had been rigged, Halfhyde swung a leg over the guardrail of the stern-walk, now somewhat battered, and led the way down to a boiling sea that took him in its grip the moment he was clear of the ship.

The great rudder was moving within its confines, violently, scraping the ropes of the three-fold purchases and the whip of the sheer-legs against the plating. Its movement was irresistible: should it touch a man's head, and never mind the wrapping of

mattresses, it would break his skull like an egg. Halfhyde, with
his six seamen around him, mostly submerged, took stock of
the situation in the beamed light of a yard-arm group, a clus-
ter of reflector-backed electric light bulbs suspended on a boom
from the head of the sheer-legs. The pintles on the rudder were
mere inches from the gudgeons and a fraction above: the lie
was favourable and Halfhyde wasted no more time. By means
of hand signals to a leading seaman posted outboard of the
stern-walk above his head, Halfhyde passed orders for both the
three-fold purchases to be hauled in together. Just a shade . . .
backed by the weight of the seamen, working largely in the
dark and suffocation of the sea's lift and send, the pintles edged
closer in towards the stern post and the gudgeons waiting to
take them. They edged closer, and moved away again—time
after time after time. Savagely Halfhyde cursed, his heart in his
mouth for the safety of the desperately toiling hands. Feeling
where he could not see, working through what seemed like a
lifetime, at long last he judged the moment with accuracy—
assisted, he knew, by good fortune. He waved up for the whip
of the sheer-legs to lower slowly. With a clang that could be
heard dully even below the water, the pintles settled into their
places over the gudgeons and dropped firm. The whip of the
sheer-legs fell slack and was cast off from the ring-bolt rivetted
to the rudder plate by the blacksmith earlier. Halfhyde signalled
for the heavy chain lashings to be sent down while two men
clamped home the nuts to join on the head of the stock, working still in water that constantly submerged them as it crashed
and swilled up against the counter. Passing the chain lashings
to prevent the pintles jumping off the gudgeons took, in the
event, longer than the final shipping of the rudder.

Halfhyde felt himself to be at the end of his physical endurance when the last of the lashings was secured and the hammock-mattress fenders cut away with knives. He was about to pass the order up for the life lines to be hove in and the seamen and himself lifted back to the stern-walk, when a sudden extra plunge of the battleship's counter-weighted forefoot lifted her stern high, and the sea drained clear of screws and rudder. In the split second in which the lower part of the rudder stood visible, Halfhyde saw a sight he would never forget: the chest and part of the head of a man, all too obviously dead from drowning or injury, was clamped cruelly by the neck between rudder plate and stern post. The top of his skull had been sliced clean away as though by a surgeon's knife.

Chapter 6

RUM WAS ISSUED to all hands who had been working on deck. While the decks were cleared up by the watch and the working-parties were rested, Halfhyde climbed with dragging feet to the bridge where Bassinghorn was waiting.

"Ship ready to proceed, sir—"

"Thank God! Well done, Mr Halfhyde. I'm grateful."

"—and a man lost, sir, hung by the neck until he was dead . . . by the judgment, as I see it, of Sir Russell Savory."

Bassinghorn stared. "I think you'd better explain that, Mr Halfhyde. What has happened?"

Briefly, Halfhyde told the captain the facts. "He was clamped in when I lowered the rudder. His head must have been taken just before, by an unfendered part of the rudder. The conditions were abominable—but I offer no excuse. I should have checked that the way was clear."

"No." Bassinghorn shook his head. "Each man has a personal responsibility for his life in such conditions. One hand for Her Majesty, one for himself. I attach no blame to you, my dear Halfhyde. A lift of the ship, a send of the sea, the thrust of one wave . . . there is sometimes an inevitability. But you spoke of Savory, and I take that point truly indeed." Bassinghorn looked out across the night-dark, heaving Bay of Biscay, cold, windswept, spray-covered beneath a starless sky; his face was set hard in the faint loom of light from the binnacle. "I take it there is positively no chance he could be alive?"

Halfhyde gave no answer: the answer lay in his expression. Bassinghorn said simply, "It was a question I was required to ask, Halfhyde. And the body. It cannot be recovered?"

"Only by unseating the rudder once again, sir. Or by sending a man down to sever the neck completely."

"Quite. Then I must ring down to put the engines ahead."

"And churn the body to bloody flesh and minced bone."

Bassinghorn rounded on him, hands clenched into fists. "Be silent, if you please! There is no need to put it into such words— such crudity! Do you not think I feel a loss as much as you, as much as any man? Do you not, Mr Halfhyde?"

Halfhyde lowered his head. "I'm sorry, sir. I know you do. I spoke hastily, and I'm dog tired. I shall be fit in the forenoon, sir, but now I propose to turn in."

"Pray do so." For an instant before he turned away, Halfhyde met the captain's eye full and square: he read unmistakably what was in it: rage, a controlled rage and a firm determination to execute his orders to the letter and even beyond. A mission that had been unpalatable had, of a sudden, become as different in the captain's view as in Halfhyde's. There was no inevitability about Sir Russell Savory: he had had no duty to steal blueprints to his own gain. That had been his decision. His hunting down had now become a personal matter. As Halfhyde went down the bridge ladder he heard the wrench of the telegraph handles and then the bells repeating from the starting-platform below in the engine-room. The captain had rung down for full power in the chase to overtake Admiral von Merkatz and his squadron. As the great screws began their thrash up to maximum revolutions, Halfhyde tried not to think about what was happening below the captain's stern-walk.

"If blood be the price of Admiralty . . ." There was much blood in Halfhyde's nightmares after sleep, a troubled sleep, had come. He saw the shattered head, the horribly staring eyes, pleading eyes they seemed in retrospect. Death was always a part of sea life, always indeed a part of the business of serving Her Majesty Queen Victoria, and a man knew what he was in for when he joined, or he ought to if he had any imagination at all. Men joined for war, and always had, for fire along the gundecks of the old sailing navy, for the cannon-ball, the red-hot shot that took the magazine and exploded the ship like a firework, or split the masts like burning twigs to bring rope and yard and sprawling canvas down upon the bloodied heads of her company. He joined for the thrill and splendour of the drums beating to quarters and the crashing broadsides as the old line-of-battle-ships laid alongside the enemy and from a matter of yards raked her decks with ball and grapeshot to soften her up for the bayonets and cutlasses of the boarding parties, seamen and marines with a deep lust for killing. Or in modern times for the thunder of the turreted guns, shards of death that sent their huge shells winging across the sea to shatter ships miles away. Death was not thought about; no man saw the writing on the gun barrels as being for himself. Yet death came, and came often enough in unsuspected ways. The man who had died that night, Leading Seaman Chegwyn, had been a married man, thirty-eight years of age. Before turning in, Halfhyde had gone forward to the man's mess deck and had talked to his mates. Tonight in Devonport, a widow and four children would be

sleeping soundly with no thought for the news that would reach
them from the office of the commander-in-chief after the *Prince
Consort* had entered Gibraltar.

In the morning Halfhyde was bleary-eyed and in a touchy
mood as he went to the ward-room for breakfast. Commander
Percy was not there, still confined to his cabin for form's sake
by the fleet surgeon. Halfhyde was glad enough not to see him:
he suspected that the commander would have had some sardonic remarks to make about the loss of life once he had gone
below. Had he made them, a flaming row would have resulted.
Halfhyde munched bacon with little appetite, bracing himself in
his chair as the battleship rolled and pitched to a heavy sea and
his plate slid away from the fiddles, spilling hot fat on to the
gleaming, starched tablecloth until retrieved by an attentive
steward.

"A weight of wind, sir."

"Yes. Thank you. Do you happen to know what the glass is
doing?"

"Steadying, sir, according to word from the captain's steward."

Halfhyde nodded absently. The deck was shaking to the
vibration of the screws and there was all the evidence still of
full power, of a desperate chase after the German squadron, a
chase in filthy weather for the *Prince Consort,* filthy weather that
von Merkatz might well, by now, have left behind him. If he
had, then he would be making excellent speed down the coast
of Portugal. The wind coming through past the after screen was
strong, damp, and salty, bringing a feeling of stickiness with it
each time the ward-room door opened to admit an officer.
Halfhyde, leaving his breakfast largely uneaten, retired with his
coffee cup to a leather armchair in a corner of the ward-room,

picking up the *Illustrated London News* on the way. He lit a cigarette, and Turkish smoke rose in a thin trail: a filthy habit but
often more convenient than a pipe. Once, as a midshipman,
when he had lit a cigarette an elderly torpedo-gunner had com-
mented, "If you go on smoking them things, Mr Halfhyde, you'll
not be worth a kick in the arse come twenty-one."

Halfhyde smiled now at the recollection: he had left the
milestone of twenty-one behind these last seven years, he was
still in fair shape, and no man had ever dared attempt a kick
at his arse anyway. He smoked on, flipping through the pages
of London society. People were getting married, Lord This and
Lady That, the Duke of Whatnot, the Honourable Eustace
Tomnoddy had escorted Lady Ermintrude to a ball at Number
One London, home of the Duke of Wellington. All very important: life went on in high circles, the guard changed at
Buckingham Palace, St James's, the Horse Guards, Her Majesty
returned in her special train from Balmoral with a selection of
her many children and grand-children, all Scottish appurte-
nances packed away in the convex-lidded trunks until next
time, and aft of the *Prince Consort*'s ward-room with its comfortable chairs and excellent service the strips of flesh and shreds
of bone grew fewer . . .

"Mr Halfhyde, sir."

Halfhyde looked up. A seaman messenger, dripping water
from his oilskins, stood incongruously on the ward-room carpet. "Yes?"

"The captain's compliments, sir. He'd like to see you in his
sea cabin, sir."

"Very well, thank you."

Halfhyde rose and stretched. He retrieved his cap from its

hook outside the ward-room, went to his cabin for his oilskin, and proceeded towards the bridge, buffeted along the upper-deck by a gale force wind blowing out of a clear blue sky. The swell had gone now as the *Prince Consort* came down upon Cape Finisterre, but a heavy sea was running, a sea rutted with high waves flattened at their crests by the tearing wind that blew them into spindrift; and the sea was coming green and heavy over the eyes of the ship to wash aft along the fo'c'sle towards the guns. In the sea cabin, crowded to overflowing that morning, two enquiries were held by the captain, and Halfhyde was concerned in both. The first, a brief and formal affair, enquired into the death of Leading Seaman Chegwyn. Bassinghorn gave a finding, duly entered into the deck log, that Chegwyn had met death as a result of an accident on duty; no blame attached to anyone. The second enquiry was longer and less straightforward—why had the rudder become unseated? Opinions were offered by Commander Percy, restored, after the doctor's rounds, from the sick list; by Halfhyde; by the *Prince Consort's* first lieutenant; and by the engineer officer, the boatswain, the carpenter, and the blacksmith. The consensus of opinion laid the blame fair and square upon Devonport dock-yard for shoddy work and poor inspection, though Halfhyde volunteered the comment that perhaps, after many years of use, even strong metal could grow tired and give up the ghost at an awkward moment, without giving any prior indication of its sorry state. This provoked smiles, tolerant or impatient accord-ing to the wearer: metal was metal, and must last till Kingdom Come. The deck log uncompromising indicated that the dock-yard had been at fault, and this would be most strongly put to the Admiralty and the commander-in-chief in Bassinghorn's written report from Gibraltar.

The enquiries completed, Bassinghorn dismissed all the officers except Halfhyde. As the others left, Bassinghorn drew a turnip-shaped silver watch from a pocket and studied it. "Close upon luncheon," he observed. "Will you take a drink, Mr Halfhyde?"

Halfhyde shook his head. The offer was no more than a polite formality: Bassinghorn himself never touched alcohol at sea, and at other times no more than one finger's breadth of whisky. Prudent officers in his company restricted their own to a little under a finger.

Bassinghorn replaced his watch. Halfhyde noted the weariness in his weather-worn face. Henry Bassinghorn was no longer of an age when many unrelieved hours on the bridge left no mark. Strain showed now in the dullness of his eyes, in the sag of bearded flesh beneath the strong chin, in the deep lines radiating from the corners of his eyes. Halfhyde said, "You need rest, sir. The ship's all right now. Why not turn in and forget it?"

"No captain can ever forget his ship, Halfhyde." Bassinghorn rubbed at his eyes. "I shall sleep soon, for a spell at any rate. In the meantime, we have matters to talk about. The past is the past—or will be when my clerk has handed my reports in at Gibraltar. We must turn our minds to the future now."

"Savory, sir?"

"More important at this moment—Admiral von Merkatz, who is well ahead of us."

"No more than around twelve hours, sir—less, since he didn't overhaul us until some while after the rudder went."

Halfhyde paused. "May I ask what speed we're making, sir?"

"Fifteen knots."

"I thought as much, largely because of the curious motion."

"Yes, she handles poorly at speed, Halfhyde—that's her rep-utation, and it's a true one. I'd be surprised if von Merkatz is making less," he added, turning to stare through a port as though willing the German ships to appear ahead. "He was making that when he overhauled us!"

"It would be too much to hope that *his* rudder will part company!"

"Too much indeed." Bassinghorn put his head in his hands for a moment, then lifted it in embarrassment that he had shown a moment of weakness to another man. "I have told the engineer officer, somewhat forcefully I fear, that we must keep steam for maximum revolutions into Gibraltar—and do our best to beat the Germans in and out again."

Halfhyde raised an eyebrow. "You think von Merkatz will enter, sir?"

"He must, for coaling ship."

"He might well make Madeira, sir, or the Canaries."

"I doubt it—at the speed he's moving, his furnaces will be eating coal. And he's already had a longer haul than us."

"And the rear-admiral in Gibraltar will give him the facility, do you suppose?"

Bassinghorn shrugged. "Our countries are not at war, Halfhyde. There is no reason to refuse, and the government at home is most unlikely to make any public announcement about Savory as an excuse for refusal."

"No doubt you're right, sir." Halfhyde ran a hard brown

hand over the length of his jaw, eyes half closed. "But the rear-admiral—if he's a man of vision, he'll put in hand delaying tactics, no doubt?"

Bassinghorn shook his head. "Rear-Admiral Latham is not a man of vision. He has a name for thick-headedness and some obduracy, and an inclination to obey the letter of the law."

"Rather than the spirit," Halfhyde murmured. "Then I suggest delaying tactics of our own, sir."

"Such as what?"

Halfhyde grinned. "Another rudder gone, this time a German one, and by design!"

"You suggest some kind of nefarious attack, while von Merkatz is in Gibraltar?"

"Scarcely nefarious, sir. We may not be at war, but it can hardly be said we're acting in concert with the Germans. I fancy we can—"

"Even so, we have the Board of Admiralty to consider, and their likely reaction."

"As ever!" Halfhyde said broodingly. "The rudder was merely an example, sir, brought to mind as a result of our own misfortune. There are other things, less obvious things."

Bassinghorn sighed irritably. "Be more precise, Halfhyde, if you please."

"I cannot, sir, at the moment. I shall be thinking." He smiled. "I have thought constructively before now, sir, as I think you'll agree. My mind is not in its grave yet, and we have some days to Gibraltar."

"Then have a care, Halfhyde!" Bassinghorn wagged a thick finger in admonition. "We were lucky in the Pacific. Luck tends to run out if pressed too far. I want no more sunken squadrons, if you please!"

"I'll bear it in mind, sir," Halfhyde said, tongue in cheek.

The bowler hat was back in place, though occasionally the wind lifted it, as though in salute to some passing chief superintendent from Scotland Yard, to fly like a round black kite and tug at its retaining toggle on Mr Todhunter's lapel. Halfhyde, descending from the captain's sea cabin, caught a sight of it as the detective inspector stood clutching at the guardrail aft on the upper-deck, letting the good clean wind blow away the cobwebs and the sickness. Mr Todhunter's face was pink and shining and his eye, when he turned it upon Halfhyde's approach, was bright and happy.

"Good morning, Mr Halfhyde."

"And to you, Mr Todhunter. A remarkable recovery!"

"Yes, I have my sea-legs, Mr Halfhyde. It's a funny thing . . . some people never get accustomed, do they? My old mother didn't."

"But," Halfhyde said wickedly, "I was under the impression she voyaged only from the Clarence Pier at Southsea to Ryde?"

"Well, yes. And back . . . Oh, a short experience, I agree—"

"Whereas you are now a deep-sea sailorman, Mr Todhunter."

Todhunter beamed proudly. "You really think so?"

"Damn it, I know so!" Halfhyde sounded hearty. "Few people recover so quickly. Why, we're not quite out of the Bay yet! I congratulate you indeed."

"Thank you, Mr Halfhyde. We shall get along nicely together, I fancy."

"I am sure we shall. And luncheon?"

"Luncheon, Mr Halfhyde?"

"Have you had it yet?"

"Why, no, I haven't, as a matter of fact, and fact is what I deal in." Mr Todhunter laughed. "Be sure I shall have it soon, Mr Halfhyde."

Halfhyde went down to the ward-room, reflecting upon the detective. He was a new Todhunter, full of bounce: after sickness, the sea air was doing him a power of good, and there was something cocky in the policeman's manner now that suggested to Halfhyde that it might not be long before he was busily instructing Sam Strawbridge upon matters of seamanship . . .

Chapter 7

THE BOATSWAIN'S calls sounded through the mess decks and flats, and blew shrilly along the upper-deck: "Special sea dutymen to your stations . . . cable and side party muster on the fo'c'sle . . . hands fall in for entering harbour, all men not in the rig of the day clear the upper-deck!" The white-helmeted bandsmen of the Royal Marine Artillery doubled aft to the quarterdeck with their instruments and on the after shelter deck a bugler stood ready to sound off in salute to the flag of the rear-admiral in Gibraltar. On the bridge stood Captain Bassinghorn, staring forward, surrounded by his bridge staff: officer of the watch, navigating officer, chief yeoman of signals, seamen boys to act as messengers, signal boys to bend on the identifying pennants as Her Majesty's Ship *Prince Consort* came below the immense frowning eminence of the Rock of Gibraltar and turned in the broad bay to make her entry. All along, there had been no sign of von Merkatz and his ships: past Cape St Vincent, past Cape Trafalgar of victorious memory, down to Tarifa and the Gibraltar Strait—nothing. Two merchant ships were sighted, liners coming through from India and China, and a gunboat wearing the Spanish ensign and crossing from Ceuta to Algeciras—that was all. But when the battleship turned to port around Carnero and came into Gibraltar Bay, all stood revealed and doubt was ended in horrible certainty. Four German naval ensigns waved flaunting defiance at the British Navy, and no less at the representative of British law still sweating into his blue serge suit though the sailors had shifted into half-whites of blue tops and white trousers. And over all, arrogantly beneath a high, hot sun, floated the flag of Admiral von Merkatz. The ships were at anchor out in the bay and appeared through a dirty haze of coal dust, targets for an unending succession of coal-filled barges under tow of tugs from the dockyard.

Bassinghorn, who had been staring through his telescope, lowered the glass and swore roundly.

"God damn them! Mr Halfhyde?"

Halfhyde moved to his side. "Sir?"

Bassinghorn spoke from behind his hand, in a low voice. "Ideas?"

"They shall come, sir. They are forming."

"Then speed them, Mr Halfhyde."

"Yes, sir." Halfhyde paused. "I have the impression they've only just started coaling, since they're relatively clean. To coal four ships from lighters will take time."

"Well?"

"Longer than it will take us, sir—that is, more especially if we're to be given the coaling wharf itself—" He broke off—a string of coloured flags was being hoisted to the mast above the signal tower in the dockyard, Bassinghorn having by now hoisted his pennants to his starboard fore upper yard-arm. The chief yeoman read them off quickly and reported to the captain.

"From the rear-admiral, sir. '*Prince Consort* is to proceed alongside coaling wharf at the North Mole. I shall repair aboard with my chief of staff as soon as you have secured. Request your full requirements in the meantime.'"

"Thank you, Chief Yeoman. Acknowledge, and make: 'Rear-Admiral Gibraltar from *Prince Consort,* I require bunkering to capacity soonest possible also divers to examine stern post and rudder. Supplies as follows . . .' you have the list from the paymaster, Chief Yeoman?"

"Yes, sir."

"Add it, then. Also any further requirements from the engineer officer. That's all."

"Aye, aye, sir." The chief yeoman turned away towards his mechanical semaphore.

Bassinghorn spoke to the officer of the watch. "General Salute, Mr Hawkins." The order was passed down: the bugle sounded stridently and the band struck up, the guard fallen in aft presenting arms from the shoulder. From the dockyard the salute was returned, and the officers on the bridge, as the ship closed the North Mole, saw an open carriage coming along from the Land Post filled with blue and white and gold: the rear-admiral with his chief of staff and flag lieutenant. Bassinghorn scowled: he was a man who much disliked being under the eyes of admirals—usually critical ones—when in the act of bringing his ship alongside. But with Halfhyde he shared a strong degree of curiosity: it was seldom that any flag officer in charge met incoming vessels in person, especially when they were to take bunkers immediately upon arrival.

Not a moment was lost: as soon as the gilded staff had come aboard, to be met at the head of the starboard ladder by

Bassinghorn and Commander Percy and taken below to the cuddy, the filthy operation of coaling ship began and the gleaming, scrubbed decks and polished bright work started to vanish under a coating of gritty, sticky black and many tarpaulins. With all ventilators closed to keep the lowerdecks free, so far as possible, of the insidious dust, the ship grew hot and stuffy. All hands were needed, officers and marines included. Gone were the smart uniforms so proudly paraded on deck for the arrival. Men now worked in collarless white duck jumpers, affairs of heavy canvas whose whiteness turned in no time to black. Some worked in a jumble of gear—shirts, torn trousers, sweat rags around necks and foreheads, anything that was functional, as the endless chain gang brought the coal baskets up the brows from the Mole to spill them in cloudy black thunder down the chutes to the greedy bunkers. Below, the stokers worked and sweated, trimming the life-giving matter as it descended in showers of dust, wielding the polished steel shovels like maniacs to keep pace. Curses and the clang of metal could hardly be heard above the roar of dropping coal as the British Navy's recurrent day of hell continued.

Even in the cuddy, whence Halfhyde had now been bidden, the coal dust penetrated somehow, though the ports had been clamped shut and the entry from the stern-walk firmly clipped down. Specks of dust showed on the officers' starched white trousers and on the white cap-covers hanging in the lobby on their hooks. There was even a scummy film on the surface of the gin and bitters poured by the captain's servant for the rear-admiral and his retinue. The servant, his back turned, was endeavouring to remove it with a nicotine-stained forefinger.

This manoeuvre was not lost upon Rear-Admiral Latham, a fat and flabby man with a bovine face that indicated some addiction to spirits.

"Captain, forgive me, but I prefer coal dust to the human finger."

Bassinghorn spoke sharply to his servant, who ceased his well-meant efforts. "Yessir. Sorry, sir. Coming up, sir." The drinks were offered. The rear-admiral, taking his, lifted it and, while the servant discreetly made his way to the captain's pantry to remain there until recalled, examined it in a ray of sunlight streaming through the closed port beside him.

"Who am I to complain," he said, "when the great von Merkatz will also be drinking coal dust in his schnapps!"

"Quite so, sir. As to von Merkatz . . ."

"Well?"

Bassinghorn said, "I take it I may speak freely, sir? That's to say, you know, of course—"

"The Board of Admiralty has found no reason not to confide in me, Bassinghorn, and I have no reason not to confide in my staff, but of course in the very greatest secrecy. That is why I have boarded you, rather than bring you ashore. Everywhere ashore there are ears—Spanish ears, Gibraltarian ears. I prefer safety, Captain." The pig-like eyes stared as if in some sort of accusation. "You may indeed speak freely aboard your ship, and indeed I shall speak to *you* shortly, for I have news to pass." He drained his gin in one gulp. "First, however, you were about to talk of Admiral von Merkatz, were you not, Captain?"

"I was, sir." Bassinghorn asked the question directly: "Do you happen to know his orders?"

"No, but I can guess as well as any man. It's clear, I think, that he is under orders to pick up that damned scoundrel Savory and deliver him to Berlin."

"And meanwhile he is being helped upon his way."

The rear-admiral lifted an eyebrow. "The coal? My hands were tied. A diplomatic incident was not wanted by Their Lordships. I'll be frank—I considered a Nelsonic blindness. But despatches are not so easily disregarded as flag hoists, and I have no great victories to quote!"

Bassinghorn caught Halfhyde's eye: Halfhyde had been growing restless, and the eye spoke a warning. Nevertheless, Halfhyde jumped in to bridge the pause that followed the rear-admiral's remark. "No victories, perhaps, sir. But you have Spanish workmen delivering the Germans' coal, have you not?"

The rear-admiral stared. "I have, Mr Halfhyde. Why do you make the point?"

"They are slow workers, sir."

"And I have not insisted that they hurry, I assure you!"

"Quite, sir. May I suggest that you now do so?"

"I beg your pardon?" the admiral said sharply, and added: "May I suggest, Mr Halfhyde, that you declare which side you are on, your captain's or the German squadron's?"

"My suggestion was a serious one, sir. I should like to repeat it most earnestly." Halfhyde's face was solemn and commanded attention. He went on, "The Spanish workmen are slow and unreliable—von Merkatz will know this. They are also temperamental, volatile, and hasty. To haze them into fast work will serve two ends: you will satisfy Their Lordships' requirement not to fracture diplomacy, and you will cause the Spanish workmen to down coal baskets—that is to say, to walk off and leave the lighters unmanned! Do you understand me, sir?"

The rear-admiral stared, his lips framing an unuttered whistle of astonishment. "By God, Mr Halfhyde, you are asking me to cause a strike, as I understand it is called?"

"I am indeed, sir."

"Gibraltar is not Britain. The Spanish are not members of trades unions."

"Then perhaps they will not call it a strike, sir," Halfhyde said impatiently, "but the result will be the same! They will walk off in a huff, and the Germans will cease taking coal—but you will have given no orders to that effect. Your yard-arm, sir, will stand clear of any criticism; the letter of the law, of the Admiralty's orders, will remain unbroken."

"Ah-ha . . ."

"In due time, sir, the dispute will be settled, and you will be rid of von Merkatz—and *we* shall be upon the African coast before him! I think you should find the Admiralty and indeed the British Government most grateful to you, sir."

"But in the event of failure, Mr Halfhyde?"

"There can be no failure, sir. The facts will stand for themselves in a clear light. Von Merkatz stays, we depart. And in no event, sir, I say again, can any blame attach to yourself, since you will have done nothing." Halfhyde, tongue firmly in cheek, looked around: he saw amusement upon the faces of the staff, and upon Bassinghorn's as well. The rear-admiral pulled at a protuberant lower lip, then at the heavy white side-whiskers that contrasted so sharply with the deep red of his face. He shook his head, then took a turn or two up and down the cabin. After a moment he began to smile himself—a happy and scheming pig-faced admiral who had hit upon something upon which he could dine out for many years in his retirement . . .

"Mr Halfhyde," he said pompously, "you have, as I understand, a reputation for unorthodoxy. Such is a two-edged sword, and frequently fails to make lieutenants into flag officers—"

"But has frequently made flag officers into commanders-in-chief, sir."

Halfhyde caught the warning look from his captain, the look that told him he was on the verge of going too far. But the rear-admiral found nothing to cavil at. He went on, "But this time, Mr Halfhyde, I believe you have it right! I wish I had thought of this myself, upon my word—I congratulate you most heartily." He turned upon his chief of staff. "Captain Thompson, if you please, speed the workmen. Haze them! Spare not the rod upon their backs! Be as rude as you wish. Threaten to withdraw all pay earned if the speed is not quadrupled—threaten to castrate those who fail to show their manhood! Tell them they shall be held aboard the lighters and not allowed home—tell them anything you like, but make *quite certain* they are pushed to the point at which they will rebel!" He rubbed his hands together briskly, eyes shining and almost popping from his red face, rotund body a-bounce upon its heels. "Oh, this is most excellent! By God, I think I shall much enjoy the Germans' discomfiture! A most splendid jape, a first-class jest to be sure!"

The news the rear-admiral had to impart was much to the point and was in fact a tribute to the sagacity of Detective Inspector Todhunter. An Admiralty cypher had been received on the telegraph from Whitehall, a most urgent message to the effect that all previous notions as to Sir Russell Savory's intended destination should be scrapped. Information had come to hand via

British agents from Northern Rhodesia operating clandestinely in Angola that Savory had doubled back upon his tracks. It now appeared evident that his true target was indeed, as Todhunter had forecast, German South-West Africa. His tracks had been picked up in the vicinity of Silva Porto, from where he was in a good position to drop down to cross the northern border of German South-West Africa, should that be his intention. Further credence was given to this theory by the fact that German troops and police had been much in evidence along their own side of that border and especially in the vicinity of the Cubango River. Mr Todhunter, when bidden to the cuddy, indulged in a little preening. He had proved more astute than his superiors and now basked in the knowledge that all Whitehall must be in the most remarkable tizzy over their miscalculation.

"I would assume, sir," Todhunter said deferentially to the rear-admiral, "that the orders are now changed?"

"Yes, to be sure they are!" The admiral turned to Bassinghorn. "I understand you were under orders for the Cape, Captain. Those orders are now in abeyance and I am directed to order you to launch Mr Halfhyde with his torpedo-boats off the mouth of the Coanza River in Angola. The river has rapids, but these will present but a small problem to shallow draught boats, and he'll be able to navigate for some 120 miles before meeting the Livingstone Falls a few miles to the west'ard of Dondo. From there, his party must proceed south towards Silva Porto, using native canoes if these can be procured."

"And the Portuguese, sir?" Halfhyde asked.

"They still have no wish to upset the Germans by arresting Savory, but they will turn a blind eye to your activities, Mr Halfhyde, so long as you are co-operative."

"In what sense, sir?"

"Do not force their blind eye to see again, Mr Halfhyde! I must stress this: they are absolutely not to be embarrassed by your presence or activities."

"Very good, sir, I shall do my best. And these agents, the men working out of Angola. Do you know what their orders are, sir?"

"They, too, will walk warily and with more than an eye to diplomatic considerations. They're keeping what one might describe as a distant watch, a surveillance." The admiral shrugged. "You may ask why they don't close and make the arrest themselves. I answer this: there is the over-riding diplomatic requirement, and also, I think, a degree of difference—to use no stronger word—between the Foreign Office, the Home Office, and the Admiralty. These agents are upon foreign soil and have no mandate."

"Mr Todhunter and I will be in a similar position, sir."

"Up to a point, yes." The admiral was sweating badly now, and was grimed with dampened coal dust. Halfhyde regarded him sardonically: he was giving orders to the sacrificial lambs, and finding it hard to justify them. "A policeman is in a different position, as is a naval officer. It is not desired that Savory's defection and threat of blackmail should become known if it can be avoided. A simple arrest by the law, with neither our agents nor the Foreign Office being involved . . . every effort is being applied towards that end . . . and I would be much obliged, Mr Halfhyde, if you would press me no further." Pointedly he turned to Todhunter. "Now, Mr Todhunter, pray do not lose your quarry!"

"That is largely out of my hands, sir."

"Don't make excuses, man!"

Todhunter inclined his head meekly, but his eyes were reproachful at injustice. "That I shall not do, sir, once I am ashore. But the business of the rudder—"

"Which was expeditiously and efficiently overcome by all concerned—another matter of congratulation to Mr Halfhyde, I gather, in particular. The rudder is at this moment being made wholly shipshape by my divers, Mr Todhunter, and you will be upon your way the moment coaling ship is complete."

"And the Germans, sir?"

"They have only recently begun coaling—a mere trickle has gone aboard, and will soon, cease, as I trust." The rear-admiral turned to Bassinghorn. "I'll be away at once, Captain, and put all matters in hand. Your stores will be seen to and your reports forwarded by the next ship for home." He paused. "I'm more than sorry about the two men lost. You'll be holding an auction of their effects?"

"I will, sir, as soon as we are at sea again and clear of the Strait."

The rear-admiral nodded, and put a hand in his pocket. He brought out four sovereigns that shone in the sunlight. "Two for each," he said abruptly. "The least I can do. In a very positive sense, they died for England." He nodded at his chief of staff and the flag lieutenant, and moved in convoy for the door, out past the marine sentry who crashed to attention, out along the after flat to the upper-deck and the grime. A blackened gangway staff saluted him over the side to his carriage, which was already thick with coal dust.

Beyond and above the haze of dust the Rock of Gibraltar loomed immense over all, threaded with galleries cut from the living rock, with lofty strongpoints to carry the great siege guns of the Royal Artillery pointing from their embrasures in powerful batteries towards Spain, beyond the neutral ground that connected Gibraltar to the land mass. The heavily garrisoned Rock spoke loudly of the imperial might of Britain. It had made in itself more than a page of British history. Halfhyde, who had known Gibraltar in the past, looked towards the pattern of brown and dusty green interspersed with the white and sand-coloured buildings of town and barracks as the rear-admiral's carriage clattered back along the mole. The very place names spoke of past glories of British arms: Chatham Counterguard, Hesse's Demi-Bastion, Cornwall's Parade, the Trafalgar cemetery where so many of Nelson's dead heroes lay shrouded in honour. Halfhyde turned away with the suspicion of a lump in his throat: for a blunt Yorkshireman he had perhaps more than his share of romanticism in his make up. But his prayer that the traitor Savory would not be allowed to sully the name of Admiralty was very heartfelt.

Within two hours word had spread throughout the ship: an altercation was going on at the end of the coal wharf, where the lighters for the German squadron had been loading. Furious shouting and gestures were aimed towards the distant flag of the rear-admiral and the Union Flag floating from the staff over Government House in Waterport Street. The British were very devils out of hell, heretics sent up from below by Lucifer to torture honest Spaniards with their crazy demands for hard work for little reward. And the Germans were as bad—must in fact be the instigators of this abominable slave driving. The sounds grew louder, the movement of the lighters grew less, and the

sea between wharf and squadron soon lay placid and empty—
as did the German bunkers. To ribald shouts of mirth from the
Prince Consort's sweat-bathed company, the Spanish work force
disintegrated into vituperative groups and poured towards the
Land Port, the gateway that led from the fortress towards their
homes beyond the neutral ground. That those bringing the coal
baskets alongside the *Prince Consort* also left their work mattered little to the British operation; unlike the Germans, the
British had no water to cross. Bassinghorn's ship's company
took the places of the Spanish workmen and the bunkering
proceeded, if a little more slowly than before. From the *Prince
Consort's* blackened bridge every telescope was turned upon the
German flagship, the splendid *Friedrich der Grösse*. It was no
time before signals began passing, the arms of the mechanical
semaphore working frenziedly. What had happened, where were
the lighters, where was the precious bunker coal? The expla-
nations from the Tower were humbly apologetic: there was a
dispute, which should soon be settled. More signals from von
Merkatz indicated that in Germany disputes would not be permitted, and if they started would be quickly settled by the bayonet. Since this dispute had been stupidly allowed to continue,
the sailors of the British Fleet should be ordered to deputize.
British sailors, replied the Tower, coaled only British ships. The
exchange went on and on. Suddenly the chief yeoman of signals burst out laughing: Halfhyde enquired the reason.

"Admiral von Merkatz, sir. He's hopping mad, sir, literally."

Halfhyde turned his glass on the German admiral's quarterdeck: von Merkatz was leaping up and down, shaking both fists
at his flag captain. As Halfhyde watched, the admiral snatched
his gold-edged cap from his head and cast it to the deck, then

jumped into the air to descend upon it with both feet, again and again, in the time-honoured manner of any senior naval officer expressing frenzy.

The *Prince Consort* completed coaling in record time: within twelve hours the bunkers were filled to capacity and beyond, with extra coal accommodated in wooden bins supplied from shore and stowed in places that brought dismay to Commander Percy, who liked a clean ship above all else. He stalked the decks and alleyways with his head held back and his nostrils dilated, hating engineers and stokers, his eyes frosty. Dark had come when, with no time lost, the captain climbed to a bridge freshly washed down and scrubbed, and the *Prince Consort's* lines were let go by the shore gang. With her engines moving astern, the battleship came off to turn in the bay and steal outwards westerly for Cape Spartel and the long haul down the coast of Africa—to the immense surprise of a ship's company that had expected an easterly haul to Malta. She steamed past the German squadron at anchor, silent and helpless ships with near-empty bunkers, ships that would not move until the rear-admiral reached an agreement with his Spanish workmen, ships that could communicate with Berlin only by the kind co-operation of that same rear-admiral. Bassinghorn gave them a wave from the darkness of his bridge.

"No doubt we'll meet again," he said. "But it'll not be yet!"

Halfhyde, standing by his side, asked, "And when we do, sir?"

Bassinghorn laughed grimly. "Von Merkatz, who will know very well what has happened, but can do nothing about it, will be looking for his revenge. If by that time I have Sir Russell Savory aboard . . ."

"Yes, sir?"

Bassinghorn turned aft and looked down into the waist at the turrets. "I shall use my guns," he said.

Halfhyde was conscious of a prickle of excitement. "You said earlier, sir, that you would prefer to bring the commander to bed than the German squadron to action! You've changed your mind, sir?"

Bassinghorn shrugged. "A captain's privilege after much thought, Mr Halfhyde. The Admiralty does not want me to use my guns—though they have not been specific, I know their mind! I *must* not use my guns, since to do so would be a kind of failure—yet it is in my view a question of balance." He paused, lifting his gaze out across the water. "The security of the construction programme affects the Navy for many, many years ahead. And we are but one elderly battleship, commanded by one elderly captain!"

Chapter 8

PAST CAPE SPARTEL, the *Prince Consort* altered course to the south, her mess decks seething with rumours until Bassinghorn passed the word as to her new destination. Halfhyde, next morning, came on deck to sniff the unmistakable scent of the African continent that he knew so well from the past. Spices, desert sand, luxuriant coastal vegetation, coconut oil, palms . . . he didn't know what all the constituents were, but appreciated the result. The sun shone brightly from a brilliant blue sky to reflect into a sea flat as a millpond. Mr Todhunter, still in his bowler hat and blue suit, and sweating profusely, was taking exercise. He pounced when he saw Halfhyde emerge from the after hatch.

"Good morning, Mr Halfhyde."

"Good morning, Mr Todhunter."

Todhunter approached closer and coughed behind a hand. "Sir Russell Savory. Have you had words yet with the captain, sir?"

"About what?"

"Why, about my man, Mr Halfhyde, what else?"

"Words, yes. The time for action is not yet, and words don't help much. All the same . . ." Halfhyde paused, musing. "Do you read poetry, Mr Todhunter?"

"Well . . . no. No, I don't."

"A pity. At times, it's apposite.

"'Sink me the ship, master Gunner—'"

"Pardon?"

"'—sink her, split her in twain! Fall into the hands of God, not into the hands of Spain!'"

"I'm sorry." Todhunter sounded irritated. "I don't follow, Mr Halfhyde."

"No? I think you will, eventually." Halfhyde rubbed his hands together. "My words with the captain had the ring of war. In certain circumstances, he intends to use his guns, by which he means the main armament, Mr Todhunter."

"Oh. Oh dear. And the Germans might fire back?"

"It would be a natural reaction." Halfhyde looked down on the bowler hat. "Have you ever been involved with gunfire, Mr Todhunter?"

Todhunter answered stiffly. "The Metropolitan Police are not normally armed, sir. Only upon the express orders of the commissioner can they be so."

"Ah, I see. And even then, presumably, not with sixteen-inch turret guns. But try not to worry, our armour belt is the thickest afloat and there's plenty of room behind it. The point I'm making is this: the captain is behind you all the way. Savory, once arrested, is to remain arrested, whatever von Merkatz may seek to do, and because of that—" He broke off before he could utter an indiscretion: there was no point in giving Todhunter an attack of sheer fright just yet. But it was in Halfhyde's mind—and it was this that had led him to lyricism earlier—that Bassinghorn was of the breed that died before surrender. The final outcome might well depend upon Bassinghorn's mental balance between Savory's potential for damage and the lives of more than five hundred British seamen. If it came to that, the captain's task of deciding would be a cruel one. Halfhyde turned the discussion to other matters. "Mr Todhunter, if you wish to become better acquainted with the British jack-tar, I suggest you attend the auction."

"Auction, sir?"

"To be held on the captain's order at four bells this forenoon. It is the custom, when a man dies or is killed, to auction his effects aboard for the highest price obtainable from sympathetic and generous shipmates, and send the proceeds to the next-of-kin."

"Admirable. And four bells is—"

"Ten o'clock, Mr Todhunter. All officers not required for duty will attend."

"By order, Mr Halfhyde?"

"By custom and desire, Mr Todhunter." Halfhyde strode away, down to the ward-room. The detective inspector proceeded to the warrant officers' mess for his own breakfast. During the meal, he raised the question of the auction with Sam Strawbridge.

"Mr Halfhyde suggested I attend. Frankly, I feel it's not my business, Mr Strawbridge."

"The hands'll not see it that way, to be sure, Mr Todhunter."

"But—"

"And you represent the Law," the boatswain went on, his tone stubborn. "It was the Law sent them two poor buggers to their deaths, indirectly. I reckon you owe them summat, Mr Todhunter—and by Christ, yes, I'm talkin' financial if you want to know." He leaned across the tablecloth, prodding a thick, tobacco-stained thumb at Todhunter. "Mr Halfhyde's advice was good. I suggest you take it."

Mr Todhunter flushed a little and concentrated upon melon

embarked with the stores in Gibraltar, followed by a slice of salty ham from the battleship's beef screen, and coffee. Then he returned to his cabin for close consideration of his orders from the Home Office and perusal of a tome on police law to ascertain whether, by his attendance at the sale of effects and donation of monies, he would in any sense be committing the Law to some responsibility in the matter of the unfortunate deaths. He found nothing precise, so could not be sure. But the man Strawbridge was very close at hand while the commissioner of Metropolitan Police was not, and Strawbridge had sounded bitter. Mr Todhunter, wishing neither to bring his force into contumely nor to risk being sent to Coventry himself by the warrant officers, made up his mind: he would attend. And attend he did, as did everyone else aboard the *Prince Consort* who was able to. Commander Percy was there, stiff and formal, but not so much so as usual. His manner was gentler today.

A combined sale of effects of both men was being held in the mess deck of the late Leading Seaman Chegwyn. The assortment of personal gear was small and sad: Number One uniforms with gold badges, lanyards lovingly scrubbed white, knives, a little money, photographs of their families, their seamen's flannels and underwear, ditty boxes, a tin of pusser's tobacco, known as Tickler's not from its effect upon the throat but from the name of the manufacturer, a pipe, a pouch, a pewter flask that had held rum; odds and ends and nothing of value to anyone but the late owners themselves. The kits fetched a little over £50 apiece from shipmates paid a pittance a day, some of them as little as one-and-fourpence, and when it was all sold, it was handed back for return to the families along with the money, and the sovereigns donated by the rear-admiral in Gibraltar. Commander Percy gave a sovereign to each, the other officers gave half-sovereigns except for Halfhyde who felt his personal involvement to the extent of two to each man. When the time came Mr Todhunter felt in his pockets. A detective inspector had to maintain his position above that of common seamen: he produced three florins. Having produced them he caught Halfhyde's eye and coughed.

"An inspector's pay is not princely, Mr Halfhyde."

"To be sure, to be sure."

"And my old mother . . . it's not nice to say it, but her funeral cost me a pretty penny, a pretty penny."

"You have my condolences."

The florins dropped with a clink into the out-held cap. The ship's company drifted away. The auction had taken time and Up Spirits was being piped by the boatswain's mates. First lieutenant, paymaster, and master-at-arms made their way below to the spirit room for the issue of the daily ration of grog, and, sadness over and done with, the *Prince Consort* swung back into noisy and rigorous routine. The ship's police began their hazing of the laggards, busy with stonachies and canes as they herded the mass of seamen, marines, stokers, and daymen towards the hatches. Todhunter, making his way aft with Halfhyde, felt rather bemused by the swift change in attitudes: Commander Percy for one was back to normal, cursing the men out of his way with sharp cries of "Gangway there, gangway, damn your eyes, clear a way for me at once!" The ship's police jumped to obey, thrusting men back into the hammock nettings and the cruel breeches of the broadside guns, adding their raucous orders to those of the commander. Todhunter observed nervously, "Such shouting, Mr Halfhyde, it doesn't seem respectful to the living, never mind the dead. Spirits . . . they'll need them, eh?"

"Up Spirits," Halfhyde said solemnly, "but stand fast the Holy Ghost."

"Pardon? That's blasphemy!"

"But often uttered aboard Her Majesty's ships of war, Mr Todhunter. We're an ungodly lot—except when it matters most."

"It must be hard upon the reverend, Mr Halfhyde."

"The reverend? Ah—the chaplain. Naval chaplains are men of the world, Mr Todhunter, and in any case the coarsest able seamen refrain from blasphemy in their hearing. Sailors have a great respect for the cloth. Largely they are nature's gentlemen— as I think you have just seen for yourself in the mess deck."

Todhunter nodded. "A charitable affair indeed—"

"Not charitable. An act of friendship and respect. In the British Fleet, Mr Todhunter, the term messmate means a very great deal to everyone. So does the more general term ship-mate." Halfhyde paused. "If we are to be brought to action, you will understand better."

At four bells in the afternoon watch, Bassinghorn called a con-ference once again in his sea cabin: Commander Percy, Halfhyde, and Todhunter attended. The captain had the charts of the tar-get area spread out on a table, together with the Admiralty "Pilot," the Sailing Directions for the relevant sector of the coast. He stubbed a finger on to the mouth of the Coanza River. "I've taken the engineer officer into my confidence—shortly, I shall speak to the entire ship's company, as to our destination, that is. I shall not mention Savory. Mr Warmsley assures me we have coal to maintain full power all the way, and I anticipate arrival off the Coanza during the middle watch on the 27th, that is, in eight days' time." He looked up. "Yes, Mr Todhunter, what is it?"

"It is too long, sir—too long!"

"You were aware of the timescale from the start," Bassinghorn said. "In any case, I can do no more than steam at full speed. I am as anxious as you are for a successful end to all this."

"Yes, sir, but such a needle in a haystack as—"

"That is not entirely so. Savory is under surveillance of a kind and his general whereabouts are known. There is another point also: his own movement is slow, much slower currently than ours. What think you, Mr Halfhyde?"

"As you do, sir—that is, if you are thinking that Savory is unlikely to reach the German South-West Africa border within our eight days—"

Todhunter interrupted. "More than eight days, Mr Halfhyde, since we have yet to navigate the Coanza River!"

"I'm aware of that. It will take far longer than eight days for Savory to reach sanctuary unless he has wings to fly with! I know the territory, Mr Todhunter. It is wild, and largely desert. There are mountains to cross, also swamps to the south of Caiundo. I—"

"Swamps, deserts, mountains that will impede us just as surely!"

Halfhyde grinned. "Not quite! We shall make good speed to Dondo at least, and thereafter I have an excellent knowledge of the tracks."

"And Savory?"

"His history shows no such knowledge likely, Mr Todhunter, as you have said yourself."

"But a guide!"

"Ah yes, a guide. That's in the lap of the gods, is it not? I think, Mr Todhunter, that we must put a little of our faith in the British agents inside Angola. Their hands are tied to a great extent, I know, but they should not prove entirely helpless." He added, "Besides, the Coanza does not stop at Dondo, even if our torpedo-boats do."

Bassinghorn asked, "What does that mean, Mr Halfhyde?"

"It means, sir, that it should not be impossible for us to pass by the Livingstone Falls to landward, and re-embark in native canoes farther up the river, as Rear-Admiral Latham suggested in Gibraltar. If we can do that—and I'll guarantee to lay hands on some canoes—then we shall travel fast by water until we are not far north of Shitembo."

"You'll not navigate all the way to the source, Mr Halfhyde!"

Halfhyde inclined his head. "No, sir. But at all events we should be able to navigate well to the south of Silva Porto, and thus cut the start that Savory will have upon us."

"Possible, possibly. Well—it's all we can do. And the torpedo-boats, Mr Halfhyde? What of them, when you take to the land at Dondo?"

"I shall have a regard for them, never fear."

"They are not to become an embarrassment to the Angolan authorities, Mr Halfhyde."

"I shall bear it in mind, sir."

"Please do. This business involves diplomacy and high affairs of state and international relations—would that it did not, and that the fish could be landed by anyone who was in a better position to cast a line!" Abruptly, Bassinghorn turned back to the chart, beckoning to Halfhyde who went to his side. "The Coanza—you see? The mouth is thirty miles to the south of São Paulo de Loanda, but that is not important, since the Portuguese have promised the eye of Nelson. What is important is the approach."

"The sand bar, sir—I know! It is dangerously liable to shifts, and there is strong surf from the South Atlantic. How far off will you lie, sir, to launch us?"

"Five miles. I'll not risk the ship closer in on a lee shore."

"And the task of the torpedo-boats made the more difficult by a night arrival!"

"I regret the necessity. It is important that our Portuguese friends—and never mind the Nelson eye—it is important that they are not unnecessarily or too openly embarrassed. You will recall that the rear-admiral was emphatic upon the point."

Halfhyde asked sardonically, "And if they become so?"

"Then they could have their hand forced against us. There is no love lost between them and the Germans, but they are under certain pressures from the southern borders. It is up to us to return co-operation with understanding." Bassinghorn tapped the chart, rested a pencil on a small cross to seaward of the river mouth and a shade to the north of it. "I shall lie off here, and you will be put overboard by the derricks. As soon as you are away, I shall take my ship to sea and steam for St Helena at slow speed. In St Helena I shall take bunkers for Gibraltar and the Channel."

"And my return, sir, with my boats' crews and Sir Russell Savory?"

"When your mission is ended successfully, you will make for Mossamedes—here, about one hundred miles north of Tiger Bay." Bassinghorn tapped the chart. "You'll contact the British consul and arrange for a telegram to be sent to St Helena. Within five days of the despatch of the telegram, I shall lie off Mossamedes to take you aboard." He paused. "Have you any questions, Mr Halfhyde?"

"At this moment, sir, none."

"Mr Todhunter?"

The detective inspector had been growing more and more restive. "Only this, sir: you and Mr Halfhyde . . . you've been talking in terms of thousands of miles—"

"Oh, come, Mr Todhunter, you exaggerate!"

"Well then, thousands of *square* miles. All bush and desert and swamp! How, sir, how, I ask you, am I ever to execute my warrant? I confess, Captain Bassinghorn, I see the business as a complete impossibility!" He threw up his hands in a gesture of despair.

Bassinghorn nodded slowly, ponderously. "You have my sympathy indeed."

"It's all very well, sir. You will be at sea, having landed me. From then on—"

"From then on, Mr Todhunter, it becomes a police matter— if with naval assistance still. It does not fall to me to criticize the Home Office and the Government, though I repeat that I could wish it had all been differently handled. You'll be aware, of course, that matters were much changed by the intelligence brought by the rear-admiral in Gibraltar."

"But boats!" Todhunter burst out, wiping sweat from his face with a vast coloured cotton handkerchief. "There is such a thing as a railway line, sir, as indeed I pointed out to my superiors in London—"

"And what did they reply, Mr Todhunter?"

"Why, sir, that boats could penetrate where as yet the railway didn't run."

Bassinghorn, catching Halfhyde's eye, suppressed a wide smile. "They said sooth, I fancy! And we have to do the best we can. Do not despair, Mr Todhunter, the British Navy is well accustomed to accomplishing the impossible. The totally impossible takes a little longer, that's all." He turned to Commander Percy. "Commander?"

"I fancy my part in this is limited," the commander said in a cold voice. "Limited, that is to say, to the safe lowering of the torpedo-boats. I take it Mr Halfhyde will be responsible for the provisioning, ammunitioning, and seaworthiness of his own command?"

"I shall be, sir," Halfhyde said. "I am already satisfied as to the seaworthiness and the condition of the engines—"

"Then I have but one question, sir," Commander Percy said, speaking to the captain. "If Mr Halfhyde is to lead his flotilla, who is to command the second torpedo-boat?"

"Do you wish to put forward names, Commander?"

"Lieutenant Portaby, sir, or Sub-Lieutenant Holmes. Both are first-class officers, and both would appreciate the experience."

"Quite so," Bassinghorn agreed. "Mr Halfhyde?"

Halfhyde said, "I prefer to pick my own second-in-command, sir. I am confident that both officers named are efficient and conscientious . . ." He paused. "I ask for time to consider both names, sir, and possibly one other whose name I shall perhaps suggest later."

Commander Percy seemed on the verge of a protest, but was waved down by Bassinghorn. "Mr Halfhyde's request is a natural one. He may take his time."

"Well met, Mr Runcorn. We have seen little of one another since leaving Devonport."

"Yes, sir." Runcorn saluted smartly, and remained at attention.

"Be easy, Mr Runcorn. You are still a shade too formal for my liking."

"Yes, sir. I'm sorry, sir." Mr Midshipman Runcorn, his white patches a dirty grey against the upstanding collar of the full whites into which the ship's company had now shifted as they came down towards the tropics, moved his feet apart into the at-ease position, and placed his hands smartly behind his back. Halfhyde looked down at him with concealed amusement. Runcorn, young for his age, was yet a good officer, eager, conscientious, and efficient. He had proved a tower of strength far beyond his years both in the Bight of Benin and in the Pacific, and he was a first-class boat handler. He, as well as Commander Percy's protégés, could do with the extra experience, the experience of command away from the ship. Besides, Halfhyde liked him; he was an old shipmate who had proved compatible, and in the days ahead compatibility was going to be of immense importance to their mission.

"Mr Runcorn," Halfhyde asked in a formal tone, "how would you like to be a captain?"

"Me, sir?" Eyes stared roundly, half suspecting a jest.

"Yes, you, sir. Well?"

"I would like it very much, sir! Very much indeed, sir! One day, perhaps—"

"That 'one day' can come sooner than you suspect, Mr Runcorn. Come with me." He placed a hand on the midshipman's shoulder, and drew him aft along the superstructure. He halted between the torpedo-boats, moved his hand from Runcorn's shoulder, and patted the hull of one of them. "A command of your own, Mr Runcorn, under the flag of Acting Rear-Admiral Halfhyde, with orders to proceed upon detached service! We're no strangers to that, Mr Runcorn, you and I. Well?"

"Sir, I don't know what to say, sir!"

"Then don't try to say too much. Yes will suffice, and I shall see to the rest."

"Then . . . oh, yes, sir! And thank you very much, sir!"

"Don't mention it. I'm glad to have you, Mr Runcorn. Stand by for orders shortly, and in the meantime, not a word to a soul."

"Yes, sir! No, sir!"

"Make up your mind," Halfhyde said with a grin. He returned the midshipman's salute and walked away to seek out the paymaster and the gunnery lieutenant to organize his requirements, leaving behind him a youth brimming over with anticipation.

Chapter 9

DOWN TO THE EQUATOR and beyond: daily the heat and the humidity grew more and more unbearable. Work became an effort, and the morning watchmen became objects of envy, for only then, as the early sun stole over the horizon and a faint breeze blew with the dawn, did life become, for a few short hours, a pleasant thing. The awnings were rigged now over fo'c'sle, bridge, superstructure, and quarterdeck—frapped each nightfall, they were spread when the sun grew strong, with the watch on deck hawk-eyed for the first sign of any wind that would cause them to be struck. Below-decks lurked a kind of hell, though all the ventilators were turned constantly to catch every slight and shifting stir of the air on deck. There was a heavy fug along the alleyways and in cabins and ward-room, and the stench of human sweat rotting the hammock mattresses and blankets in the mess decks. If there the heat was stifling, in the stokehold it was truly infernal. On the advice of the fleet surgeon, the stokers now worked for no more than twenty minutes at a stretch before being allowed on to the upper-deck for a merciful spell before returning to the clanging shovels and coal dust and furnace mouths. With von Merkatz now likely to be coming up behind once more, the captain urgently wanted a constant full head of steam in all his boilers; and this was maintained within a pound or two, about which small drop Bassinghorn made no overt complaint. It was left to Commander Percy to sniff superciliously at the coal-grimed stokers in their deplorable vests and sweat cloths who were sullying the scrubbed alleyways and leaving trails of their calling behind them upon the fo'c'sle.

He took the fleet surgeon aside. "The stokers are entitled to fresh air, of course; but quite so much, and quite so often, Doctor?"

"I've already told the captain, I regard it as the minimum essential."

"In your opinion?"

"Naturally, in my opinion!"

The commander made a grimace. "Sometimes, Doctor, I find myself doubting the worth of your opinion. Before Gibraltar, I was most positively not sick!"

"The thermometer told a different story, Commander. In any case, the stokers must have proper rest from such continual sweating—it drains a man's body and leads to total collapse. You appear not to think the stokers are human beings."

Percy put his head back and looked the fleet surgeon up and down, coldly, seeming to concentrate his gaze upon the red distinction cloth between the three gold stripes on the shoulder straps of the white uniform, non-executive cloth that, in Percy's view, robbed its wearer of proper authority. Then he turned on his heel and stalked away, back towards the quarterdeck still clean and free of stokers. Glancing up as he went past the heavy battery in its twin turrets, he saw Halfhyde on the superstructure above, making a final overhaul of the torpedo-boats with the boatswain and gunner now that they were beginning to near the Coanza River.

He halted, hands behind his back, and called up. "Mr Halfhyde?"

Halfhyde looked down. "Yes?"

"A word, if you please."

"I'm all attention, sir. Pray proceed."

The commander flushed. "I do not propose to bawl from here, like an urchin at play. Come down at once, Mr Halfhyde!"

Halfhyde opened his mouth, but shut it again before any indiscretion should emerge. He turned away from the guardrail and clattered down the ladder to the gundeck. "Now, sir, what is it?"

Percy was looking angry. "I gather you have had words with the captain, in regard to who shall command the second torpedo-boat. I understand you have asked for—"

"Runcorn, sir. That is correct. I believe the captain is favourably disposed?"

"He is," the commander answered shortly, "but I am not, and have said as much. However, the choice has been made and there is no more to be said, except this: there are many dangers to be faced ashore in Angola and you must expect casualties. If you yourself should become one, then in my view Mr Runcorn has not the age or experience to assume command of the expedition. In the event of any subsequent enquiry, I shall make it very clear what my views were. That is all, Mr Halfhyde."

Commander Percy stalked away. Halfhyde stood for a moment glaring at his departing back, then swung away with an angry laugh. Age came only with the act of growing older; but experience came from taking part, from learning to take charge, and was a more positive attribute than age; and it did not come from cotton wool or mothballs. Nevertheless there was truth in the commander's words, especially as regarded age. Mr Midshipman Runcorn, as Halfhyde had reflected earlier, was indeed young for his years. When Halfhyde had told him the facts about Sir Russell Savory and their mission, Mr Runcorn's reaction had held a hint of the fifth form and never mind his years in the training ship *Britannia* and his subsequent sea-time as cadet and midshipman. Mr Runcorn, in spite of being prepared by certain rumours that had swept the ship via the galley wireless and the attentive ears of the captain's servant, had been scandalized into a schoolboy's crimson blush. To him, a traitor was almost unbelievable, the lowest possible thing to crawl upon God's earth. Mr Runcorn was young enough not to appreciate the pull of money and power—but he would mature. As to the rest of it, Halfhyde knew that Bassinghorn himself had had his doubts about the possible risk, but had been swayed by Halfhyde's insistence and by the fact of the previous partnerships between the lieutenant and the midshipman that had achieved success. Halfhyde went back to the torpedo-boats, frowning and preoccupied. Success was more than ever important this time in Bassinghorn's interest: Commander Percy had uttered a carefully concealed threat to the captain as well as to Halfhyde.

It was night now, and the hour was almost come: The boatswain was imparting last-minute advice.

"Not the blue serge, Mr Todhunter."

"You think not?"

Sam Strawbridge, sweating his fat away into the tightness of his white uniform, was positive. "It is hot now, and God knows how you stand it! On an African river, you'll melt like a pusser's candle on the galley stove. You must dress for the country you're in, Mr Todhunter. Surely you were told?"

The detective inspector nodded, and drew away from a cockroach that had invaded the mess. "Yes, to be sure, but . . . well, I suppose I must adapt. I've brought white shirts, of course, and trousers of a less heavy material—"

"Then wear them, and go coatless in the daytime, and leave the bowler hat aboard." Strawbridge pulled out his watch. "There's not long to go now. You'll have a rough trip through the surf and over the sand bar, but don't worry too much. From what I've seen of Mr Halfhyde, you'll be in good hands, Mr Todhunter."

"Yes, yes. He inspires confidence, I fancy."

"Aye, he does that." Strawbridge chuckled. "So does gin. You'll take a tot?"

Todhunter shook his head. "No, thank you." He glanced around the warrant officers' mess, deserted at this late hour except for the torpedo gunner, sound asleep in a leather armchair. Todhunter felt a twinge of regret at being about to leave. The mess had become home, and was a firm link with England and the more familiar world of the Metropolitan Police. The foreseeable future held strangeness and alarm. Mr Todhunter was a good police officer for whom criminals—murderers, swindlers, thieves—held no terrors. The arrest of Sir Russell Savory, if ever he was caught up with, would be no problem to Mr Todhunter—but Africa itself was a different kettle of fish. Africa was a place he had read about only in books—extensively read about of late, on account of his mission—and the reading matter made much of crocodiles, elephants, lions, spiders, snakes, and poisonous fish. And there was a great deal of disease: malaria, blackwater fever, yellow fever, beri-beri. Mr Todhunter tried to find comfort in the undoubted fact that white people did manage to live in Africa without succumbing, but this thought led him inevitably towards the large number of white people who, in succumbing, had never returned to England. Mr Todhunter broke out into a fresh sweat: he would be immensely glad to set foot aboard the *Prince Consort* again in due time. He thought about his blue serge suit. He was fussing and he knew it, but the blue serge represented the authority of the Law of England. He had always worn blue serge, on duty and off—always! Without it he was naked, stripped bare of his inspectorship; it was his uniform, his respectability in the eyes of his fellows and of his criminal adversaries. He would take it with him, just in case, in his gladstone bag; it would offer comfort and could even be a talisman against ill luck.

Bassinghorn, dead-reckoning from his last position obtained by star sight from the navigator's sextant, the chronometer, and the *Nautical Almanac,* approached his determined area for the launch. Halfhyde, with him on the bridge, stared through his telescope towards the distant shore, picking up the white, luminous line of the breaking surf. A light wind, on to the shore, capped the short waves with small white horses. That wind was warm and moist and sticky, bringing no comfort with it. A curious quiet now permeated the whole ship; Bassinghorn had ordered the engines to slow some while before, and the machinery sounds were muted, as though the very engines were holding their breath in anticipation. Men moved quietly about the decks. Orders were given in low voices or by hand movements, as the lowerers of both watches moved to their places at the mainmast boom for swinging out the torpedo-boats from their crutches under the direction of the first lieutenant and Sam Strawbridge. Runcorn, filled with eagerness, was standing by his command importantly, assuring Mr Todhunter that he would take the water without mishap, for the detective inspector had been somewhat alarmed by the order that both boats' crews should wear lifejackets for the launching, and indeed for the whole passage inward until they had crossed the bar in safety.

From the bridge a few minutes later the captain passed the order: "Stop engines, wheel amidships."

The telegraph and repeater bells rang, the ship slid on in her silence, gradually easing her way as the screws died to stillness. The onshore wind sighed eerily through the standing rigging. The captain turned to Halfhyde. "There we are, Mr Halfhyde. You may swing out the boats as soon as you wish."

"I'm ready now, sir."

"Very well." Bassinghorn turned to the officer of the watch and gave a brief order. A boatswain's mate went down the ladder, piping for all seamen to clear the lowerdeck and man the ropes of the great four-fold purchases that would lower the torpedo-boats, after lifting them out over the water. "Good luck, Halfhyde, and a safe and speedy return. And a successful one."

"Thank you, sir."

There was a whimsical smile on Bassinghorn's large face, visible in the glow from the binnacle lamp. "Take good care of the strong arm of the law, Halfhyde. When he took his leave of me, I fancied I detected signs of strain and anxiety!"

"A fish out of water, sir. When the time comes for him to

act as a policeman, he'll shape up as though he were back in Scotland Yard. It's bred in the bone, like seamanship—they run true to type, our British bobbies!"

"I trust so." Bassinghorn held out a hand, which Halfhyde took and gripped warmly, and then turned away down the ladder to the superstructure. Already the hands were mustering, waiting to take the ropes and back them up when the order was passed to lower away the first of the boats from the boom which was now raised on its topping-lift. No time was lost: as soon as Halfhyde and Runcorn had reported their respective boats' crews present and correct, and the steadying lines had been bent on fore and aft, the first lieutenant ordered the coxswains, bowmen, and sternsheetsmen aboard. The remainder were ordered to go down the whips of the blocks once the boats took the water. At this there was a protest from the detective inspector.

"Oh, dear, I'd really rather not!"

Sam Strawbridge came up and spoke to the first lieutenant, quietly. Mr Todhunter was given permission to embark from the gundeck. Cautiously, he prepared to do so. Sam Strawbridge moved to his side and slid something hard and flat into his hand. "A flask o'whisky, Mr Todhunter."

"Oh, no—"

"Take it! You may have a need of it, who knows?" The boatswain grasped his other hand. "Do every one of us a favour and get that perishin' traitor, eh?"

"What? I've never said—"

"No, you haven't said a thing, Mr Todhunter, but you know there's been rumours. Loud voices, like, and big ears—it had to come out. And I never did hear the like o' what the bugger's done. Low enough to crawl under a snake's arse with a tall hat on, he is! The whole ship's behind you. Goodbye and good luck, old mate!"

"Mate?"

"That's what I called you," Strawbridge said gruffly. "D'you mind? Meant for a compliment it were."

Todhunter nodded, and pressed the boatswain's hand. There was quite a lump in his throat and he found he couldn't utter. But the next moment he almost uttered a most unpoliceman-like scream: the torpedo-boat, as he stepped on to the gunwhale to be taken into the arms of the coxswain, had swayed alarmingly between the steadying lines, and had it not been for the coxswain he would have fallen between it and the ship's side and dropped sheer down into the unfriendly black of the South Atlantic Ocean. Gasping a little, and clinging to his gladstone bag until it was taken from him, he stood teetering on the gunwhale. He tried hard to summon up enough nerve to step down into a kind of cockpit set amidships between a shallow compartment forward and an equally shallow cabin aft.

"Mr Todhunter," the first lieutenant called sharply. "Smack it about, if you please."

"What?"

"*Hurry,* Mr Todhunter!"

"Oh." Pulled by the coxswain, Mr Todhunter hurried. He was stood on his feet in the midships wheelhouse and asked to remain still and silent while the torpedo-boat was lowered. It was a nasty sensation as they travelled downwards and there was a jolt and a splash as they took the water . . . Todhunter mopped at his face and looked upwards. Halfhyde, with the rest of the boat's crew, swarmed down the rope falls and landed easily upon the narrow deck inside the guardrails. Led by Halfhyde and a torpedo-gunner's mate, they dropped down amidships. The ratings vanished into a canopied compartment leading off forward, while the bowman and sternsheetsman remained to bear off from the *Prince Consort*'s side with long boathooks. Halfhyde waved up to the deck, and the falls were slackened away for the blocks to be cast off the ring-bolts. As soon as this had been done, the hands on deck backed up the falls and hoisted the blocks clear, and the main boom was swung away to put Runcorn's boat into the water. Halfhyde passed his first order to his miniature engine-room:

"Engine slow ahead. Wheel ten degrees to port."

They were away. Mr Todhunter mopped his forehead as two thin funnels set abreast of each other before the cockpit began belching thick clouds of smoke. Mopping, he came into contact with something hard. From force of long habit, and despite the advice of Sam Strawbridge, he found his bowler hat in place.

"We proceed in line ahead, the junior boat taking station two cables' lengths astern," Halfhyde explained. "When we reach the surf, it's each boat for itself. Shortly before that, Runcorn will shift station abeam. All right, Mr Todhunter?"

Todhunter nodded, looking astern with longing. His boat had been joined by Runcorn's off the battleship's port bow, and both had turned for the distant shore. The moment they were on their proper course, the *Prince Consort*'s huge black bulk had swung away, turning to starboard to head for St Helena. She left behind her a starkly lonely feeling. The thrust of her screws sent back a turbulence that brought queasiness to the policeman's stomach—the torpedo-boat smelled unpleasantly oily, and the after cabin would be fuggy, he was certain; and the short, sharp motion was unlike that of the battleship. Bile rose in his throat, but he fought it down.

"What is the surf like, Mr Halfhyde?" he asked.

"Nasty, but you shall soon find out in some detail."

"And dangerous?"

Halfhyde laughed. "Think not about danger, Mr Todhunter! Forget it, and concentrate your mind on the future instead." He brought up his telescope and stared ahead: the line of surf stood out clearly, washing the shore with spray-capped rollers, surging across the sand bar into the river mouth. The passage of the surf was their first obstacle, and a nasty one: the West African surf was normally best navigated in native dugout canoes manned by skilled blacks from the coast-dwelling tribes. Halfhyde gripped the rail ahead of him until his knuckles stood out white in the darkness. He had made this kind of passage before, and so had Runcorn. He must have faith in the judgment and skill of both of them, and he must never falter. As the torpedo-boats came within a half mile of the first of the lines of surf, he trained the boat's battery-operated signal lamp on the vessel astern, and gave two flashes. At once Runcorn turned to port, and, as Halfhyde slowed his engines momentarily, came up on the beam of the leader. Halfhyde put a hand on his coxswain's shoulder.

"Take it steady, Cox'n. Hold her ahead, come what may."

"Aye, aye, sir." The coxswain, a three-badge petty officer, solid and dependable, chewed steadily on a quid of evil-smelling ship's tobacco, his eyes attentive to his course. Halfhyde ducked down and shouted below the canopy of the forward compartment, warning the seamen to hold on for their lives. He gave a similar order to Todhunter, advising him to cling fast to the brass rail in front of him and to brace his body back against the after bulkhead with his feet against the forward coaming.

"Take your weight on the cheeks of your arse, Mr Todhunter," he shouted above the rising roar of the surf. "It's soft and pliable and has no bones to break!"

Todhunter's voice was high, desperate. "Shall we not be dashed to pieces, Mr Halfhyde?"

Halfhyde shook his head. "I think not—I trust not! We're too far off the beach to do what I would otherwise do, which is to drop two anchors and veer in on my cables, with the rudder unshipped. But have no fear, Mr Todhunter, I shall bring you through in one piece rather than many!"

A moment later they were into the rearing rollers and all hell had broken loose. To Halfhyde it felt as though the craft were bouncing to destruction on some appallingly hard surface, a surface that must surely smash the bottom-plating. When this ceased for a while there was a curious and unnerving lift of the bows, so much so that the boat seemed to stand upon her stern, up-and-down like a mast. Steadying for a mere fraction of a second, she disappeared into a great flurry of spray that dropped aboard and swilled her below like a hundred deck hoses. Then her head went down and she plunged into the deeps before being checked with a jolt that threatened to break her back and dislodge the men that were clinging like so many leeches inside her belly. After this came a short, very short, period of calm before the second surfline gripped her and hurled her ferociously forwards towards the still distant beach. As if by a miracle, Petty Officer Rawlings held her steady and safe to Halfhyde's yelled orders. The roar of the surf deafened them all, as did the attendant sound of solid water and spray dropping aboard to drench and flood. Flood was a very present danger; in such awesome conditions it was impossible for any man to spare a hand for the pumps. In the tiny stokehold, the furnace doors were clipped tight shut to prevent burning coal flying out. The bunkers, filled to capacity as they were, shook and clanged like a shipyard with a million rivetters at work together. Mr Todhunter's eyes were as tight shut as the furnace doors, and his lips moved rapidly in prayer, at least until the horrible gush came and cruelly parted them into a great round o like the runaway pipe of a battleship's bilge. After what seemed hours, there was a great shout from Halfhyde, a shout that carried across the tearing racket of the surf:

"River mouth dead ahead, by God's good grace!"

They plunged on, every piece of metal and timber shrieking in agony, bumping, bouncing, climbing, sliding, jerking. As the boat sped through the last line of the surf, a difference in the cufuffle beyond indicated the approach to the sand bar. Beyond this was comparative calm, no spray leaping luminously against the dark of the land.

Halfhyde called, "Engine to slow ahead, steady as you go." Then a moment later, a sudden yell almost at the extremity of his lung power as he saw the shoal ahead: *"Hard a-starboard, engine full astern!"* As the boat swung to safety, Todhunter gasped, and reached out to seize Halfhyde's arm in an urgent grip. Halfhyde shook him free, furiously. Then he saw what had disturbed the policeman—away on the starboard beam, widely separated now from the leader, was Runcorn's command, lying on her beam ends and spilling men into the boiling inshore surf-line.

Chapter 10

"I'M SORRY, RUNCORN. To use a sailing term incorrectly, I was in irons. Had I turned right across the surf, more men would have been lost. As it was, I very nearly grounded on the bar."

Runcorn nodded: he was dumbstruck, suffering the misery of losing a boat beneath him, of losing lives—of the seamen and engine-room ratings under his personal command, four were unaccounted for. A fifth body, head down and sluggish in the pounding surf, had followed Halfhyde's boat across the bar and lay in the less turbulent waters of the river mouth. Halfhyde, leaving his command in the care of his coxswain, had plunged over the side and, at risk of his life, had fought back through the surf to give what help he could. The torpedo-boat was a total loss, already breaking up under the impact of the rollers, but the survivors were now safe aboard the leader.

Runcorn found his tongue. "I'm sorry, sir."

"No apologies, Snotty. It was the luck of the game. It could have happened to me, and nearly did. I take it you took the sand?"

"Yes, sir."

Halfhyde said solemnly, "It was a miracle that any of us got through. But with God's help, the Navy is well capable of performing miracles, at least in the view of Their Lordships who issue the orders for their performance!"

"But I failed Their Lordships, sir, and you as well."

Halfhyde put a hand on Runcorn's shoulder. "Not so. We're in the river and we're a force in being, and that's what counts! Cheer up, lad, and don't dwell on misfortune, or misfortune will most positively dwell on you like a flea on a dog." Halfhyde looked about him, straining his eyes through the dark. A fitful moon peeped through heavy cloud. At this time of the year the seasonal rains of the tropics seemed to come and go according to their whim. Now, the moon's light showed Runcorn's torpedo-boat in its death throes. There was nothing to be done about that, nor about the vanished bodies that by morning would have been cast up along the beach. There was no time for a lengthy search, and little point in it either. The Portuguese authorities must suffer an unwanted embarrassment at a British landing that could not now be disguised, and Halfhyde could only hope for as small a fracture of diplomacy as might be pos-sible. Fleetingly, there came into his mind the thought that Commander Percy would sneer many I-told-you-so's when the news reached him that Mr Midshipman Runcorn had made a monkey's arse of his job . . . but these unwelcome thoughts were quickly put aside, for sneers could be transferred into official reports and made permanent; and it behove a naval officer upon a dangerous mission to think success and not failure. For now, there was one thing that could be done, and therefore must be. Halfhyde said, "Mr Runcorn, the poor fellow who came in astern of me. He is caught in the reeds ahead. He at least shall be decently buried, and not left to rot in the open air."

"Yes, sir."

"Then stir yourself, Mr Runcorn, and detail hands for the

work. We have an urgent need for speed now." He added, "The
ground is soft, and there are shovels in the engine-room."

The dead man, a leading stoker, was buried some twenty yards
back from the Coanza river's bank by a burial party whose
members pushed through the reeds and trod the oozing mud
and sand with care, fearful of what horrible crawling creatures
they might disturb. As the grave was filled in Halfhyde murmured prayers, his hand at the salute before they all turned
away and trudged back, no one speaking a word. They went
aboard the now overcrowded torpedo-boat as silently, impressed
by the desolation of the burial, by the act of leaving a shipmate
in slimy mud on a foreign shore, a less clean ending than sailors
would normally expect. It was Detective Inspector Todhunter
who broke the grim silence.

"I'm very sorry, Mr Halfhyde and Mr Runcorn. I know how
you feel. Not long ago I lost a constable, also drowned while
following his duty. In the Thames, the result of a fracas and a
knife thrust. One feels it personally."

"You're right, Mr Todhunter—right indeed! I thank you for
saying so."

"It was sincerely said, Mr Halfhyde."

"I don't doubt it." Suddenly, on an impulse, Halfhyde held
out a hand. "I've not been as friendly as I should have been.
You police . . . yes, you also have an often dangerous duty, more
often than many people realize, I fancy. From now on, we shall
work well together."

"Nice of you to say so, Mr Halfhyde." Todhunter looked
away in some embarrassment. "We're often figures of fun, too,

the butt of jokes. It's natural, no doubt; the British do not take kindly to men in uniform poking their noses in . . . and the image of the Bow Street Runners persists still."

"Then, since they had a reputation for getting their man, Mr Todhunter, we shall let it persist 'til we catch up with our friend Savory." Halfhyde turned to the midshipman. "Mr Runcorn, you shall be my commander, my navigating officer, and currently my officer of the watch also. Take the boat up river, if you please, without more delay."

"Yessir!" Runcorn saluted smartly. Moonlight revealed the return of eagerness in the young face and eyes. "Engine slow ahead, Coxswain, and helm ten degrees to port." The torpedo-boat moved out with a belch of smoke from her twin funnels, and pointed her bows up river for onward passage to Dondo. Runcorn gave his orders decisively and needed no help from Halfhyde in keeping the torpedo-boat on a safe midstream course clear of obstructions from the banks, assisted by a lead-ing seaman acting as leadsman and making constant casts of his line. As Halfhyde had discovered in the past, Runcorn was a born boat handler, and he already had his confidence back now that he was being trusted and seen to be trusted in the eyes of the ratings. Halfhyde let him have the watch for an hour. Then he sent him below to the after cabin—the tiny space that served as ward-room and in which it was impossible for even a short man to stand up—to find what sleep he could in a sea-soaked bunk. Halfhyde himself remained on deck throughout the night, conning the torpedo-boat on her journey around the twists of the river, seeing, as the dawn came up, the occasional crocodile sliding scalily into the cover of reeds and tall grasses, seeing now and again a startled and incredulous native staring from behind trees and undergrowth at the smoking, chugging monster on the waters. As the light grew stronger and they began to come beneath the shade of overhanging trees on the fringe of thick jungle, Todhunter came on deck wearing his bowler hat, the headgear that he had managed to keep safe and sound all through the tempestuous surf passage of the night before.

"Good morning, Mr Halfhyde."

"Good morning! You're up bright and early, Mr Todhunter."

"I found myself quite unable to sleep. It's remarkably stuffy below-decks, and most wet."

"It'll be close up here as the day moves on."

"I don't doubt it." Mr Todhunter's roving and interested eye lit upon a black-skinned figure watching, like the earlier natives, from the bank. "Goodness me, Mr Halfhyde, what's that?"

"A local inhabitant. They're largely fishermen round here, with a leaning to the water rather than the land like the up-country tribes. But equally warlike."

"He seems to be carrying a weapon of some sort, Mr Halfhyde."

"Yes. A bow and arrow."

Mr Todhunter was much surprised. "Good gracious! Of course, I knew they were primitive." Smiling, he waved an arm in a vigorous and friendly gesture at the native. A second later, though he had been scarcely aware of any movement on the native's part, there was a buzz as of a bee above his head and his bowler hat fell to the end of its retaining toggle, spinning rapidly. "What was that?"

"An arrow, Mr Todhunter. When you waved, an act which I trust you will not repeat, he thought you were hurling something at him."

"Good gracious! Upon my soul!" Todhunter drew his body down below the gunwhale and examined his bowler: there was a nasty rip in the cloth. "When mother waved from the Clarence Pier at Southsea—"

Halfhyde laughed loudly. "Different ships, different long splices. The natives are not the same out here."

"Quite—quite. Forgive me. A stupid thing to say, as I realize, of course. It was an association of ideas."

"A natural comparing of your two seagoing experiences," Halfhyde said, his eyes glinting with suppressed laughter. "If I were you, Mr Todhunter, I'd refrain from demonstrative motions until decently friendly relations have been established."

"I most certainly shall!" Todhunter went below: stuffiness was better than arrows that might even be poisoned.

Halfhyde's command was capable of eighteen knots at full power, and, knowing the overriding necessity for speed, he drove her as fast as the river navigation allowed. By his reckoning he was making around fifteen knots over the bottom, but there were unavoidable delays to be faced and overcome. Fallen trees across the way had to be cleared—at some risk from the slithering tree snakes. On one occasion striking a half-submerged crocodile produced an impact that sent men staggering and swung the torpedo-boat off course while the angry brute flailed away down the side. Many times the water intake to the boiler became clogged with foul weed, and had to be cleared before navigation could continue. Rocks and rapids had to be negotiated carefully at dead slow speed on the engines. Thus, in spite of his good speed, it was late afternoon before Halfhyde heard the roar from ahead, the warning watery thunder of the Livingstone

Falls. At once he brought the engine down to slow and warned
the leadsman to report instantly when his lead-line began to
incline for'ard as the boat was taken astern by the rush of river
water from the falls. The moment it did so, he steered in for
the bank. The bowman and sternsheetman jumped ashore with
their lines, which they made fast to tree trunks. A sustained
rush of water from ahead gave the stationary torpedo-boat a
bow wave as though she were still under way. Runcorn asked,
"What now, sir?"

"For the moment, journey's end, Mr Runcorn. And some
projection into the future with Mr Todhunter."

"The time factor, sir—"

"Is urgent! You need not remind me. I have it well in mind.
But the human body must eat. You may pipe the hands to an
early supper, Mr Runcorn, and inform the ward-room steward
that we shall be ready to partake in half an hour's time. First,
I think, we shall consider the bar open."

Runcorn looked surprised. "The bar, sir?"

"You heard my orders," Halfhyde answered briskly. "Attend
to them at once, if you please, Mr Runcorn."

"Aye, aye, sir!" Runcorn passed the order to the coxswain,
who nodded at a seaman acting as boatswain's mate. Over the
unlikely surroundings of jungle and river, over the harsh cries
of brightly coloured birds and the muddy stirrings of crocodiles
on the farther bank, the metallic voice of Her Majesty's Navy
was heard as the boatswain's call shrilled and the order was
passed: "Hands to supper. Cooks of the mess to muster at the
galley." Halfhyde rubbed his hands pleasurably: Todhunter,
emerging from the apology for a ward-room, gaped in astonishment.

"I fancied for a moment I must be dreaming, Mr Halfhyde, and that I was back on board the *Prince Consort*."

"Excellent!" Halfhyde said. "That's the idea! Small we may be, but we wear the White Ensign, Mr Todhunter, and it is to be lived up to constantly."

"But have your men—"

"Slackening routine leads inevitably to sackening morale. The men are accustomed to routine from the moment they join the training ships, Mr Todhunter, and are lost without it. Myself, I have the reputation of being an unconventional naval officer, yet even I am forced to recognize certain immutable facts."

"At Scotland Yard—"

"I see no paving stones, Mr Todhunter, no charge rooms, cells, nor racks of truncheons. What I see is one of Her Majesty's ships of war in full commission and under my command." Airily Halfhyde waved a hand. "I shall not insist that you dress for dinner, Mr Todhunter."

"Well, I never," Todhunter muttered, and shook his head.

Halfhyde clapped him on the shoulder, smiled, and ducked down into the ward-room whose restricted space was almost completely filled with a table flanked by two bunks, the mattresses now dried out in the tiny boiler room and covered with standard issue blue service counterpanes bearing the naval crown in their pattern. In this space the seaman detailed as ward-room messman was struggling with a once starched white tablecloth: seizing one end of it, Halfhyde lent his assistance.

"Thankee, sir."

"That's all right, Holleyman. When you've done, there's whisky and glasses in the cupboard beneath Mr Runcorn's bunk. Or have you already made this discovery?"

"Yessir, I have, sir."

"I trust you've drunk none of it, Holleyman?"

"Me, sir?" The reply was indignant. "Dear me, no, sir, I wouldn't do that, sir!"

"I'm glad to hear it. Let us consider the ward-room bar open. A glass, if you please, and two fingers of whisky. No water, since we shall need our stocks if the rains and pools fail us. I should not wish to drink the river water! And for you, Holleyman, messman's perks."

The seaman knew the drill and responded with gratitude. "Thankee, sir, much obliged indeed, sir."

"*One* finger."

"Yessir, o' course, sir."

When the whisky was brought, Halfhyde sat in silence, sipping the raw spirit absently. A moment later Todhunter came down and sat himself upon the other bunk. Mr Runcorn, coming aft from checking the mooring ropes, sat upon the step leading from the midships cockpit. Both refused whisky, and Halfhyde did not press them. Closing his eyes, he pondered. Todhunter, he was convinced, would have no ideas to offer at this stage. Once within, as it were, detective track of his quarry, Todhunter would start functioning mentally again. As for himself, his duty was clear and, in the saying thereof, simple and direct. He must lead his small ship's company, with their rifles and bayonets and the three heavy-calibre service revolvers issued aboard the *Prince Consort* to himself, Runcorn, and Todhunter, south towards Silva Porto and the tracks down to the frontier of German South-West Africa. Just that. All at once the needle-in-a-haystack element struck Halfhyde like a blow between the eyes. Up to this moment he had been too busy, too occupied with ship matters and navigation, to worry. But Africa was immense, a brooding and very dark continent filled with extravagant dangers and pitfalls, and the Germans would be on the watch. And with equal suddenness Halfhyde saw the British agents, those shadowy men working inside Angola and keeping their checks on Savory's movements, as being so insubstantial as to be virtually worthless . . .

The messman came back, bearing plates of food from the stove shared by officers and men—bully beef from a tin, overlaid with thick gravy, and some uninteresting potatoes. Halfhyde stirred and opened his eyes.

"Filthy," he observed. "But no doubt nourishing. Clean plates afterwards, if you please, gentlemen. This promises to be our last civilized meal for a while. And you'll not be sleeping in your bunks tonight, either."

Runcorn looked up. "Not, sir?"

"Not, Mr Runcorn. We march tonight, since time presses. After dinner, you will fall in the ship's company ashore, with all their equipment and stores for the river passage, leaving a leading seaman and two ABs as shipkeepers, also a stoker. They are to remain—" He broke off, holding up a hand for silence. From the distance a thin cry was heard, a cry that became a scream of terror, followed by two rifle shots in quick succession, and then another scream. Then silence.

Chapter 11

HALFHYDE was out of the ward-room in an instant, thrusting Runcorn aside. He called down to Todhunter to bring the revolvers from their stowage beneath his bunk. From the midship cockpit he looked around. He saw nothing living, only death. On the river's surface, moving downstream on the rush of water from the falls, was a crocodile, belly uppermost, dead, but with a man's body still clamped in the teeth.

Halfhyde swore. At his side, Runcorn said suddenly, "There, sir. A man . . . in the trees." The midshipman pointed. "He's coming out now, sir!"

"So I observe, Mr Runcorn."

"What shall we do, sir?"

"We shall let him come. He's white."

"Perhaps German, sir. And he is armed, sir."

"I think British, sir. There is no look of the German race." Halfhyde studied the man as he approached; the rifle was held like a sporting gun, beneath one arm and pointed downwards. The man was tall and very thin with a walrus moustache. He was dressed in a full-skirted khaki bush jacket, torn and dirty but worn with an air of authority, and a white pith helmet of non-military pattern and equally dirty. Large sweat patches showed darkly on the fabric of the bush jacket. Lifting an arm, the man waved and called out in a loud, carrying voice,

"Lieutenant Halfhyde, I presume?" He laughed. "If so, then well met by Livingstone Falls!"

"Well met indeed—perhaps," Halfhyde answered, his fingers around the trigger of the revolver passed to him by Todhunter. "May I enquire, sir, who you are?"

The man came closer, and halted by the torpedo-boat's after mooring line. "Certainly. Major Forbes, at your service. Forbes of Rothiemay, and of the 93rd Highlanders."

"The Argyll and Sutherland?"

"As now known." Major Forbes doffed his helmet, and bowed. The last of the sun fell on white hair—he was a good deal older than Halfhyde had at first thought. "When the army reorganization in '81 brought change, I arranged my secondment to the West African Frontier Force."

"A considerable change."

"A considerable change indeed. May I come aboard?"

"One moment," Halfhyde said. He gestured down the river. "That man—that crocodile—"

"Both dead. I shot them. I am a good shot. You will have seen, perhaps, that the man was white. I committed murder as an act of mercy."

"A friend, Major?"

Forbes smiled, showing very white teeth for a man of his years. "A German. There may be others. I think I should come aboard quickly, if you don't mind."

There was a gasp from Todhunter. Halfhyde said, "First an explanation. How do you know who I am?"

Forbes shrugged. "I'm in touch with the British government from time to time. I happen to be a British agent working in Rhodesia, and I have occasional contact by telegraph."

"You've heard from Gibraltar?"

"No. From Whitehall. Allow me to substantiate myself: your captain's name is Henry Bassinghorn. His brother is a country parson in Cambridgeshire. His second-in-command is named Percy—one of the Northumberland Percys—"

Halfhyde laughed. "All right, Major! You may come aboard." He reached out a hand, and assisted Forbes across the gap of water. The Scot had a grip of steel, and his body, whatever his age, was hard and wiry. He was in excellent physical shape, his back straight as a ramrod, his eyes bright in a mahogany-brown face.

He said, "As you'll have gathered by now, I am under orders to make contact with you and the man from the London police." He looked around. "Which is he?"

Todhunter removed his bowler hat. "Detective Inspector Todhunter, sir, and very pleased to meet you."

"How d'you do." Forbes surveyed the headgear. "I really had no need to ask, had I? Stupid of me. But to go on . . . I fell in with a German, a man in plain clothes but obviously a soldier. *He* fell in with a crocodile, not by my agency since I would have wished to question him, but such is life in Africa. The point is this: as I said, there may be other Germans around, and—"

"Upon a mission similar to your own, Major—to find us?"

"Exactly! I don't know what your plans are, but I advise you to remain with your boat for the time being."

"I intended looking for native canoes beyond the falls."

Forbes nodded. "I thought as much. I am here to assist you in that, as a matter of fact. Meanwhile I suggest you remain here a little longer. I doubt if I'm known to the Germans, but your boat is somewhat obvious. If there are any more in the vicinity, they may attack. You can sustain an attack better aboard, I fancy."

Halfhyde pondered. "They may decide to wait until we go ashore. If we allow them to lay siege to us, and delay us, we shall not find Savory." He paused. "Major, do you suppose the Germans have some knowledge of my movements? Or is their presence here merely fortuitous?"

"I can't say. I understand the German naval authorities had intended despatching ships under Paulus von Merkatz, but—"

"He was delayed in Gibraltar!" Briefly, Halfhyde outlined the facts. Forbes, away from his base for many weeks, had heard nothing of this, and was vastly amused. Halfhyde asked, "What of Savory? Do you know his whereabouts?"

"Well south," Forbes said. "I can offer nothing more specific. You spoke of delay. Delay is certainly to be deplored, but if you and your men are wiped out tonight, the delay will pass into infinity, will it not?"

Halfhyde lifted an eyebrow at the detective inspector. "Mr Todhunter?"

Todhunter cleared his throat and seemed to be taking a grip on his obvious fears of the African bush; there was a new light of determination in his eye. "Well, Mr Halfhyde, I suppose the decision's yours. But my duty's clear enough, and so were my orders. I have to execute my warrant, sir, and never mind the risk. I'd rather get on with it."

Halfhyde nodded. "Bravely said, Mr Todhunter. You will prove tough meat for any cannibal's cooking pot—"

"Oh, my God." Todhunter went pale.

"Merely a joke, Mr Todhunter, and I apologize. Major, do I understand you can lead me to some canoes?"

"I can, if that's what you want."

"I do, Major. But we'll not march yet—we'll wait till full dark, and see what we shall see in the meantime. For now, dinner awaits us—and you also, of course. There is whisky as well."

Forbes rubbed his hands together. "Is there, by jove! Damn it all, you fellows live in the lap of luxury!"

After doubling up the watch on deck and leaving Runcorn in charge, Halfhyde led the way through the entry to the wardroom. The food had grown cold, but neither Halfhyde nor Todhunter was in a mood to care. A plate was brought for Forbes, who ate with a ravenous hunger and made no bones about accepting a second helping. The whisky went down his throat like water, brightening his eye even more but having no other visible effect. He talked much about Savory.

"A swine, sir. A damn blackguard! Though I'm a soldier first and foremost, I make no bones about saying the Navy is our first line of defence. Storm-tossed British ships—and all that! Napoleon Bonaparte, who was not given to praising the British— said they stood between him and the dominion of the world. He was right. Yes, my dear fellow, thank you." He held out his glass in response to Halfhyde who had lifted the whisky bottle in his direction. "Thank you, that'll do. I'm told if those blueprints reach Berlin, we may as well start learning how to kiss the Kaiser's backside."

"You don't exaggerate, Major."

"And we can't have that." Forbes leaned across the small table, his eyes luminous in the electric light that had now been switched on overhead, powered by the torpedo-boat's dynamo. "What do *you* know of Savory, Halfhyde? And you, Todhunter?"

"For me," Halfhyde said, "only what I was told before leaving Devonport, and that was to remain between my captain and myself."

"Then I shall not ask you to break a confidence," Forbes said at once. "Todhunter, my dear fellow?"

Todhunter started on his official formula of date and place of birth, origins, career. Forbes cut him short. "Yes, yes. I refer to the man himself—his desires and ambitions, his personality. I gather he's never quite reached the heights he intended, and has seen the end of the road ahead. He's highly placed, of course, but is unlikely to achieve the summit."

Todhunter nodded. "In Germany he will seek to attain what he sees as denied him here—even though it is said that no country appreciates a traitor."

Forbes murmured, "And truly said, I think! Which suggests to me that he may have friends, German friends, in high places. A mere supposition, of course, but worth mentioning perhaps. It would account for the curious risks he's taking." He changed the subject abruptly. "We shall see, we shall see. Your boat, my dear Halfhyde. What do you propose to do about it?"

"My shipkeepers will have orders to remain in case I have need of the boat, Major, but after seven days to proceed to the river mouth and wait for the *Prince Consort,* which will lie off after she has picked me up from Mossamedes."

Forbes nodded. "I'll give you some assistance. After we reach my landing, I'll come back and take up more comfortable quarters aboard—with your permission, of course?"

"I'll be grateful," Halfhyde said. He looked around. "Well, gentlemen, it's dark enough now and we must be on our way, and risk the Germans."

Disembarkation was carried out in silence, with no boatswain's calls to disturb the brooding darkness of Africa. Equally silently the hands melted towards the jungle with rifles and equipment, including all the food and water that could be carried. Once again the moon was fitful, but remained clouded until they were safely into the trees and making their difficult way along the track indicated by Forbes, who marched ahead with his rifle, seeming to know his way blindfolded. The men marched in single file with Halfhyde and Todhunter behind Forbes and a torpedo-gunner's mate behind Todhunter. Runcorn and the second torpedo-gunner's mate brought up the rear. Each man held on to the shoulder of his next ahead, so that they wound along the narrow, twisting trail like a snake, flicked and lacerated by branches, feet sinking into swampy mud until they put distance between themselves and the river. The dugout canoes, Forbes had said, were some six miles' march ahead, a flanking march around the great Livingstone Falls whose thunderous roar could be heard more clearly as the line of men moved on. The darkness was total, the atmosphere thick and humid and stinking, and even breathing seemed difficult. Mr Todhunter made his way fearfully, thinking of snakes and spiders; every now and again he uttered a stifled yelp as feet or hands touched possible unpleasantness, perhaps mercifully concealed from his gaze. He felt it to be a miracle that he was not eaten or poisoned in the first mile; and saw another miraculous intervention by the Almighty insofar as no Germans had manifested themselves—it now seemed likely that the German killed by the shot from Forbes's rifle, or by the teeth of the crocodile, had been a mere chancer, or at any rate alone. Suddenly Major Forbes, in the lead, stopped dead, a cannoning effect shot down the line, and Todhunter found himself viciously squeezed flat between Halfhyde and the torpedo-gunner's mate, whose rifle butt dug hard into his kidneys.

Forbes whispered: "Someone ahead, I fancy."

"Someone," Halfhyde asked, "or something?"

"Human. Gone too still for an animal of any size. Get your men off the track, into the trees—scatter, as wide as possible."

Halfhyde passed the order back, mouth to mouth. He took Todhunter's arm. "Keep with me," he whispered. "Down on all fours, and move left." He pulled and thrust. With the rest of the party, they wriggled into the undergrowth. It was wet and smelly, slimily unpleasant. Something like a great fat slug landed upon the flesh of Todhunter's neck, and he almost screamed. He pulled himself together. It was probably, he thought, a bloodsucking leech. Feeling behind, he removed it, his flesh cringing. With their bayonetted rifles at the ready, the seamen lay still and silent, ears straining through the darkness. For a while nothing happened. Then there was a loud report and a flash of fire, from ahead and a little to the left, and, almost in the same split second, another from closer at hand: Forbes. Forbes was still standing, as Halfhyde saw in the brief flash, and his aim had been true. A strangled cry indicated a hit, and after it Halfhyde heard the major's crashing progress through the jungle. He got up and followed the sounds, his revolver cocked. He cannoned into Forbes, who cursed him.

"I apologize, Major."

"Oh, never mind. We have another dead 'un."

"German, by any chance?"

"Hard to say, in the dark! Have you a match?"

"Yes," Halfhyde struck it cautiously, shielding the flame with his hand so that it lit upon the dead man's face and upper garments. A bush jacket similar to the major's but white. What was left of the face could have been Germanic, but there was no certainty. Blood and brain matter drooled. The match went out, and Halfhyde stood up. "There could be more around, couldn't there?"

"I doubt it. They'd have joined in the fight by now. Let's get on, shall we?"

"By all means! I'll be happier when I'm back on the river, frankly." Halfhyde quickly passed the word for the men to come out from cover and resume the march. They were not far off the Livingstone Falls now, he judged—the roar was tremendous, seeming to shake the very earth. As they made progress past, it lessened again. In such country the march was of necessity slow. The dawn was already touching the treetops, though it had not yet begun to penetrate lower down, when they reached the end of the track and came out once again to the river bank and Forbes's encampment by the landing. Forbes had a biggish entourage: upwards of twenty native bearers and an astonishing array of packing cases.

"Ammunition and stores," he explained. "If asked, I'm on a hunting trip, with authority from the Portuguese administration." He waved a hand towards the river, where four native canoes lay alongside the bank. "There you are, my dear fellow. Your fleet! All shipshape I think you'll find. And if you're short of stores, I can assist there too."

"I'm very grateful, Major. As to stores, I'll not need to deprive you—I have plenty. In addition, I know how to live off the land."

Forbes said, "As a seaman, I find that interesting."

"A seaman from Yorkshire, Major, and of good farming stock—yeoman stock. And with personal knowledge of Africa."

"So I was told in Salisbury. Now, I suggest you take some rest, my dear Halfhyde—it will pay dividends, though I'm well aware of the dangers of delay."

"Rest need not delay us," Halfhyde said briefly. "We shall leave at once, and take our rest on passage."

Forbes shrugged. "It's up to you, of course. You know the country, so you know the dangers of taking too little sleep—it weakens a man, and makes him the more susceptible to disease."

"I have quinine and I shall see that it is taken." Halfhyde swung round on the midshipman. "Mr Runcorn?"

"Sir?"

"The canoes. Embark the men and the stores if you please."

"Aye, aye, sir."

"We shall cast off the moment they're aboard. Speak to the torpedo-gunner's mates, and arrange a watchkeeping rota of paddlers, four to each canoe until we find out what speed that will give us."

"Aye, aye, sir."

"Then carry on, Mr Runcorn." As the midshipman doubled away, Halfhyde thanked Forbes for his assistance. "Good service indeed, Major, and I'm most grateful."

Forbes made a gesture of deprecation. "There will be further assistance up river," he said. "You'll be expected in the vicinity of Silva Porto. A canoe will be waiting at a landing on the east bank, with a good Portuguese friend, a man who prefers us British to the Hun. I think you will find him of value, and he is entirely to be trusted. His name is Bernardino Antunes. He's a short man, very fat, who smokes the most revolting cigars I've ever smelt. He has a dago moustache and exceptionally bad teeth. If that's not enough, there's a password."

"Yes?"

"As you approach, he'll hail you from the landing. He'll say, in English: 'Up river a very large alligator is lurking.' You'll reply, 'Alligators are not normally found in Africa.' He will say, 'There is a first time for everything.' To that you'll respond, 'Let us hope this one is rendered harmless.' You understand?"

Halfhyde repeated the formula and then nodded. "After that exchange, I approach this Portuguese?"

"Yes. He'll mention my name. From then on, it's up to you. Take great care, Halfhyde. As you drop down upon the border, you'll find German soldiers on both sides—they won't be particular about frontier etiquette until Savory's safely in their hands—as they hope!" Forbes held out his hand. "Good luck, my dear fellow. Britain will be depending upon you and your detective."

While Halfhyde, feeling a strong aura of cloak and dagger that was worlds away from ship routine and the roistering atmosphere of the home ports of Devonport and Pompey Town, saw his men aboard the canoes, Forbes vanished into the jungle fringe with one of his packing cases and two native bearers.

When he reappeared he was a different man: he could have been upon the parade ground in Stirling Castle. Gone was the khaki bush jacket, gone the white pith helmet and the mud. Forbes was resplendent in full regimentals, not of the West African Frontier Force but of the Argyll and Sutherland Highlanders—kilt, sporran, doublet, spats, diced hose, black feather bonnet with white hackle, an incredible sight but somehow moving in its very incongruity on the fringe of the African jungle. Behind Forbes came a native bearer, his coal-black face beaming and shining beneath another feather bonnet, legs like trunks of ebony beneath the kilt. Upon his left shoulder was a set of bagpipes. The two figures marched solemnly to the river bank. At first Halfhyde felt a strong impulse to laugh but he restrained himself. As he passed the order for his miniature fleet to proceed, the black piper puffed air into his instrument. It uttered the wail of a dying pig, and the hand of Major Forbes quivered to the salute. Standing up precariously and against all the tenets of seamanship, Halfhyde returned the salute before plumping back in an undignified flop to his seat in the canoe. They were piped away to the stirring notes of "The Campbells are Coming." Halfhyde found himself murmuring some of the words: "Great Argyll, he goes before, he makes the cannons and guns to roar . . ." He caught Todhunter's eye. "Prophetic, would you say, Mr Todhunter?"

"Possibly." Todhunter paused. "The tune has changed. It is more dirgeful now."

"It is indeed," Halfhyde said after listening for a few moments. "It's 'The Flowers of the Forest,' a Highland lament for the slain at Culloden."

"Well," Todhunter said glumly, "I trust that'll not be found prophetic too." They slid up river, four war canoes whose paddlers had already had to be reinforced to maintain way against the flow of the Coanza River towards the falls close behind. It was a strange progress in the growing heat of the day, with the overhanging branches of the trees scraping their heads, the powerful stench of the river assailing their nostrils, and the haunting notes of the piper still stealing down upon them from the receding landing.

Chapter 12

REST AND SLEEP were taken in the bottoms of the canoes between spells at the paddles. During the mealtime halts—brief ones—the canoes came together by the river bank for the distribution of rations and water under the supervision of Mr Midshipman Runcorn and the two torpedo-gunner's mates, both petty officers. So far as possible, even now—inspired perhaps by the pipes and the regimentals of Major Forbes—Halfhyde was maintaining some semblance of naval routine. He made medical rounds at sundown, accompanied by a leading seaman with a metal box containing quinine and ointments and bandages, and attended to bites and grazes before they could turn septic. The paddling was kept up throughout the night, the set watches changing at hourly intervals. By dint of only the briefest halts, Halfhyde expected to reach the vicinity of Silva Porto in a little over four days from his departure point, even though he had to take into his reckoning the fact that on many occasions he would need to bring his fleet ashore and manhandle the canoes overland through thick jungle to avoid cataracts and other obstructions. With a distance of around four hundred miles to go, this would mean an average speed of between four and five knots over the bottom—not an easy task and one that would reduce the strength of his men considerably.

"Nevertheless," he said to Todhunter, "we shall travel very much faster than friend Savory!"

"Unless he, too, uses the river, Mr Halfhyde."

"Which he will not. He must expect pursuit for a certainty, and he'll know it will be by river." Halfhyde gave a harsh laugh, a sound with no humour in it. "By this time, be assured of it, word will have been passed by telegraph to many places from Admiral von Merkatz!"

Todhunter said, "Not from his ships, Mr Halfhyde. And the rear-admiral in Gibraltar—"

"Not from his ships, of course. And we don't know what the rear-admiral will have permitted to be telegraphed in the German cypher. But I have a feeling he may have put into Santa Cruz de Tenerife, or Las Palmas. If so, I doubt if the Spaniards will have seen any reason to impede his messages!"

Todhunter nodded glumly. They might be in Africa, but Admiral von Merkatz was not written off yet, not by any means . . . Todhunter shifted about uncomfortably in the bottom of his war canoe, feeling most unwarlike, his bowler hat upon his head and his gladstone bag between his knees, guarded like the crown jewels since it contained his all-important warrant. He scratched and rubbed and squeezed. Everything in Africa had bitten him and he was all lumps, and he had prickly heat as well in unmentionable places. None of his companions appeared quite so badly affected, though none was unscathed. The voyage up river was proving to be purgatory, and the pace was being kept up solely by the selfless efforts of Halfhyde, Runcorn, and the petty officers, who exhorted and made jokes that seemed to Todhunter the essence of daftness but which were appreciated by the sailors. And they sang seafaring songs, too, to keep all hands going—songs with words that Mr Todhunter could not bring himself to utter since they were more obscene by far than anything heard at even all-male police functions. Sailors, he reflected as he scratched himself sore, were at least inventive wordwise even if their tunes were largely those of hymns. Halfhyde's voice broke into his thoughts, and he said, "Pardon?"

"Must you scratch, Mr Todhunter? Why not leave it to the ointment?"

"It seems to have little effect, I'm sorry to say. Perhaps more bandages would—"

"You are virtually a mummy already, Mr Todhunter, and I must conserve my stocks. Try to bear the itch, which will go the quicker if unmolested."

"Unmolested!" Todhunter repeated with extreme bitterness, and gave a hollow laugh. The dreadful voyage proceeded. Soon night came down, thick and black and ghostly, its brooding silence too often broken by dismal jungle sounds, hootings and scufflings and slithers, sometimes a sharp cry, sometimes even a distant roar. Todhunter felt a sense of desperation and claustrophobia in the bottom of the canoe, even silently cursed his gladstone bag for its leg-restricting bulk. If only he could stretch out flat! Just that would be a kind of heaven. His bites nagged at him and brought him a headache to add to everything else. All at once he remembered Sam Strawbridge's gift of the flask, and his eyes shone in the darkness. No drinking man normally, he did feel in need of a nip now. It would do him good, but he decided it should be done clandestinely, since his brief sojourn aboard ship had told him a fact of naval life: no officer was permitted alcohol in his cabin any more than the ratings of the lowerdeck were permitted to bottle their daily issue of rum. Officers drank only in their mess, the captain being the sole exception, since he visited the ward-room only by invitation of its members. Todhunter had no wish to bring about trouble for Sam Strawbridge, and he bided his time for his nip, indulging himself only when the paddlers fore and aft of him had settled into their rhythmic motions and were half asleep from sheer weariness. Then, negotiating the gladstone bag, the tumble-home of the canoe's side, the movements of the paddlers, and his own leg cramp, he brought out the flask from his trouser pocket, unscrewed the top, and had his nip. He felt instantly better and began to relax.

Runcorn's voice came from astern, urgently, a little after the full dawn had broken upon a heavily clouded sky. "Native canoes, sir, coming up fast!"

Halfhyde turned sharply. He saw six war canoes, making good speed up the river behind, their paddles flashing in perfect unison, sending up spray. Each canoe, manned by more than a dozen warriors, had a bone in its teeth, a bow wave to show its speed through the water.

Halfhyde shouted, "With a will now, my lads! We're being chased, and if we're caught we're likely to be scalped and sent to the cooking pots. Paddle for your lives!"

Every man put on an immediate spurt. From each canoe, the coxswain called the time, faster and faster; but even so the native craft were seen to be closing the gap. Halfhyde sweated blood: to be overhauled would be fatal, not only to his boats' crews and Todhunter but to their whole mission. Even if they were by some miracle not put to death, the pursuing natives would be unlikely to release them in time if at all. Halfhyde turned to look again and see how quickly the pursuers were gaining: in the churning water astern, he saw a number of small spouts. Arrows or other missiles, so far failing to reach the aftermost boat. Halfhyde made his decision, and cupped his hands to relay it to all the boats. "In to the bank, starboard side, and smack it about! Leave the canoes and fade into the jungle with all your arms and equipment, d'you hear?"

No time was lost. The paddlers worked like maniacs, sweating and straining for the bank. The canoes took the side at full speed, tumbling their occupants about. The disembarkation was fast but orderly nonetheless. In Halfhyde's boat only Todhunter remained, snoring. Halfhyde, cursing, shook him vigorously. "Wake up, Mr Todhunter! Out for your life, man!" There was no response: the detective inspector's face was pale and he was sweating profusely in his slumber—or his unconsciousness. Halfhyde looked up at Petty Officer Thomas, one of the torpedo-gunner's mates. "A hand, and quickly! He's got the malaria or I'm a Dutchman."

"Aye, aye, sir. You there, MacInnes." Thomas bent to his task and with MacInnes lifted Todhunter to the canoe's gunwhale and tumbled him inertly ashore. Halfhyde saw to the fast despatch of his armed seamen and stokers into the shelter of the jungle, with the pursuit now only some six cables'-lengths away. In the canoe Petty Officer Thomas bent to retrieve an object that, being now clear of Todhunter's body, reflected a dull metallic gleam. Then he and his helper seized the detective inspector and bundled him hastily into the thick jungle growth like a flaccid sack. A little way back from the river bank, they found Halfhyde mustering the remainder of the hands. Thomas, dumping the policeman, approached and saluted.

Grinning, he said, "You're a Dutchman, sir—in your own words that is, sir."

"What the devil d'you mean?"

"Mr Tod'unter, sir, has not got the malaria. I found this." He held out Sam Strawbridge's flask. "Then there's the smell, sir, to corroborate like. Mr Tod'unter's as drunk as a fiddler's bitch, sir."

Halfhyde spread the seamen and stokers out with their rifles, a fast manoeuvre that produced a long line of men, each one separated by three yards from his neighbour. In line he moved them stealthily back towards the bank, halting them while still in cover but within about four yards of the water, every man well concealed. He was just in time: they reached their firing position as the six war canoes touched the bank. The natives were given no chance. Before they had time to disembark, Halfhyde shouted the one order:

"Open fire!"

At once and as one, every rifle crashed out, firing again and again until the magazines were empty, when fast reloading took place. It was wholesale slaughter, with not a man escaping, not a man, indeed, left alive. As the echoes of the firing died away Halfhyde strode alone through the gunsmoke to the bank. It was a bloody scene, with bodies lying in the canoes and draped over the sides or floating head down in the scummy water. His face stiff, Halfhyde turned to find Runcorn beside him. Solemnly he said, "It was us or them, Mr Runcorn."

"Yes, sir. I understand that, sir. But pursuit is natural to them, isn't it, sir?"

Halfhyde glowered. "Are you questioning the correctness of my action, Mr Runcorn?"

"Oh, no, sir—"

"Oh, yes, sir, you are! Kindly remember your status. A midshipman is . . . what, pray, is a midshipman, Mr Runcorn?"

"Sir, the lowest form of animal life in the Navy, sir—"

"Precisely, you have it." Halfhyde dropped a hand on the youth's shoulder. "I like it no more than you. They are the local inhabitants, we are the interlopers. It's the way of the world, Snotty. The business of great nations over-rides the interest of primitive peoples. One day, perhaps, they'll be primitive no longer, for I sense the stirring of creeds different from those that have so far held sway."

"Do you, sir?"

"I do, but we'll not concern ourselves with that at the moment." Halfhyde looked down once more at the bodies. "In the meantime, console yourself with this thought: they died as warriors, not as old grey men. Look upon mass death, Mr Runcorn, and see in it a release from old age and the workhouse, or sick kraal or whatever."

"Yes, sir." Runcorn hesitated. "Shall I detail burial parties, sir?"

Halfhyde shook his head. "We have not the time. Nature will disperse them quickly in this climate, Mr Runcorn." He looked up at the sky: there was much rain up there, and they would have a dismal day's river trek. "Get the hands aboard, if you please, Mr Runcorn, and we shall get under way directly."

"Aye, aye, sir. And Mr Todhunter, sir?"

"Mr Todhunter will need to be carried. Have him dumped in his usual place in my canoe, and make sure his wretched gladstone bag is safe."

• • •

The detective inspector was no longer as drunk as a fiddler's
bitch. He had been thoroughly soaked when the lowering skies
had burst open, and he had come to his senses—though he felt
desperately ill. A working lifetime of conscientious performance
of his duty made him reach for his gladstone bag as soon as he
was able. It was, and he thanked God, safe—but not quite
sound. There was a hole in it, as if made by something like a
native spear, and the rain had entered as he could deduce
detective-wise from the sog and splosh. Todhunter gave a sick,
sad groan: God alone could tell what had happened to his warrant! He tried to sit up, but a wave of nausea overcame him
and he fell back.

"You are recovering, Mr Todhunter."

Halfhyde's voice: Todhunter thrust out a swollen tongue and
licked at dry lips. His mouth was worse than the proverbial
bottom of the parrot's cage. He managed to say, "Yes, thank you,
Mr Halfhyde. I really don't know what happened."

"I do," Halfhyde said grimly. "You were as tight as a drum."

"I apologize! . . ."

"So I should think. You have proved a brave man so far, Mr
Todhunter, but bravery is not all. Sobriety, too, is needed in
such a situation as we are in."

"Unpolicemanlike . . ."

"And unseamanlike! You could have upset the canoe by having to be lifted out like a dead porpoise."

"It'll not happen again."

"Indeed it will not, since there is no more whisky, at least
not in your possession. You are a disgrace to your cloth, Mr
Todhunter."

At this injustice Todhunter burst out with indignation. "Have you never been the worse for drink, Mr Halfhyde?"

"Frequently," Halfhyde answered with a grin, "but not as worse as you were earlier! At sea, one learns to control the results of indulgence. And you, Mr Todhunter?"

"And me—what?"

"Your first such experience, I take it?"

"Well, yes." Todhunter lifted a shaking hand to his brow. "And the last. Mind, I was never a teetotaller. A glass of beer, maybe a gin and water. I've been a bit sort of, well, giggly."

"Have you indeed?" Halfhyde suppressed a wide smile. "Then I advise nothing more than giggles in future, Mr Todhunter, and more water than gin. Meanwhile, fortunately, no harm's been done except to your own head and liver. We shall say no more about it—after all, as you suggested just now, I've transgressed myself, and I understand."

"Thank you, thank you indeed."

Halfhyde waved a hand. "Now you shall concentrate on a speedy restoration to health. And when you are better, you shall take quinine."

Todhunter shuddered. "I'd rather not."

"The feeling of malaria, Mr Todhunter, is worse by far than the feeling of drink taken." Halfhyde turned his attention ahead. Now the canoes were coming into a broad part of the river, with a wide bend looming through the teeming downpour, and the little fleet was holding to a midstream course, well clear of the lush growth of the banks. In spite of the coldness of the rain itself there was a sticky heat-fug, a most uncomfortable combination that made the paddlers sweat heavily beneath their oilskins, and made Todhunter sweat beneath the tarpaulin that had been thrown over him. Halfhyde noticed the increasing shake in the policeman's body. He was shivering badly and could do with some exercise to circulate his blood and drive away the fumes of alcohol. When next the paddle watch was changed, Halfhyde ordered Todhunter to take a turn. There was no protest, but the result made for poor navigation, with the canoe tending to turn round in circles until Todhunter began to get the knack. After that he paddled reasonably well, pulling his weight manfully until after an hour's spell Halfhyde relieved him.

"You are tiring, Mr Todhunter."

"No, no—"

"Yes, yes! I appreciate what you have done, but I shall not drive you too far. Muscle is best built up in easy stages. And I think you will dry out soon. I see signs of better weather ahead."

The better weather came. The heavy cloud grew thin, then faded away beneath a hot sun. Oilskins were shed and the hands dried out as if by magic. Spirits rose. When the canoes were ordered in to the bank as evening approached once more, and rations were issued, Halfhyde, with an eye partly to Todhunter's need for a hair of the dog, authorized an issue of one mouthful per man of the ward-room whisky, taken straight from the bottle. This done, he passed the order to move out yet again. They proceeded on up river, back once more in a narrow part with the overhanging trees brushing their heads and the jungle sounds close and eerie. Along one branch a tree snake lay, its coils wound round the wood and its head lowered, eyes bright black and tongue moving like forked lightning only inches away. Todhunter made as though to fend it off with upraised gladstone bag, but then they had passed below the creature's belly in safety, gliding on through the scum of driftwood and dead animal bodies and leaves, a scum whose stench seemed in some way concentrated and increased when the night fell. Halfhyde, impatient as he was for speed and more speed, did not haze the paddlers: they were doing their honest best, and they were not far off exhaustion.

Halfhyde turned and shouted down the line of canoes: "Landing ahead, Mr Runcorn! I fancy it's our next stage, since we should now be level with Silva Porto."

"Yes, sir. Orders, sir?"

"Hold your course for the time being. I shall draw level, and we shall see what we shall see."

"Aye, aye, sir."

"Stand by for further orders as the situation develops, and be ready to go alongside the bank."

"Yes, sir."

Halfhyde turned ahead again. At the landing there were dugout canoes drawn up on the bank itself, high and dry, and two more in the water but unoccupied. There was no sign of life at first, but as the fleet drew closer Halfhyde saw a figure come into view from the jungle behind. The man stood for a moment shielding his eyes with one hand before turning back into the cover of the trees. Shortly after this, he reappeared, this time with a rifle held loosely across his body.

An instant report came from Petty Officer Thomas: "The man's armed, sir."

"So I see. It's natural. But have all men ready, Thomas."

"Aye, aye, sir."

Halfhyde brought up his telescope, looked through it, and knew he could relax. The man was swarthy and moustached, so short as to be stunted. He was fat, and was smoking a cigar. It must be Bernardino Antunes. Halfhyde felt like giving a hearty cheer as he headed his craft in towards the river landing. Once within hailing distance, he slowed the paddles and stood by to give the password. A moment later the man on the bank cupped his hands around his mouth, cigar and all, and shouted: "Up river a very large alligator is lurking."

Grinning, Halfhyde gave the reply: "Alligators are not normally found in Africa."

"There is a first time for everything, Senhor."

"Let us hope this one is rendered harmless."

The Portuguese smiled widely and waved an arm in welcome. Halfhyde turned aft and signalled to Runcorn, then turned more sharply for the bank. Just as he did so there was a commotion ashore—another man, a white man, tall and angular, rushed suddenly from out of the jungle growth, waving his arms like a windmill and shouting. Halfhyde saw the Portuguese swing round and bring his rifle up. A shot rang out, but the wild man ran on for the bank, gesticulating towards the approaching craft, and Halfhyde picked up the excited words:

"Awa' wi' ye—get the bloody hell oot, fast as ye can row. Awa', ye daft silly buggers! Yon bastard—"

Very suddenly, the shouting stopped. The Portuguese had got his aim, and the Scot went down with a crash and lay rigid. As more men, both blacks and whites, came running out from the jungle, Halfhyde found his own voice in a roar down the line of canoes: "Give way fast, do as the man said! Follow me up river for your lives!"

Urging his own boat's crew to all possible speed, Halfhyde swung fast away from the landing as a rapid and sustained fire broke out from the bank. Bullets sang and buzzed like bees. The paddles flashed in the sunlight, sending up spray that sparkled like diamonds. Then a cry came from astern. Halfhyde looked back and saw the last canoe in the line beginning to founder, settling in the water as the river rushed in through the holes left by the bullets, with Runcorn still shouting hoarsely, urging his men on to paddle the sinking boat to safety.

Chapter 13

"LEAVE HER, SNOTTY! Abandon ship—I'm coming back for you. We live to fight another day. Petty Officer Thomas, your shirt."

The torpedo-gunner's mate looked astonished. "Sir?"

"Up with it, man, on a paddle—and wave it!"

"Surrender, sir?"

"Surrender. And smack it about! An order, Petty Officer Thomas."

"Aye, aye, sir." His whole bearing reluctant and disbelieving, Thomas pulled off his shirt, stuck a paddle through the neck, hoisted it, and waved. The rifle fire died away and stopped. The canoe nearest Runcorn's had already turned to give assistance, and Runcorn's spilled-out crew were gripping the gunwhales—but only two of them. Five bodies were drifting up river, along the line of canoes, and Halfhyde cursed savagely. He detested surrender, but he knew he had no option. He would not leave Runcorn or any other man behind to be mown down, and in any case a pursuit would have caught him up as surely as the grave. He looked towards the bank as his fleet made slowly, reluctantly inshore. The bank was lined with men, many of them white, all holding rifles or revolvers. Halfhyde had a bitter taste in his mouth as his canoe took the bank and was gripped in by some of the men.

The fat Portuguese approached, grinning, his rifle trained on

Halfhyde. "You are Lieutenant Halfhyde, of the British Navy?"

Halfhyde scowled. "I am."

"As lily-livered as your flag of surrender."

"Not lily-livered. There was no choice. I do not send men to an unnecessary and certain death. I assure you, you shall not hold us long!"

The man jerked his short neck and head forward, and spat. Saliva landed stickily on Halfhyde's trousers, but he took no notice. He merely stared back at the Portuguese, haughtily, with his head thrown back. "You, I take it, are Bernardino Antunes, turned traitor?"

"No. I am not he. Bernardino Antunes lies dead, very dead. I resemble him."

"A clever subterfuge—"

"That brought you alongside as planned—yes!" The fat man smirked. "Now, please, come out of the boat. You and all your men. Give no trouble, or you will be at once dead men like Bernardino Antunes."

"And the Scotsman who tried to warn us—who was he?"

The fat man shrugged. "An employee of the Scotsman Forbes, whom you will have met. A soldier of his regiment once, lately attached to Bernardino Antunes. Come out to the shore, Lieutenant Halfhyde." The Portuguese turned and spoke obsequiously to a hard-looking white man. He was armed with a revolver, and had the stamp of the military about him with duelling scars running down both cheeks. "Hauptmann von Arnhem, the Englishman is yours."

The German nodded, but said nothing. He advanced to the bank as Halfhyde disembarked, and made a stiff bow. "Lieutenant Halfhyde, you are my prisoner," he said in guttural

English. "You and your men will be correctly treated so long as you give no trouble. As one officer and gentleman to another, I promise this. Have I your promise of no trouble?"

There was a glint in Halfhyde's eye. "Parole, Hauptmann von Arnhem?"

"Parole, yes. Your word—"

"There will be no parole given, Hauptmann von Arnhem," Halfhyde said in an even tone. "I am here to do my duty—you know what that duty is, I think. I intend to do it, in the name of Her Majesty."

Von Arnhem shrugged. "That is at all events honest. No parole, no freedom of movement, Lieutenant Halfhyde. There is a compound, and in it you will all go."

Halfhyde grinned nastily. "From here to eternity?"

"For as long as is necessary."

"Until the traitor Savory is safely inside German South-West Africa?"

"I have no comment to make on this, Lieutenant Halfhyde."

"You have no need to. I take it you are a flunky of Admiral von Merkatz, who may or may not still be coal-less in Gibraltar, and dancing in a stupid rage upon his quarterdeck and his cap—"

"That is enough. You will be silent." Von Arnhem's face had darkened. "The high-ranking officers of His Imperial Majesty are not to be insulted by—"

"By officers of His Imperial Majesty's British grandmother?" Halfhyde laughed in von Arnhem's angry face. "Do you imagine that Her Majesty will sit idly by upon her throne in Windsor Castle, and allow her seamen to be held helpless in the African jungle? If you do, you will be making a very great mistake!

Perhaps it has escaped your notice that we have land forces in South Africa?"

"I am naturally aware of the British military and naval dispositions, my friend, and I am not especially concerned, since they will not know what has become of you and your party of seamen. Who is the person in the bowler hat?"

Halfhyde turned: Todhunter, looking formal but fearful, was behind him, clutching his gladstone bag with both hands. Behind again, the naval ratings were being disarmed by a squad of natives under the orders of the German soldiers, as Halfhyde took them to be in spite of their ragged mixture of apparel. Todhunter answered von Arnhem's question: "Detective Inspector Todhunter, from the Metropolitan Police."

"Ah yes, I was told a policeman was to be sent—"

"You know a lot, it seems," Halfhyde interrupted. "May I take it you have your spies in Whitehall?"

The German shrugged. "You may take it how you wish. It is true I know a lot, but I do not know all. You shall tell me what I do not know, Lieutenant Halfhyde, and here is the first question." He reached forward and tapped Halfhyde's chest. "Your ship, the battleship *Prince Consort.* Where is she now?"

"I'm afraid I've no idea, Hauptmann von Arnhem." Coolly, Halfhyde took out a handkerchief and dusted down his uniform where the German's fingers had touched it. "I think you'll have to ask the Admiralty."

"Insolence will not help you. What are her orders, and what are *your* orders in regard to rejoining her? Come, Lieutenant Halfhyde, please do not be foolish, and put me to the disagreeable business of extracting the information I ask!"

"I've nothing to say, and in no circumstances will I put nothing into words."

Von Arnhem frowned. "What is this, double Dutch?"

"Call it what you will," Halfhyde answered with indifference. "I've said all I intend to say."

The German officer's nostrils flared, his mouth thinning in anger to give his face an expression of sadistic hate. "I advise caution, my friend. You must not forget I can do what I wish with you." He looked at Todhunter, who returned his stare manfully. "The bag. It contains secrets, perhaps?"

"Not secrets, sir. My private possessions."

"You are a man who is possessive in regard to his private property?"

"Pardon?"

"You clutch your bag tightly, in case it runs away." Von Arnhem laughed. "I think it contains secrets, and I shall look inside it."

"You will not, sir." Todhunter clutched the gladstone bag even tighter, and glared back at the German. "You have no right to touch a person's private property, sir, and you know it. I shall insist—"

"There speaks the British policeman, the peeler as I think you say, or bobby, or flatfoot. I remind you, you are not now upon your beat, twirling your club and your moustaches at the housemaids in Eaton Square—"

"I am a detective inspector, sir. It is the constables who carry truncheons. And not clubs. There is a difference."

"Very well, truncheons. Now I shall honour your exalted rank."

"Pardon?"

Von Arnhem, losing his patience, snapped: "The inspection, Detective Inspector! The bag." He advanced upon Todhunter; at the same time two of his soldiers also came forward and took Todhunter's arms. Von Arnhem seized the bag and pulled it from Todhunter's grasp as the soldiers twisted his arms viciously. Stepping back a few paces, von Arnhem opened the bag and turned it upside down. Out fell the blue serge suit, which in truth almost filled the inside. Out came the empty flask, a pair of woollen socks with suspenders attached, a striped flannel nightshirt, a pair of combinations, and the handcuffs, Mr Todhunter's total equipment for the bush. Out also came the all-important warrant for the arrest of Sir Russell Savory, limp from the ingress of water. Todhunter's face was crimson with mortification, fury, and alarm. Von Arnhem gestured at one of his soldiers, who bent to pick up the warrant. As the document was handed to him, von Arnhem stirred Todhunter's possessions with a foot, seeking more secrets. Finding none, he read the warrant, slowly and carefully, then looked up.

"This is your authority, Detective Inspector?"

Todhunter nodded dumbly.

"Without it you are powerless—that is to say, even more powerless than you are already?"

Todhunter licked at his lips, seeking Halfhyde's eye. "In a legal sense, yes," he said.

"I have always heard that the British have stodgy minds bound in with paper formalities and stupid routine procedures, and that they must never act without due authorization. A foolish race and an unresilient one." Von Arnhem turned to Halfhyde. "What do you say, my friend?"

Halfhyde smiled. "You put it admirably, a very concise description of the German people, Hauptmann von Arnhem, if I may say so."

"You will regret that remark," von Arnhem said, "before the day is finished." He snapped his fingers at the man who had picked up Todhunter's warrant. "Lucifers," he said. Matches were brought and struck. The flame was applied to the warrant, which at first resisted. Then the fire overcame its lingering damp and it curled around von Arnhem's fingers until he dropped it in a flurry of ash.

Todhunter's face was a study in shock and disbelief.

"Try not to worry about it," Halfhyde said wearily from the darkness. They had all been marched away to a mud hut and now lay on the earth floor with their hands tied behind their backs. In Todhunter's case, von Arnhem's heavy sense of irony had led to the use of the detective inspector's own handcuffs. "It's no more than a scrap of paper when all's said and done."

"I'm surprised you should say that, Mr Halfhyde."

"You must remember this is not England. We've been accused of lack of resilience, of inability, in effect, to react to changed circumstances. The warrant's gone—we must act without it. It's not a capital offence to do so, Mr Todhunter!"

"No, but nevertheless, I have no standing without it."

"Nonsense! In any case, even if you haven't, I have. Be assured that when we catch up with Savory, he'll be duly arrested. If you like, the responsibility for acting without the proper authority of the Bow Street stipendiary will be mine entirely—"

"Not the Bow Street stipendiary—"

"Oh, well, whoever it may be—and frankly I don't give a damn!" Halfhyde said irritably.

"I think, sir, you miss the point," Todhunter said in an aggrieved tone. "It's not that the warrant didn't exist, it's not that it won't be, as it were, *honoured* in London. It's that I now have nothing to show to any authorities we may encounter— consuls and so on—"

"Then we shall show them Sir Russell Savory," Halfhyde said with an air of finality. "And now, if you please, Mr Todhunter, pipe down. I've heard enough, and my head aches abominably. Mr Runcorn?"

The voice from the darkness seemed to encompass a verbal salute. "Sir?"

"Crouch at ease; Mr Runcorn, you're still too formal. We have to consider how to get out of here. Have you any ideas?"

"No, sir, I'm sorry, sir."

Todhunter said, "If we try to get out they'll shoot us. The sentry—"

"Yes, yes. There's always a risk in war, and to an extent we're in a war situation now, with the Germans as the aggressors. I propose, from now on, to disregard all past adjurations to be tactful and diplomatic."

Runcorn asked, "What have you in mind, sir?"

"Walls," Halfhyde said, "have ears. Wriggle closer and I'll whisper in *your* ear rather than that of the wall." Scuffling noises could be heard from the darkness as Runcorn approached. When the midshipman was alongside, Halfhyde continued. "I've half a mind—no decisions yet—to drop the search for Savory, in a direct sense that is, and make with all speed for Mossamedes.

I'm assuming we can break out first, of course, and I'll back myself to achieve that, once the camp's turned in for the night."

"And in Mossamedes—"

"In Mossamedes we have that telegram sent to St Helena. We bring the *Prince Consort* in with her battle ensigns flying, Mr Runcorn! How does that strike you?"

"Well, sir, it's a sight I'd like to see. But what would the captain *do,* sir, upon arrival?"

"I can't answer for the captain, Mr Runcorn, but what I shall suggest is that the captain picks us up and stands out again to sea—to await Admiral von Merkatz upon his departure from German South-West Africa for the Channel and the Fatherland, with Savory aboard."

"I see, sir. And then, sir—"

"Then the German squadron is brought to action upon the high seas!"

"Yes, sir." Runcorn paused, then went on tentatively, "One ship, sir, against four?"

"You shrink from action, Mr Runcorn?"

"Oh, no, sir, certainly not, sir! But surely, the odds would be against all the rules of naval tactics, sir?"

Halfhyde frowned. "Schoolroom stuff! Rules are to be learned but not always blindly followed. Surprise can enter tactics, Mr Runcorn, and to the best of my knowledge Nelson never shrank from engaging the enemy more closely, nor indeed from engaging superior force."

Halfhyde's voice had risen a little more than he had intended. A response came tartly from the detective inspector. "You appear to be positively enjoying this, Mr Halfhyde."

"Danger sharpens the mind admirably, Mr Todhunter, and I've got out of much tighter spots than this in my time."

"That may be. But do you suppose Captain Bassinghorn is likely to agree to open fire upon the ships of a friendly power?"

"Friendly my arse, Mr Todhunter! Think of your desecrated warrant, and the impertinent use of your own handcuffs!" In a sober voice Halfhyde added, "Think, too, as I have thought, of the murder of five of my seamen. Captain Bassinghorn will take that much to heart."

There was no further word from Todhunter or Runcorn. They all lay silent, each busy with his thoughts and anxieties in the enclosing privacy of the dark hut. They heard the footfalls of the armed guard, softly muted on the earth of the jungle clearing, and heard the clink of rifle slings. The only other sounds were of scratching and muffled cursing as an army of insects explored and tickled and bit, invading every part of the sweating bodies. Halfhyde reflected with an increasing sourness on his so-far unhatched plans. It was true enough that Bassinghorn would be highly reluctant to be the first to open fire, and it was equally true that von Merkatz would not precipitate action once he had Savory safe aboard his flagship. In that event it would be no more than a procession of ships towards the Channel, with the *Prince Consort* merely shadowing, an impotent laughing stock for the German admiral, a helpless tail-end Charlie tagging along behind. Halfhyde scowled and smashed a fist into his palm in sheer frustration. The whole matter had now moved far, far beyond the ken of Scotland Yard or the Home Office, was way beyond the arm of the British law, and had to be coped with as such. Bassinghorn would surely see the issue plain: if war did not come now, it would be a hundred times worse when it did come, with Savory's blueprints and personal knowledge providing the basis for the build-up of a mighty German High Seas Fleet to overtake the Admiralty's construction programme and sweep the British Navy from the world's oceans.

Chapter 14

THE EXPECTED QUESTIONING came after almost three hours' confinement in the hut—Halfhyde fancied he had been intentionally left to stew, to soften up. He was brought out into the strong sunlight of noon, his hands still tied behind his back and a native standing guard with a rifle. The German was seated on a folding camp stool beneath a large striped umbrella held by another native. A second camp stool stood empty, to which Von Arnhem gestured. "Be seated, Lieutenant Halfhyde."

"Thank you." Halfhyde said. The umbrella's shade failed to cover him, and he pulled the camp stool inwards until stopped by von Arnhem. He was, it seemed, to remain in the noon sun. He made no protest and waited for the German to start the conversation.

Von Arnhem drew a cigar case from a pocket and slowly selected a Havana, slicing off the end with a silver cutter. The attendant native struck a match, and von Arnhem puffed smoke luxuriously. "Now, Lieutenant Halfhyde, you know my questions; the answers, please."

"There will be no answers, Hauptmann von Arnhem."

"No?"

"No."

"I advise you not to be hasty with your refusals. There will be ways of persuasion, ways you will not like."

"Really? What ways?"

Von Arnhem frowned. "You sound flippant. Later, you will wonder how you ever came to find flippancy possible . . . but I shall satisfy your curiosity, Lieutenant Halfhyde, and indeed you are wise to ask in advance." He blew smoke over his prisoner, a welcome fragrance. "You like cigars yourself?"

"Yes."

"Then you shall have as many as you can smoke, once you have told me what I wish to know. If you do not, then the other things wait. There are the matches, for instance."

"Matches?"

"But not to light cigars! To thrust beneath fingernails, and light. There is the water torture, when water is dripped down the nose and the mouth held shut—it sounds not much, but is truly terrible, with the effect of drowning. There are the *anomma*. With your knowledge of Africa, you will know of the *anomma*, the dreaded driver ants of—"

"I know the *anomma*, Hauptmann von Arnhem."

"They overwhelm all in their path—vegetation, animals, humans. They cannot be resisted except by flight."

"They would find me tough meat to chew!"

"But tough meat spreads well with syrup. I have syrup, and I have driver ants in biscuit tins, many biscuit tins. Staked out in the sun and covered with my syrup . . . yes, you would talk very quickly, Lieutenant Halfhyde!"

"I wouldn't wager on that if I were you."

"No?" Von Arnhem laughed quietly. "However, you and I— we are officers and gentlemen, are we not? Torture is for lesser persons to inflict and receive. There is no reason why we should not behave in a civilized manner, and that is why I am offering you the chance. On the other hand, if you refuse the chance, then . . ." He shrugged. "I need not repeat what I have said, I think?"

"You needn't." Halfhyde had been thinking fast, his mental processes much hastened by the looming threat. He had little doubt that extreme pressure would be applied, and that von Arnhem might well go to the lengths he had described. The German looked both dedicated and sadistic. As for himself, he could not say with certainty how far he might go before breaking. Every man, it had been truly said, had a breaking point somewhere along the line, no matter how strong he might feel himself to be. That point could not be ascertained in advance, and things could be forced from a man's lips when the point was reached. Often duty was better served by subterfuge . . . Halfhyde appeared to be pondering the situation in some fearfulness, and after a decent interval said tentatively, "It's possible, no doubt, that some accommodation can be reached between us, Hauptmann von Arnhem?"

"A compromise?"

Halfhyde nodded. "Some give and take, perhaps."

Von Arnhem's eyes gleamed behind his cigar. "Mutual help— is this what you suggest?"

"Perhaps. I would prefer not to be too specific."

"Unless you should incur displeasure from your Admiralty! Be easy—there are no listening ears from the hut—your men shall not know. I think I understand very well, Lieutenant Halfhyde. Tell me how I may assist, please."

"It's not easy to put it briefly."

Von Arnhem waved his cigar, and smiled. "You may take your time. I shall not hurry you. Please compose your thoughts."

"Thank you. The fact is, I begin to see my mission as becoming impossible. That is why I make my suggestions. I'm by no means scared by your threats of personal violence."

"But of course not." Von Arnhem's eyes gleamed again, this time with amusement.

"But I've never been given to banging my head against brick walls, if you understand me?"

"Perfectly."

"And sometimes the inevitable has to be accepted. There is a certain inevitability about being taken prisoner, Hauptmann von Arnhem—and such captivity leads to delay. Delay in its turn makes it likely that Savory will reach the German South-West African frontier before I can reach him."

"This is indeed so."

"Of course, one can always attempt to escape," Halfhyde said reflectively. "But then there would be casualties—on both sides."

"Mostly among you British, I think. Escape will be found quite impossible, Lieutenant Halfhyde."

"I have many men, as you know."

"And all unarmed, as *you* know! It would be most foolish to make any such attempt."

"It's my duty to try, nevertheless. If I should so decide, then I can promise that your men will not come out of it without casualties!"

The German made a gesture of impatience. "I do not understand you, Lieutenant Halfhyde. I do not understand what you are asking for."

"I'm not asking you to accept a further surrender, that's for certain. I'm asking for an accommodation, as I said." Halfhyde leaned forward, speaking quietly and earnestly. "When a mission reaches the point at which reasonable people would consider it to have failed, there is no need to invite casualties to one's men." He paused, then went on with a particular emphasis. "Equally, when success is seen, why should the winner invite unnecessary risks?"

"Then you are saying, Lieutenant Halfhyde, that unless there is an accommodation, you will attempt a break-out?"

Halfhyde smiled. "You have it precisely, Hauptmann von Arnhem!"

"You will be the loser, not I."

"*Quod est demonstrandum,*" Halfhyde said with a shrug. "Which is yet to be demonstrated—"

"I also understand the Latin tongue, and would reply that the correct quotation happens to be in the past tense. I think I have already demonstrated my superior force." Von Arnhem sent twin trails of cigar smoke from his nostrils. "However, I am willing to listen to any proposal that will save us both the necessity of unpleasantness." He added, "It is true that the Fatherland does not wish to make unnecessary trouble, and has no wish to kill you British—"

"No?" Halfhyde's eyes blazed. "The Fatherland's wish has not been heeded, then. Have you forgotten that I lost five men killed by your rifles?"

Von Arnhem waved a hand. "Necessary casualties, since you were attempting to get away. I am sorry for them, and my hope and the Fatherland's is that there will be no need for more. I repeat, there is no desire for trouble and death."

"In other words, you are under orders to be diplomatic in your conduct of the affair?"

"I did not say that," von Arnhem retorted sharply, apparently regretting a small indiscretion. "Your proposal, if you please?"

Halfhyde smiled again, a sour smile. "Very well. Down river of the Livingstone Falls, I have a torpedo-boat waiting. I would like to rejoin it, with my seamen. I would be willing to accept an escort, and to make the journey unarmed—down river, it should take no more than three days, I fancy. And you would be rid of an embarrassment, Hauptmann von Arnhem."

"Indeed? And you?"

"I would go to sea and rejoin my ship, and report the facts."

"The facts that you were prevented from making an arrest and that the affair now passes into a *fait accompli?*"

Halfhyde shrugged. "You put it reasonably well."

The German showed no immediate reaction. He sat deep in thought, cogitating along lines at which Halfhyde could make a fair guess. He, Hauptmann von Arnhem, would have brought off an almost bloodless victory, handling an awkward situation with tact and diplomacy to the gratification of the Fatherland and the enhancement of the German emperor's personal position. Honour would be well satisfied and orders obeyed. There would be no clash with the British Fleet, which would be unwilling to provoke a war; that fleet would slink home with its tail between its legs, a perpetual laughing stock to all German warships in the future. The light of victory glinted in von Arnhem's eye as at last he uttered. "Another quotation from the Latin, Lieutenant Halfhyde: there must be a *quid pro quo*. Before I agree to your accommodation, I for my part wish to know the whereabouts of your ship, the *Prince Consort*. If I give way a little, then so shall you."

Halfhyde nodded slowly, seemed to consider awhile, then shrugged in resignation. "Very well. I dare say there's nothing to be lost now. My ship's on passage south for Simon's Town."

"Are there not nearer ports?"

"Not in British territory. My captain is under orders to enter only a British colonial port, and I am under orders to rejoin at Simon's Town."

"With Sir Russell Savory?"

"Such were my orders."

"A long land journey, Lieutenant Halfhyde."

"I have good legs. So have my men. Assistance would have been available once I had crossed into Rhodesia, and legs would have been needed only as far as Salisbury and the railway line to the Cape."

"And now—that is, should I agree to have you sent under guard to your torpedo-boat? What then?"

"As I said. I shall rejoin, but by sea and not by land. As a seaman, I prefer the sea."

Von Arnhem got to his feet and stood staring down at Halfhyde, his eyes cold. "I thank you," he said, "for at last answering my questions. I trust the answers were truthful. If they should prove to be false you shall suffer, and your men also. On that you have my promise. As to the rest . . ." The German spat at Halfhyde's feet, disdainfully. "You must take me for a fool! I know your British Navy and its officers. I pay you the compliment of knowing you do not give way easily and that what you propose as an accommodation is out of character with your stupid, hidebound race! You seek only to divide my command, knowing that I must keep many of my men here. You seek to turn upon your escort and then resume the search for

Savory. Unlike most British, Lieutenant Halfhyde, you are full of subtleties—and with me they do not work!" Drawing himself up, he snapped an order at the armed native and stalked away. Halfhyde was pushed ahead of the man's bayonet, back again to the darkness and indignity of the prison hut.

Halfhyde was in a surly mood, hugging failure to himself as he sat with his back against the mud wall. The heat and the fug inflamed him as much as had the disconsolate questions of Todhunter and the respectful ones of Mr Midshipman Runcorn; as indeed did the unspoken ones of the petty officers and other ratings that seemed to emanate like accusing fingers from the silent figures in the darkness. Halfhyde had passed the word via Runcorn that he had parleyed to no effect, and had been quite curt when the midshipman had asked whether he had been interrogated about the movements of the *Prince Consort.* He had no wish to explain his mendacious revelations; the fewer who knew, the fewer those whose tongues, entering into indiscreet discussion in the hut, could reveal his lies to any listening ears outside.

"You should not presume to question your elders and betters, Mr Runcorn. You are told what you should be told, and no more."

"Oh, but, sir—"

"Hold your tongue, Mr Runcorn, if you please."

Runcorn had moved away; Halfhyde guessed his cheeks would be flaming, and was sorry. Now, in the enclosing dark, he cursed all Germans, Sir Russell Savory, the fools in the Admiralty who had not discovered earlier the purloining of vital secret papers, and the bigger fool who had appointed him,

St Vincent Halfhyde, to this wretched mission. It had been, he thought furiously, doomed from the start—a wild goose chase *par excellence*. And he had made a monkey's arse out of a wild goose! On his return he would get a tongue lashing from the whole majestic assembly of Their Lordships, as would Bassinghorn. Bassinghorn might get away with that verbal onslaught, but Halfhyde never. He had come up against the Board of Admiralty too often before, and revenge would be sweet to them. Obloquy would follow him into civilian life: he would be forever known henceforward as the bungler—or worse, the coward—who had lost Savory. Thus his thoughts rioted. But as the afternoon wore on towards evening and mentally he came full circle, his mind settled to one certain fact: if he was no better off than before his interview with von Arnhem, he was no worse off either. Escape remained as a line of positive action and must be undertaken as an act of duty. Thankful for a decision reached, he called for the midshipman.

"Mr Runcorn?"

"Sir?" The voice came from the far end of the hut.

"A moment," Halfhyde said acidly, "if you can spare the time."

"Oh—yes, sir!" Scurrying sounds indicated Runcorn's approach. "Here I am, sir."

"Good. We shall break out, Mr Runcorn."

"Yes, sir." The response was prosaic, unsurprised. "When, sir?"

"Tonight, one hour after full dark. You will inform all hands, quietly."

"Yes, sir. But our wrists are tied, sir!"

Patiently Halfhyde nodded. "It hasn't escaped my notice. But you're young, Mr Runcorn, and no doubt you have sharp teeth. Like a rat—my apologies—you shall gnaw. You shall start with me, and when I am free I shall untie you, and together we shall untie the others, and hope we're not disturbed by any guards."

"Yes, sir. Mr Todhunter, sir, is—"

"In handcuffs—I know. He'll have to suffer them. You'll detail two men to take him in charge and keep him safe from harm when we break out. When all the rest of us are untied, we shall lie low in our places with our wrists concealed behind us. When the time comes, I shall give the word and we shall muster quietly on either side of the doorway. At the right moment we shall rush the doorway, overpower the guard, and take his rifle. If this can be done in silence, so much the better—if not, we shall need to take on the entire outpost. I do not minimize the risk, but we have orders to obey. In either case, we run for von Arnhem's native canoes and make our escape down river to Dondo and the torpedo-boat. My intentions are as I indicated to you earlier—to rejoin Captain Bassinghorn. We make certain that we take all the available river transport. Is that understood, Mr Runcorn?"

"Yes, sir."

"Good! You're not scared?"

The reply was indignant. "Oh, *no,* sir!"

Halfhyde grinned. "Liar! You're as scared as I! I have no wish to stop any German bullets with my head, chest, or stomach! But we shall never let that sway us, shall we?"

"Certainly not, sir."

"Good," Halfhyde said again. "Gnaw, if you please, Mr Runcorn—gnaw hard, and fast!"

• • •

The ropes were not easy to gnaw, and the business took a long time. Runcorn spat blood after a while as he strove to pull Halfhyde's binding rope through its knots. But there was no intrusion from outside and at last the job was done. Halfhyde let out a long sigh of relief as he stretched his arms and flexed his fingers, rubbing life back into his wrists. After dealing with the midshipman's rope he moved silently across the hut and assisted Runcorn in the task of freeing the other men, a job that was quickly completed. Todhunter was, not unnaturally, aggrieved.

"The detective," he said, "to be the only one still not free! I hope this'll not be made known at Scotland Yard, Mr Halfhyde."

"I shall try not to include it in my report," Halfhyde said solemnly. "What you report is your own affair."

"And my warrant burned in front of my nose!"

"Like the singeing of the king of Spain's beard—you may yet go down in history, Mr Todhunter, as the only detective to execute a burned warrant! Keep your spirits up—the British Navy never thinks in terms of defeat." Leaving the detective inspector's side, he moved across towards the doorway, which was secured with reeds bound to a heavy framework and held in place outside with a cross beam. A little daylight was still filtering around the edges. Tentatively Halfhyde prodded with a finger, easing it through the reed thatch. That thatch was penetrable, as he had suspected. It would need a sudden firm movement at the last moment, but it could be done—an arm thrust through to lift away the holding beam, and they would pour out to rush the guard. Halfhyde, motionless by the door, listened for the soft footfalls of the armed sentry, approaching, fading away to the end of his beat, coming back again . . . a close eye on the sentry's timing should tell him when the man's back was turned. All in all; there was a fair chance of success.

Halfhyde remained in his station by the door, observing the edges and the thin, fading streaks of daylight. He watched the onset of the dark, and saw the flicker of camp fires after a while. The fires, he fancied, might be of some help. A few brands thrown on the huts should create a useful panic and diversion . . . thinking thus, he heard movement outside, and went back fast to his place on the floor, lying down with his hands behind his back. The beam was lifted, and men came in bearing food, which could be seen in the light of flares. They had bowls of fruit and berries, and earthenware water pots. These were taken round and the men were fed individually. There seemed to be no suspicions in the minds of the natives or the German guard, whose rifle was slung from his shoulder as though he saw no need to carry it more alertly. Nothing was said by either side. The feeding took a fair time, and before it was completed Halfhyde noted that it had become full dark outside. He pondered: would it be better, perhaps, to redraft his plan, rally all hands now with a cry, bound to his feet, and assault the guard inside the hut? Perhaps not. The men would not be fully ready for a change of orders, and there might well be a sentry still outside in addition to the guard. He was weighing the pros and cons when a fresh sound was heard from the distance: a monotonous drumming, the beat of tom-toms, drawing closer. A sudden tension was felt in the air, and the armed German snapped orders at the natives, who at once withdrew. The German followed them, shutting the reed door behind him and slotting the beam back into place. The tom-toms ceased as suddenly as they had begun, and silence fell. But soon Halfhyde heard, faintly at first, the sound of song, a curious dirge approaching the encampment, then the closer sound of many men coming through trees and undergrowth. His heart sank to his boots and he called for Runcorn.

"Sir?"

"Negative, Mr Runcorn. It's too late now. We must wait for a better time."

"Yes, sir. Who do you think is coming, sir?"

"How the devil should I know?"

"No, sir. I'm sorry, sir."

Halfhyde sank back against the hut wall, feeling bitter. Much disappointment was in the air: the hands had keyed themselves up, and the sudden and unexpected release of tension left a sourness behind. There was a lot of noise outside now: moving men, and conversation in German. Halfhyde wondered, but came to no conclusions. The sounds faded; the men were left alone and uninformed in the prison hut. Then, at last, after some two hours of guesswork, the doorway was opened up and von Arnhem himself came just inside. Beyond him, Halfhyde could see rifles and bayonets, many of them, forming a strong guard.

"You will all come out," von Arnhem called. "In single file, and carefully, or you will be shot."

Halfhyde stood up. "Do as the Hauptmann tells you," he said in a loud voice. "*All hands* together. I repeat, all hands." Sweating blood, he waited, hoping the hint would be taken. It was: every man got to his feet with his hands in place behind his back, as though tied still. Halfhyde led the way out past von Arnhem, with Runcorn and Todhunter behind him. As they

emerged, the armed men fell in on their flanks, directing them
to a circle of light in the centre of the compound. In the middle of the flares a man stood, a man who looked at the end of
his tether, dressed in once white shirt and trousers, his face
drawn and unshaven, his eyes haunted pools that reflected
hunger, hardship, and a deadly weariness of body and spirit.

Halfhyde, staring, felt the pressure of Todhunter's fingers on
his arm. "Well?" he asked in an impatient whisper. "What is it?"

"I recognize the man from his description and photographs,
Mr Halfhyde. It's Savory!"

Chapter 15

VON ARNHEM strode up the line of British prisoners and confronted Halfhyde. "Very clever," he said. "I congratulate you, Lieutenant Halfhyde."

"Upon what?"

Von Arnhem gestured towards Halfhyde's wrists. "The removal of the ropes. By scraping against some sharpness in the hut, no doubt?"

"In a sense, yes."

"A wasted effort! The first man to move a finger is as good as dead." The German officer called an order, and from the shadows beyond the circle of light, natives ran for fresh rope to re-secure the seamen's wrists, while the rifles of the guards held steady beneath watchful eyes.

Halfhyde said conversationally, "You have Sir Russell Savory, I see."

"I have."

"He was expected?"

Von Arnhem nodded. "There was a rendezous with one of my patrols, in a native kraal." He turned, looking down the line. "Where is your policeman, the detective?"

"Here I am," Todhunter said.

"Ah yes! Look, Herr Detective, at your intended victim! It is the last you will see of him, and—"

"What do you intend to do with him, Hauptmann von Arnhem?" Halfhyde interrupted.

"He will be taken south tomorrow, into German territory."

"He doesn't look fit to march another step."

"He will be carried when necessary, and there are other ways than marching." Von Arnhem smiled. "You need not fear for his health. We shall look after him most excellently. He, as well as his blueprints, will be of much value to Germany—but this, of course, you realize, I think!"

"Yes. Will you allow me a word with him, Hauptmann?"

Von Arnhem spread his hands. "It can do no harm. Walk ahead between the flares, Lieutenant Halfhyde. You alone, no one else." Once again he smiled. "You will perhaps be satisfied afterwards that Sir Russell Savory has no intention of returning to England."

Halfhyde nodded and walked ahead. He stared at the discomfited figure in its dirty clothing, repelled yet fascinated by his first contact with a traitor. Savory, he felt, failed to look the part of a man who had shaken the core of government and high command. He was almost nondescript, physically small and scraggy, though he might fill again after a decent meal and some sleep had clothed his bones and smoothed away the haggardness of his cheeks. No doubt there was brain there—the forehead had the domed look popularly ascribed to professorship and learning, but the mouth was pinched and mean. Formally, coldly, Halfhyde stated his position. "I am a British naval officer, ordered to find you and return you to London. You confirm that you are Sir Russell Savory?" he added.

"Yes." The eyes were downcast, humiliated. There was no arrogance in the man, no attempt at brazenness.

"I ask you this: is it your intention, if allowed, to go of your own free will to Germany, in the custody of Hauptmann von Arnhem, or do you wish to give yourself up to me and the police officer from Scotland Yard, and stand trial in London?"

Savory shook his head. "No. I'm committed. I wish to go to Germany."

"And your blueprints?"

Savory held up a bag similar to Todhunter's. "They're here."

"And you'll hand them over in Berlin?"

"Yes. To Chancellor Bismarck, in person."

"Ex-Chancellor, since 1890."

Savory nodded. "Yes, that's right, but he's still a man of influence and importance in Germany, and it's been agreed that I shall be taken to him immediately when I arrive in the Fatherland."

"Oh, so it's the Fatherland already, is it?" Halfhyde recalled Forbes's words: the soldier had believed Savory to have some influential connection inside Germany, a category into which Prince Bismarck most undeniably fell. "Is this to be a comeback, then?"

Savory stared. "I beg your pardon?"

"I mean, is this a private arrangement with Prince Bismarck, who may emerge from his retirement once he is in possession of the means to greater power than ever?"

Over Halfhyde's shoulder, Savory sought the eye of von Arnhem, who strode forward and laid a hand on Halfhyde's arm. "That is enough, Lieutenant Halfhyde. Go back to your men."

"I have more questions yet to be asked."

"I have said, that is enough. I shall not say it a third time." The eyes of both men met and held. Halfhyde, feeling blind anger rise, had a mind to swing round upon Savory, take his neck in his hands, and whirl the man round and round his head until the neckbone snapped. But this was no time for senseless heroics; Savory would certainly be rescued before he could be killed, and Halfhyde turned away in obedience to the German's order.

"You may have the swine," he said loudly. "He's too dirty to set foot on English ground again, and—"

"Just a moment," Todhunter interrupted, equally loudly.

"What is it, Mr Todhunter?"

"I have my duty to do, Mr Halfhyde. I have no warrant, and I am handcuffed, but I must utter the arrest."

"Nobly said, Mr Todhunter, but the scene is set against you, and against me too! I advise a decent acceptance of the current facts, and of *force majeure.*"

"That won't do, sir." There was a new obstinacy in Todhunter's voice. He spoke with determination, directing his speech beyond Halfhyde to the man still standing in the circle of light from the flickering, naked flares. The formal tones, the traditional phrases of the law of England, sounded incongruous in the African jungle.

"Russell Spencer Savory, knight . . . I arrest you in the name of Her Majesty the Queen by the authority vested in me by signed warrant of Her Majesty's principal Secretary of State for the Home Department, on the grounds that you are in process of committing a treasonable act. Do you wish to say anything in answer to the charge? I must warn you that whatever you say will be taken down in writing and may be given in evidence."

Halfhyde's mind flickered on to the absence of pen and ink.

There was a silence, a curious silence in which Halfhyde felt almost embarrassed for Todhunter's sake. It was Todhunter himself who broke the silence, lamely. "It was my duty, Mr Halfhyde. I've always done my duty."

"Of course. You are quite right, Mr Todhunter."

"Well, I've said it, I've presented the charge, haven't I?" Todhunter sounded bellicose now. "If the Germans take him after this, it's an act of interference with the law, in my book. They're taking an arrested man out of my custody!"

"Yes indeed, Mr Todhunter. If I were you, I'd—"

"Hauptmann von Arnhem, sir, you've heard what I said. I expect you to take due note."

The German bowed gravely, clicking his heels together. "Prince Bismarck will naturally be informed of the great danger he is in, Herr Todhunter. He will tremble. And now, if—" He broke off sharply. "Lieutenant Halfhyde, what is this you are doing?"

"A last word with Sir Russell Savory," Halfhyde answered. He was already moving back into the circle of flares. Savory had placed his bag of blueprints on the ground, apparently too weary to go on holding it.

"You will come back at once," von Arnhem called.

"I shall not!" Suddenly, Halfhyde put his head down and charged for Savory. He knocked the man flying with his shoulder, got down on hands and knees and seized the bag in his teeth. Up in a flash as the guns opened fire, he raced for the bank. Dropping the bag, he swung his right leg back as bullets whined past his body, and gave a mighty kick. The blueprints sailed out over the river, there was a splash and a sparkle of spray was visible in the light of the flares. In the same instant, also clearly visible, a huge scaly tail thrashed the river, and immense jaws clamped tightly over Savory's leather bag. As von Arnhem, beside himself with rage, directed heavy rifle fire towards the robber of his nation's destinies, the creature slid swiftly down river on the current. A moment later something struck Halfhyde heavily on the side of his head, and he crashed unconscious to the ground.

On regaining consciousness, Halfhyde found himself water-borne. He was sick and giddy and his head ached as might Mr Todhunter's after a whole gallon of Sam Strawbridge's whisky. When he was able to open his eyes, he saw that he was in a native canoe and that Runcorn was alongside him. Runcorn's hands, like his own, were still tied behind his back.

"Mr Runcorn—"

"Sir! Thank God, sir! You're all right, sir?"

"An overstatement," he groaned, "but it will pass. Tell me what happened, Mr Runcorn."

"Yes, sir. You were struck on your head, sir—"

"That much I have deduced. What about the blueprints?"

"Consumed, sir, I believe. At any rate, taken down the river and no doubt well chewed."

Halfhyde murmured, "I have an idea that that excellent crocodile has saved the British Fleet!"

"Well, sir, not quite, sir. There's still Sir Russell Savory, sir. He's still in German hands, and going south."

"And us?"

"North, sir. Down river, sir, to the Livingstone Falls, under guard."

"Back to the torpedo-boat, Mr Runcorn?"

"Yes, sir. And really, sir, I don't know why." Runcorn shook his head in wonder as the canoe, with others behind containing the British seamen, glided down river beneath a high moon. "Why did Hauptmann von Arnhem do in the end what you wanted all along?"

Halfhyde eased his head; there was a feeling of dried blood and he was very sore, but the worst had passed. He pulled himself to a sitting position, and felt as he did so the nudge of a rifle barrel in his back. He looked around; the guarding escort was strong. Answering Runcorn's question he said, "It's simple enough, I would have thought. Von Arnhem, as you said, has Savory now!"

"Yes, sir, but—"

"So home we go, our tails between our legs! Earlier, von Arnhem was simply procrastinating, putting me off until he had our traitor actually in his grasp."

"Yes, sir, I understand," Runcorn said after a pause. "But will he not—"

"But, but! You are as full of butts as a nanny goat, Mr Runcorn." Halfhyde paused. "The men. Have we any casualties?"

"No, sir, apart from yourself, sir. It was done so quickly, sir. And before there was bloodshed, sir, Mr Todhunter and I had words with Hauptmann von Arnhem, sir."

"What words?"

"Sir, I threatened him with exposure. He seemed to want to take revenge for what you had done, but I pointed out that to act coldbloodedly would not only be pointless but might lead to war, sir."

"Well done, Mr Runcorn! And Todhunter?"

"Mr Todhunter spoke of Scotland Yard, sir. In the end,

Hauptmann von Arnhem ordered all hands aboard the canoes. I believe, sir, he saw he had no other alternative than to hold us prisoner, which might have proved an embarrassment."

"Indeed it might," Halfhyde said. "But to go back to what you were asking, Mr Runcorn. I perceived the nub of your question: will not von Arnhem realize that the *Prince Consort* is liable to make an attempt at seizure on the high seas—is that not it?"

"Yes, sir, exactly. So why did he let us go, to report the facts?"

"Because he will have come to the conclusion that the *Prince Consort* will do no such thing! And he may well be right, for there is very considerable danger to naval careers inherent in such an attack."

"Then, sir—"

"Don't fret about it, Mr Runcorn. I am not well enough, and there are many more ways than one of killing a cat! In the last resort Captain Bassinghorn is not a man to be put off doing what he sees as his duty by the equivocal dictates of the miserable clerks who infest the halls of government! We must consider ourselves fortunate that Hauptmann von Arnhem has close knowledge neither of myself nor of Captain Bassinghorn." Halfhyde paused. "How is Mr Todhunter after all the excitement?"

"He's all right, sir, but he's still handcuffed, sir."

"We are *all* still tied, are we not?"

"Yes, sir, but Mr Todhunter must remain so until we can find a blacksmith, sir. I saw Hauptmann von Arnhem throw the key into the river before we left, sir."

•   •   •

The canoes reached the vicinity of the Livingstone Falls inside three days. Upon arrival all the British except Todhunter were freed of their bonds and put ashore under cover of the rifles. The canoes were turned round to head back up river with the German guards. Halfhyde led the seamen overland to where they had left the torpedo-boat. Coming out from the jungle track to the water's edge they found Major Forbes hanging his newly washed khaki jacket out to dry on the forward guardrail. Forbes waved, delighted and relieved to see them.

"Welcome back aboard, my dear fellow! Your command is intact, and I formally hand over." His eyes narrowed. "Where's that damned traitor?"

Briefly, Halfyde explained. Forbes was greatly saddened by the news of Bernardino Antunes's murder, also by that of the Scot who had tried to give a warning in time. "Sar'nt Campbell," he said, shaking his head. "A good soldier, and a good Scot. We served together in India. God rest his soul." For a moment Forbes closed his eyes, standing gaunt and silent in the sunlight. *"Ne obliviscaris,"* he said, and opened his eyes again.

"I beg your pardon, Major?"

"Never forget. It's the motto of the Dukes of Argyll, the Chiefs of Clan Campbell." He took a deep breath. "Well now, Halfhyde, we face the future without forgetting the past. At least you've despatched the blueprints! What do you intend to do now?"

Halfhyde outlined his intentions. "We're going to run short of coal before we can reach Mossamedes," he said. "I'll have all hands ashore at once, to chop wood. It must be stowed in every available place and we must just accept the discomfort until it is burned." He looked towards the guardrail and its draped laundry. "Your washing, Major. Ashore upon a tree, I think?"

"Just as you wish, of course, but it's doing no harm, is it?"

"It's not seamanlike, Major, not shipshape. This is one of Her Majesty's ships of war, not a Chinese laundry." Halfhyde clapped Forbes on the shoulder. "You'd not allow it upon the flagstaff at Stirling Castle, I fancy!"

Aided by the fuel-conserving flow from the Livingstone Falls, they were down the river in a little under ten hours. All hands were ordered on deck so that their living quarters could be stacked to capacity with wood chopped from the jungle trees. Halfhyde had ordered life-lines to be rigged on deck; and, clinging to these life-lines and to the guardrails, the torpedo-boat's company made the outward passage of the sand bar and the lines of rolling, crashing surf. Outward passages through surf were always easier than inward ones, since the waves were breasted instead of run before; and, like half-drowned rats, shivering with the cold of the seas and a teeming rain, they came through in safety and set their course to the southward for Mossamedes. A consuming impatience gripped everyone aboard. Halfhyde was in a taciturn mood, frowning out ahead continually, driving himself hard. There was little need to drive the men: a full head of steam was kept up and the seamen willingly backed up the stokers, helping to relieve the watches below at the furnace. Savory was not going to get away with it now, nor was the arrogant von Arnhem. Todhunter, still in his shackles, inhabited a space in the ward-room now cleared of wood, and caught up on lost sleep; when awake, he hugged his grievances and his disappointment. He was convinced, now, that Savory was gone for good. Forbes, who had asked to come with them since he had business in Mossamedes—where he promised to be of assistance—tried to reassure the detective inspector that all was not lost. But he talked in vain.

Two days out from the mouth of the Coanza River, Halfhyde entered the small port of Mossamedes. He proceeded ashore at once, minus his uniform cap and tunic, and with Forbes reported at the office of the British consul, an elegant Portuguese named Fernando dos Santos, known to Forbes. Most of the talking was done by Forbes, since he had an excellent command of Portuguese, while the British consul suffered a sad lack of English. "Very small lot of sheeps, Senhor," the latter said apologetically to Halfhyde. "Breetish sheeps come leetle and I no spik."

Halfhyde waved a hand. "No matter. We shall be brief but pointed. Major, the important thing is the telegraph to St Helena. No delay, if you please."

Forbes nodded, and addressed dos Santos in a rapid flow of words, answered with nods and smiles and gesticulations and more words. It was a wordy morning. Outside again, Halfhyde asked for clarification.

"The message will go at once, my dear fellow. He was most cooperative, and will see that the authorities turn a blind eye to your use of the port."

"He's to be trusted?"

"I think so. In any case, we have no alternative, have we?"

"No. Has he placed any stipulation upon my use of the port?"

"He'd rather no one was allowed ashore. And he'd like you to be away within 24 hours. That's all." He added, "This was suggested merely as a wish, but in my view you'd do well to comply."

"And comply I shall! You asked about stores and coal, did you not?"

Forbes nodded. "A ship's chandler is to report to you for orders, bringing a man with a hammer to strike away poor Todhunter's handcuffs."

"Damn it, I'd nearly forgotten about Todhunter! Thank you, Major, for all you've done to help. And now goodbye." They shook hands. "As soon as I've taken stores and bunkers, I shall go to sea on a westerly course and then remain on station outside the port to await the *Prince Consort's* arrival—and keep a weather eye open for Admiral von Merkatz at the same time."

It was a dirty, uncomfortable night. The torpedo-boat bucked and rolled and pitched, hove-to on Halfhyde's decision to conserve vital bunkers. There was a fug below in the coffin-like ward-room, which was battened down against spray and the occasional wave that swept right over the plunging vessel. Todhunter's stomach was once again playing him up and a wash-deck bucket had been placed beside his bunk, secured with rope in a position handy for his mouth, since the man with the hammer in Mossamedes had failed to shear the chain of his handcuffs and the detective inspector was not in full control of his destinies. British steel and Scotland Yard between them produced the world's strongest handcuff chains, which was some small consolation to Mr Todhunter's pride, of which he was now feeling stripped naked.

In the midship cockpit, Halfhyde and Runcorn shared the

watch. The *Prince Consort* could not be expected for a matter of days, but Admiral von Merkatz might proceed to sea at any time after Savory had been handed over. By Halfhyde's estimate Savory could be expected to cross the frontier into German South-West Africa within three to four days of leaving von Arnhem's camp if, as was virtually certain, the greater part of his journey was to be made by river—the Cubango, the Cuito, the Cunene, all were available. That meant he could be inside German colonial territory already. Admiral von Merkatz and his squadron of heavy ships were most probably lying in Walvis Bay. On the other hand von Merkatz could be lying off the coast well north of Walvis Bay, near the frontier itself and ready to take Savory off in his boats; and that would mean he would get to sea the quicker. All night the telescopes had watched to the southward for the white masthead lights and the red and green sidelights that would tell of approaching ships. Many had been seen, but each time the lights had turned out to be those of northbound merchantmen coming up from the Cape. At the first of the sightings Runcorn had regretted the absence of their torpedoes, removed from the tubes before the launch in the interests of safety while negotiating cataracts and rapids.

"You are warlike, Mr Runcorn."

"Yes, sir. Would you not have used them, sir, against the Germans?"

Halfhyde shook his head, smiling. "I fancy I would not. There are more subtle things than torpedoes, Mr Runcorn."

"It wouldn't matter, sir, if we killed Sir Russell Savory, would it?"

"Not in the least, since he'll never serve Her Majesty again, but it was not him I was thinking of saving!" Halfhyde brought up his telescope again and continued the fruitless search. After the dawn they sought not lights but monstrous shapes, the fighting-tops and smoke-belching funnels that might at any moment loom through the overcast. But none came, and Halfhyde remained on station, ceaselessly watching, waiting as the grey day wore on, ready to melt with his tiny vessel into the wastes of sea upon sighting von Merkatz, and then wait again for the arrival of the *Prince Consort* to pick him up and turn into the wake of the German squadron. Worms of doubt niggled at his mind: perhaps he had run things too close, for if the gap between the arrivals was long, then von Merkatz might well make a German port before he could be brought to book.

Bassinghorn paced his navigating bridge, hands behind his back, beard outthrust, eyes hard. Halfhyde's message from Mossamedes had been a bald confession of failure, and failure had to be turned into success as the eleventh hour approached. Immediately upon receipt of that message, Bassinghorn, with his bunkers full again to capacity, had taken the *Prince Consort* to sea and was now steaming at full power towards the coast of Africa, his sweating stokers slave-driven by the petty officers to keep the hungry, roaring furnaces fed with coal. On deck, the wind tugged at the standing rigging, sang through the wires and ropes like a hundred demons, sent the White Ensign out stiff and straight, and blew a heavy spray up over the eyes of the ship to lash back in spindrift upon the bridge personnel, even over the lookout at the foretopmast head, an oilskinned able seaman straining his eyes through the murk. The battle-ship, with her company at cruising stations, had steamed with half her armament manned as she began to near the rendezvous position. As they came now into the area for the pick-up, the lookouts were double-banked and warned to be continually alert, to sweep their arcs constantly for a sight of Lieutenant Halfhyde or the German squadron.

Commander Percy climbed to the navigating bridge, his face stiff. Bassinghorn turned at his approach. "Ah, Commander. We should make the rendezvous within the next hour, I fancy. You're all ready to hoist the torpedo-boat?"

"Yes, sir,"

Bassinghorn lifted his telescope, stared ahead of the battleship's track, then to port and starboard in a long sweep of the glass before lowering and snapping it shut. "By the look upon your face, Commander, you have something to say. Kindly say it."

"Yes, sir." Percy gave a cough, then cleared his throat. "I have bloodshed to speak about, sir, and very heavy casualties to offi-cers and men. This is no light matter." As the captain made no answer, Percy went on, "I trust you have fully considered the implications, sir, of interfering with a foreign warship on the high seas—*all* the implications?"

"You may rest assured I have," Bassinghorn answered coldly.

"To be precise, sir, *four* foreign warships. I would advise fur-ther thought."

"I have scarcely stopped thinking, Commander, since Mr Halfhyde's message reached me. I am well aware of the odds, but we have heavier guns than von Merkatz—that is, if he cares to use his! I have a suspicion, Commander, that the very fact of a sea battle would make it impossible for Germany to hold

Savory, simply because the whole thing would be brought into the open. As to the act of interference, as you call it, I am only too well aware of the consequences of failure—the consequences to the future defence of Great Britain!"

"The future is not yet with us, sir. The present is—and the *immediate* future lies not far ahead." Percy coughed again. "Their Lordships are customarily more concerned with closer matters than with projected uncertainties that may or may not come to fruition."

"Nonsense! And if they do, then they behave as ostriches!" Bassinghorn snapped.

"Perhaps, sir, perhaps. But—"

"My orders from the Admiralty were clear on just one point, Commander. Perfectly clear. Sir Russell Savory was not to reach Germany! In this case, Their Lordships cannot in fact be accused of not looking a decent distance ahead."

"But with discretion."

"Yes, with discretion—exceedingly imprecisely stated! It is within my province to interpret it, and that I propose to do."

"By engaging Admiral von Merkatz." The commander shook his head. "An extreme act, sir . . . and one with which I have now decided I should not care to be associated in the minds of Their Lordships."

Bassinghorn swung round sharply. "I beg your pardon, Commander?"

"I mean, sir, that after full consideration I wish to state a formal protest, and would be glad if you'd be kind enough to note it."

The blood drained from Bassinghorn's face, leaving it deathly grey. His hands shook, the fingers clenched and unclenched. "It is noted. I have made no firm decision yet to engage von Merkatz, but shall not hesitate to do so if I think fit in the circumstances as I find them. I trust my ship is in all respects ready to clear for action?"

"Yes, sir."

"And you will obey such orders as I may give, unless you wish to find yourself in arrest and confined to your cabin. You spoke of consequences. May I remind you of the consequences of refusing to obey your captain?"

"I shall obey your orders, sir, never fear." Without waiting to be dismissed, Percy turned on his heel and went down the ladder, his whole manner and bearing a protest in themselves. Bassinghorn simmered, eyebrows drawn down in a heavy, scowling line of grey bush. His anger at disloyalty was increased by the knowledge that there was truth in what Percy had said. Bassinghorn was walking a tightrope between duty and expediency, and another between concern for his country's interests which could lie in two directions—a world-shaking incident now, or the build-up of a rival empire's naval strength for the future. It was a hairline decision, and it was his alone to make; but it was not unreasonable to expect wholehearted support from his subordinates.

"Ship on the port quarter, sir!"

The shout came from right alongside Halfhyde, from Petty Officer Thomas. Halfhyde, steaming to the west currently to keep himself well out from the shore, swung round and followed the torpedo-gunner's mate's pointing arm. "Do you identify?"

"Not yet, sir, but I fancy it's a warship."

"Then—" Halfhyde broke off, feeling excitement flood

through him like a tide as he saw the approaching mastheads and fighting-tops of a battleship. From that quarter, it could scarely be the *Prince Consort,* which would approach from dead ahead, or at most a little on either bow. Then through the gloom and the rain he saw the naval ensign of Germany flying out abaft the mainmast head, and astern the loom of another vessel. "It's von Merkatz," he said. He blew down the bell-mouthed voice-pipe to the engine-room. "Full speed!" he ordered. "I want everything you've got." Turning to the helmsman he ordered the course to be maintained to the west.

Runcorn emerged at the rush from the ward-room. "What are we going to do, sir?"

"For now, Mr Runcorn, we do as was intended and fade into the rainy wastes! We hope we fade unseen, and we hope the *Prince Consort* is not too far to the westward!" The torpedo-boat gathered way, lurching heavily into the restless seas, bows rising and falling and water coming aboard in great gouts. Halfhyde brought up his glass and looked out astern: faintly as they increased the distance he saw the German squadron steam past on its northerly course in line ahead, rolling heavily to the beam sea, four mighty ships awash with water, the great tubes of their guns pointing ahead to the Fatherland.

Chapter 16

CONTACT WAS MADE within the hour. Once the German squadron had vanished, Halfhyde turned his command away from the west, going back on his tracks, reckoning it was wiser to lie closer off the approaches to Mossamedes in case he should miss the *Prince Consort* in the wider seas outside. And just as he came within sight of the coast, his lookout reported the British battleship coming up on the port beam. Halfhyde turned towards her, and as she stopped engines semaphore signals were exchanged. Within minutes the torpedo-boat was hooked on to the blocks swinging from the main boom and the hands on the battleship's deck were starting to hoist her inboard and settle her into the crutches. The captain was himself waiting on the upper-deck to take Halfhyde's report as he stepped aboard.

"Well, Mr Halfhyde, welcome back aboard. I understand you have sighted von Merkatz?"

"I have, sir, steaming north as expected." Halfhyde swept water from his face with his hand. "I judged him not to be steaming under full power, sir, most likely so as to conserve his coal." He laughed. "He'll not be wanting to enter Gibraltar again, at all events, though no doubt the Canaries are at his disposal."

"By which time, perhaps, I shall have overtaken him. We shall lose no time now." Bassinghorn turned to Commander

Percy. "A messenger to the fleet engineer, if you please. When I ring down for the main engines, I shall want full power maintained for overhauling von Merkatz—I wish the engine-room to know the facts. Mr Halfhyde, to my sea cabin, if you please. I—" He broke off, staring. "What is the matter, pray, with Mr Todhunter?"

"He has arrested himself, sir, I fancy! But that's unkind—it was forced upon him. May I suggest he is taken below to the blacksmith's shop for release?"

"Bless my soul! Oh yes, very well, have him sent below." Bassinghorn turned away and strode forward. Halfhyde followed him to the bridge, where he ordered the engines ahead again and indicated the course; then to the sea cabin, where Bassinghorn gestured to a chair and poured him whisky, asking for his full report of all that had happened ashore. Concisely, Halfhyde gave it. The captain listened without interruption. When Halfhyde had finished he said, "At all events the blueprints are gone and that's something. But Savory himself remains and will be able to reconstruct them when he has German drawing boards at hand." He stroked his beard. "This involvement of Prince Bismarck. Do you give that particular weight, or not?"

"I do, sir. Very much so!"

"In what direction?"

Halfhyde repeated what Forbes had said originally, and added his own interpretation: "A comeback into active political life may not be too wide of the mark, sir."

"Yes. I share that view—or I tend to. I had some conversations in St Helena, most interesting ones. They have a link with what you have just told me, though at the time I saw no such link, I confess. Now . . . I wonder!"

"Sir?"

Bassinghorn got up and stared out of the port. He said slowly, "I met a certain Frenchman—his name is of no moment now—a gentleman recently retired from the French diplomatic service. He spoke of strong rumours that Bismarck was, indeed, anxious to re-emerge as Chancellor of Germany—and was seeking something to use as a lever."

Halfhyde smiled. "Sir Russell Savory! Those were the lines my mind was working along."

"So when we meet von Merkatz, such knowledge may prove useful."

"Yes, sir. But it's still supposition rather than knowledge, of course."

"True. But let us, as an exercise, suppose a little further, Halfhyde." Bassinghorn turned away from the port, and sat again, his elbows resting on the arms of his chair and his fingertips held together in a parson-like manner. "Let us suppose this: Savory is in touch, not with Germany as a nation—not with the Kaiser or his ministers, that is—but with Bismarck directly. If this is so, then we may be correct in assuming that von Merkatz is as it were, committed to Bismarck's camp. Do you follow? He is acting for Bismarck."

Halfhyde nodded, eyes narrowed. "I follow indeed. But the despatch of a naval squadron is a matter for the German Admiralty, not for a retired Bismarck."

"Oh, I agree certainly. But Bismarck is not without influence still, and has friends in high places. A little jiggery-pokery could, I believe, result in certain orders to von Merkatz."

"Possibly, sir, if improbably—in my view, that is. In any case, I confess I don't see the point insofar as we are concerned."

"The German emperor is known, is he not, to be unfriendly towards Bismarck? Two strong personalities—the one exacting and imperious, the other expecting to retain all his old power when the new emperor was proclaimed in '88? There has been more than a degree of hostility, and Admiral von Merkatz, as a Bismarck's man if we're right, is standing into dangerous waters *vis-à-vis* his emperor!"

"Who may not be party to Bismarck's machinations?"

"Exactly!" Bassinghorn smacked a fist into his palm. "You have it, my dear Halfhyde! Von Merkatz will have his emperor to answer to if he makes a monkey's arse of his mission. And in the German Navy, failure is as much to be condemned as it is in the British Navy."

"Undoubtedly. In which case, he'll do his best *not* to fail, sir!"

"Ah—there we part company! There are different forms of failure. There's an element of risk in it, but I believe von Merkatz, in the circumstances, may perhaps prefer to let Bismarck down rather than fail in such a way that leads his emperor prematurely into war. Remember, the Germans have not yet built their splendid new fleet!"

Halfhyde frowned and pondered. He said, "Your point has sunk home, sir, but I am not wholly convinced of its validity, to be frank. No doubt time will tell—"

"Yes, indeed. And I propose to hasten time along as soon as I have overhauled Admiral von Merkatz!"

"How, sir?"

"By using my guns, Mr Halfhyde, and bringing the Germans to action—or, at any rate, the threat of it, I've an idea that'll be enough." Bassinghorn paused, looking intently into Halfhyde's face. "Shall I have your support, in addition to your obedience?"

"You shall, sir, though at the same time I would advise caution. We are but one ship against four, and in fact our chances would be slight—and our casualties heavy—"

"The British fleet, Mr Halfhyde, did not attain its pre-eminence by shying from the odds."

"Indeed not, sir. I only suggest we do not rush our fences. While I'm not convinced of your theory in regard to von Merkatz and Prince Bismarck, I would remind you that I gained the impression from Hauptmann von Arnhem that he was under orders to be diplomatic in his handling of the Savory affair ashore. It's more than likely von Merkatz has been similarly instructed. And I think we must wait and see."

"I note your advice," Bassinghorn said in a coldly formal tone. "Is there anything else, Mr Halfhyde?"

"One thing more, sir: if you should use your guns, then the avoidance of failure on your part will be a pre-requisite to the avoidance of court martial!"

"That, too, I have considered." Bassinghorn stood up, large and formidable, filling the small sea cabin with his physical bulk and with an emanation of his resolve, his determination to do his duty as he saw it. "If necessary, I shall still bring Admiral von Merkatz to action!"

The chase continued in filthy weather, with a curious cold fug below-decks behind the deadlights now closed over the ports, and solid water washing back from the fo'c'sle head, swilling aft in a grey and urgent stream, breaking in spray from the bower anchors at the catheads to send spindrift flying over the bridge and the guns. Tension could be felt along the mess decks and flats, a keen anticipation of a taste of war. The word had now been passed down from the captain via the commander and the divisional officers, informing the ship's company of Bassinghorn's intentions. And already the *Prince Consort* was cleared away for action so far as was consistent with the prevailing weather conditions—the tampions were still in their places in the gun muzzles of the heavy armament and the canvas covers were still in place, but these could quickly be unshipped when the order came. Awnings, themselves long since struck, now had their stanchions unpinned and laid flat to give the guns a clear field of fire, and all the ship's side guardrails had been removed. Movable upper-deck gear had been shifted; and below-decks all was secured and battened down against the shaking and pounding that would reverberate through the ship if the great sixteen-inch guns opened above. Though the ship was still at cruising stations and would remain so, with her action parties not yet closed up, until the German squadron was overhauled and in sight from the bridge, the fire parties were being exercised in what they might be required to do if German shells ripped and tore through the *Prince Consort's* sides above the armour belt that should, in theory at least, protect her magazines and engine-room and boilers. Halfhyde, with no particular shipboard responsibilities for the present, walked through the lowerdeck, having a word with the men here and there. In the tiller flat he found Sam Strawbridge with a carpenter's mate, overhauling the emergency steering gear that would be brought into use if the navigating bridge and wheelhouse were put out of commission.

"All sound, Mr Strawbridge?" he asked.

Strawbridge straightened. "All sound, sir." He paused. "I understand you met the man Savory personally, Mr Halfhyde?"

"I did."

"A pity you didn't shoot the bugger, sir!"

Halfhyde grinned. "I had a mind to, but the circumstances were against me. How's the feeling in the ship, on the lowerdeck?"

"Plenty of spirit, sir. They take it personally. It's their Navy, sir—*our* Navy, like. They won't let him get away with it. They want to see him swing for treason."

"They're behind the captain?"

"There's not a man as isn't, sir, and never mind the odds."

Halfhyde nodded. "As I thought. And Mr Todhunter? How is he?"

"As well as can be expected, sir." Sam Strawbridge grinned. "A period ashore, and a period in a small boat, has robbed him of his big-ship sea-legs for a while!"

"And the prospect of action?"

The boatswain wiped the back of a hand across his forehead, then reached out to steady himself as the compartment lurched to a heavy wave that battered outside and added more noise to the intermittent clatter of the steering engine. "He has guts, sir. All the same, there's a touch of the squitters in the offing. London criminals are no soft option and I'm the first to admit it, but a battleship clearing for action is a bit different till you get used to it."

"And Mr Todhunter is a man of some imagination, I think, or he would not have become an inspector." Halfhyde paused. "Mr Strawbridge, have I your permission to penetrate the fastness of the warrant officers' mess—that is, if Mr Todhunter's there?"

"You have, of course, sir, and he is. He'll have to leave shortly, no doubt—the WOs mess is the after casualty clearing station in action."

"Yes, indeed. Thank you, Mr Strawbridge." Halfhyde turned away and climbed back through the ship to the warrant officers' mess on the port side. Before he reached the door his nostrils were assailed by a smell of medicaments, antiseptics, and rum that would ease the pain of men wounded in action. Sick berth attendants had mustered with stretchers, piles of bandages, plasters, blankets coloured red to conceal blood, and other adjuncts of their calling. Mr Todhunter, looking green, was lying at full stretch upon a leather settee beneath the deadlights and staring with a fearful fascination at the medical apparatus being produced, which included sharp knives, scalpels, probes, and clamps.

"Good afternoon, Mr Todhunter."

"Good afternoon, Mr Halfhyde. Has the German admiral yet been sighted?"

"Not yet, but he will be—our speed is excellent." Halfhyde sat on the settee beside the detective inspector, whose forehead was bathed in sweat. "Have you had your orders for action, Mr Todhunter?"

Todhunter nodded, his face set. "I've been told to report to the captain's sea cabin and remain handy."

"To make your arrest?"

"That's correct, Mr Halfhyde. I am to be sent across in a boat. I don't relish the idea, I may say."

Halfhyde suppressed a smile. "That was the captain's order?"

"No. I insisted. It's my duty, Mr Halfhyde, though at first Captain Bassinghorn didn't see it as such. But only I can make the arrest. It's what I'm here for, isn't it?"

Halfhyde nodded. "Of course. You're a brave man, Mr Todhunter, as I've had occasion to remark before—"

"I don't know about that. As a matter of fact, I'm feeling quite queasy." Todhunter stared towards the surgical array filling the mess. "Those blankets, Mr Halfhyde. Why are they red?"

Halfhyde told him. "Blood in quantity has an alarming effect upon wounded men, sometimes—but if I were you, Mr Todhunter, I'd not think about that. As for me, I've come to talk about something different, and that is the *avoidance* of action."

"Avoidance?" Todhunter stared from his recumbent position, looking surprised. "I thought—"

"Savory has to be removed from the Germans, we're all agreed about that. But I'm concerned about my captain. I have a very high regard for him . . . I'd not like to see him made to suffer when we reach Plymouth Sound. Their Lordships are difficult people to satisfy, to appease—and often they find post captains handy sacrifices. Do you understand, Mr Todhunter?"

"I think I do, sir, yes. To some extent we suffer the same in the force."

"I'm sure you do. You'll understand my anxiety." Halfhyde shrugged. "Action is what I wanted, once we'd lost Savory to Hauptmann von Arnhem, and I don't deny that it may become essential. But I don't want to feel responsible for any trouble that may strike Captain Bassinghorn due to my having botched my part ashore. You see, I have certain possibilities in mind, Mr Todhunter."

"What are they, sir?"

Halfhyde said, "Savory may already have passed some of his secrets to Admiral von Merkatz. Vital notes may have been made, notes that will be concealed if the German is boarded. Also it's possible, isn't it, that the blueprints in fact reached Berlin by some separate route? We have only Savory's own word that his bag contained his documents. If not, that unfortunate crocodile will have suffered indigestion to no avail!"

"Eggs," Todhunter said thoughtfully, "in two baskets rather than one?"

"Exactly—well put, indeed! If that's the case, then bringing the German squadron to action cannot of itself make our mission successful, and will rebound upon the head of Captain Bassinghorn."

Todhunter shook his head. "Myself, sir, I doubt your hypotheses, I doubt them most strongly."

"Why so?"

"Well sir, had you been conscious after the crocodile had grabbed the bag, I think you would have deduced that the bag did indeed contain the documents—Hauptman von Arnhem was quite beside himself. Also, as you know, I've made a study of Savory—we spoke about it on passage towards Gibraltar. His ambition, his seeking of prestige—"

"A perverse prestige, I think you said?"

Todhunter nodded. "Quite right. But he will act it right the way through, I'm certain. No one else will be permitted to steal his thunder. Britain has disappointed him, Germany offers hope. It is essential to him, to my way of thinking—and I'm far from inexperienced—to carry his mission to a conclusion *himself*. He'll not be side-tracked, nor would he have accepted being left to wither without his blueprints."

"You sound convinced enough, certainly."

"I *am* convinced." Todhunter lifted himself on one elbow. "Consider Savory's conduct since he made his demand—he would not take the easy course, Mr Halfhyde, and hand over his secrets in Chile. He preferred the difficulties, the hardships, the dangers. Now he's within a stone's throw, as it were, of his goal, he'll not alter his approach!"

"Well, not willingly, perhaps, I'll grant you that. But could he not be forced?"

Todhunter pursed his lips and scratched at his face reflectively. "I can't deny the possibility. On the other hand, I can't see the point of von Merkatz doing that. Can you, honestly?"

Halfhyde shrugged. "His own self-aggrandizement. Or a means to success without risking war! Milk Savory first, then hand him back with apologies. Have you not considered that, Mr Todhunter?"

"Well, I must admit, as a matter of fact, I have. I've argued with myself—and convinced myself like I said. I believe the Germans will see a need for Savory in person. Much of his value lies in his head, in his day-to-day presence at the side of the German naval constructors. You can't put all a man's thoughts and brainpower down on paper, Mr Halfhyde. Not if it's to be really *useful* when problems arise. You need the man himself. I've no doubts about that at all."

"Perhaps. It's a chance either way." Halfhyde shook his head and sent out a long sigh of frustration. 'What I'm looking for is a stratagem—something short of a full-scale confrontation that will yet hoist von Merkatz—" He broke off. A boy seaman had entered the mess and was standing at his shoulder with an urgent look on his face. "Yes, what is it?"

"From the captain, sir. The German squadron is in sight ahead, sir."

"Thank you, I'll be on the bridge directly." Halfhyde jumped up, his eyes alight. Despite all he had said, the close prospect of action was an invigorating one. He looked down at Todhunter. "Good luck, and don't worry, we shall come through with flying colours, Mr Todhunter!" He turned away from the detective inspector's glassy-eyed, green-faced stare, and left the warrant officers' mess at the double, tall body bent against the low clearance of the deckhead with its snaking steam pipes and cables and tubes. As he went through the flat outside he heard the buglers of the Royal Marine Artillery sounding for action, and the tattoo of the drummers as they beat to quarters. It looked, now, as though the die were cast.

On the bridge Bassinghorn closed his telescope with a snap and used it as a pointer. "There we are, Mr Halfhyde! Still in line ahead, with the *Kaiser Wilhelm* last of the line."

"Yes, sir." Halfhyde stared through his own telescope. The great counter ahead was heaving to the seas, pouring water down the plates as she rose and fell to a heavy pitch. So far as he could tell, the after guns were as yet unmanned; the German naval ensign was streaming out, flauntingly. Excitement and anger rose in Halfhyde's throat. It would be marvellous to bring that arrogant ensign down with a well-placed shot, to lie in ignominy upon the German decks, or trail over the side in the heaving West African waters! Closing his glass, he asked formally, "Your intentions, sir?"

"To close, steam up the line to starboard four cables' lengths clear of the squadron, and take station on the admiral's beam."

"And then, sir?"

"First, an exchange of signals, Mr Halfhyde."

"Asking for the handing over of—"

"*Demanding* it, Mr Halfhyde! Why should I ask for my own? I shall make no bones about it."

"And if the answer is . . . unhelpful? What then?"

"I shall fire a warning shot, which will act also as a ranging shot for my gunners."

"And action," Halfhyde murmured, "to follow."

"If necessary, Mr Halfhyde. I am not to be trifled with, and Admiral von Merkatz must learn that." He paced the bridge back and forth for a while, then came back to Halfhyde and stood with him, staring ahead as they closed the stern of the *Kaiser Wilhelm.* Von Merkatz, it seemed, was not increasing the speed of his squadron. Bassinghorn said, "It's still possible action may be avoided."

"How so, sir?"

"I can try ordering him into Gibraltar, Mr Halfhyde."

"An arrest of his ships, sir—a seaborne Todhunter in a boat, flourishing handcuffs and hoping that this time he'll not become locked in them himself?"

"I dislike witticism of that kind, Mr Halfhyde."

"My apologies, sir," Halfhyde said gravely, his lips twitching. "I fear Admiral von Merkatz might prove to be a resister of arrest—since I think we have neither the authority nor enough ships to enforce it if we had!" He paused, frowning, thinking. "On the other hand . . ."

"Well, Mr Halfhyde?"

"Second thoughts . . . Why not try it, sir? I'm sorry I spoke as I did. It was hasty. A little bluff can work miracles on occasions, I fancy!"

Bassinghorn looked sideways, sharply, staring at Halfhyde. "I know you to be an officer of devious mind—and I don't mean that in any unpleasant sense. What are you suggesting now?"

Halfhyde smiled. "The beginnings of a stratagem, sir, which may not work. I would prefer to keep my own counsel until we see how matters shape. The exchange of signals may yet prove helpful, who knows?"

Bassinghorn gave a short laugh. He was about to speak again when there was a whistle from a voice-pipe. A side-boy bent to answer it, then reported: "Captain, sir, Detective Inspector Tod'unter present as ordered, sir, in your sea cabin."

"Thank you. Warn Mr Todhunter that there may be much noise presently, and he would do well to guard his eardrums."

"Aye, aye, sir." Saluting, the side-boy withdrew back to the voice-pipe. From the bridge, everyone watched the German squadron draw nearer. As they came abeam of the *Kaiser Wilhelm,* they could see telescopes trained on them, oilskinned figures of German naval officers and ratings on the bridge, and clustered, curious figures dotted about the upper-deck. Still the guns did not appear to be manned. Admiral von Merkatz, Halfhyde fancied, had decided to play the game coolly, almost to pretend that there was no point of issue between himself and the British battleship. Up the line they went, slowly overhauling the next, the cruiser *Königsberg;* then the *Nürnberg,* and onward to come abeam of the flagship *Friedrich der Grösse* flaunting the splendid flag of Admiral Paulus von Merkatz.

Bassinghorn, with his glass once again to his eye as he

scanned the flagship's bridge, called across the wind and rain for his chief yeoman of signals.

"Sir?"

"Chief Yeoman, make by lamp to the flagship: 'Admiral von Merkatz from *Prince Consort,* I request you to heave to immediately in the name of Her Majesty the Queen and to permit my officer of the guard to board you.'"

"Aye, aye, sir." The chief yeoman saluted, and turned away to start rattling out the signal on his shuttered projector. As the bridge personnel waited for the German response, the commander climbed the ladder and approached Bassinghorn. He asked, "Do you not intend to salute the admiral's flag, sir?"

"I do not."

"An act of courtesy, sir?"

"To hell with the niceties, Commander!" Bassinghorn burst out. "On our last meeting, did von Merkatz return my salute? He did not! He shall get none now." Brusquely, he turned his back. The shorts and longs of the Morse code stabbed across towards the wallowing German flagship. Halfhyde, watching through his telescope, studied the figures on the bridge. Admiral von Merkatz with his flag captain, commander, navigator, and officer of the watch. He saw them clearly, and noted the superior smile on the lips of von Merkatz; he saw him turn aside to his flag captain, utter some remark, and then bellow with laughter in which he was joined by the others as the signal from the British battleship was read. Within a minute of its reception, the answering flashes were coming through.

Halfhyde lowered his telescope and glanced at Bassinghorn's set face. Everyone on the bridge was listening to the voice of the chief yeoman as he read off the message for the benefit of a leading signalman scribbling on a signal pad: his report to the captain was superfluous.

"Captain, sir. From Vice-Admiral Commanding German Special Service Squadron to *Prince Consort:* 'I am unable to consider your request and do not recognize the authority of the Queen of England upon the high seas.'"

Bassinghorn snorted. "Damned impertinence!"

"But only to be expected, sir," Halfhyde murmured. "At least, by me!"

"What's that, Mr Halfhyde?"

"His is a normal reaction, sir. And he is correct. Would we recognize the authority of the German emperor?" Halfhyde smiled. "I think not!"

"But you agreed, eventually, with my proposal, did you not?"

"Subject to a plan that I'm composing, sir, and which is not yet fully complete. For now, nothing is lost, I assure you, and my stratagem will wait."

Muttering angrily to himself, Bassinghorn turned away and paced the navigating bridge, back and forth, like a caged, frustrated tiger, cruelly aware of the amusement at his predicament that must be gripping the officers and men of the German squadron. His hands shook. He gripped them all the harder behind his thick back. With all his being now he wished to open fire and resolve the matter in smoke and flame and the whine of shells. Yet now that the twelfth hour was upon him, he was forced to recognize the truth—that to do this could lead only to the death of his command and all her company and the flouting of the Admiralty's unspoken orders. To himself he cursed Commander Percy, whose words had dropped like the poison of cowardice and indecision into his thinking, yet at the same time, when coolly appraised, held common sense. Yet again, the wars and sea battles of the past had not always been won by the application of undiluted common sense, or even by strict obedience to orders!

Bassinghorn stopped his restless pacing. "Mr Halfhyde, have Todhunter sent up, if you please."

"Aye, aye, sir." Halfhyde bent to the sea cabin voice-pipe, and whistled. "Mr Todhunter to the bridge, and quickly." He replaced the brass cover, and turned as the captain spoke again.

"Mr Halfhyde—you had, I think, a stratagem?"

"Yes, sir."

"Then now is the time to propound it, since the exchange of signals has scarcely helped!"

"Yes, sir. I suggest you make another signal in accordance with your own proposal—tell von Merkatz that you are arresting his squadron and that he is to steam for the Channel and is to enter Plymouth Sound—"

"My proposal was for Gibraltar, Mr Halfhyde, was it not?"

"Yes, sir. And mine is for the Lizard."

"Pray explain why," Bassinghorn said tartly.

Halfhyde smiled, and caught sight of Todhunter from the corner of his eye. "Because, sir, von Merkatz is scarcely, in my opinion, likely to obey in any case—"

"Then surely to God—"

"And you will be made to look a fool, sir, with respect, when he continues northward past the Gibraltar Strait. On the other hand, since we shall be going the same way as he, we shall be in a position to continue the theoretical arrest until we are in soundings—inside the Channel, sir, and not far off Plymouth."

Bassinghorn fumed. "A mere charade!"

"But a charade that could turn into reality for Admiral von Merkatz. What think you, Mr Todhunter? What, in your opinion, would your chief superintendent say?"

Todhunter opened his mouth, then shut it again and waved his arms. He was flummoxed, and said so. "This is off my beat, sir. I'm not experienced in the laws of Admiralty. I doubt, however, if an arrest would be legal."

"Even though there is a British subject held prisoner?"

"Not prisoner, sir. Savory is willing. He said so himself."

"Under duress, Mr Todhunter."

Todhunter shook his head. "I think not, Mr Halfhyde—"

"And I say you are wrong, Mr Todhunter!" Halfhyde interrupted, tongue in cheek. "In my opinion—and of course it's no more than an opinion, but we're well entitled to act upon it—in my opinion, Savory was under duress. I believe we are entitled to make an attempt to rescue him." Halfhyde turned towards the captain, lifting an eyebrow. "Well, sir? Will you make the signal? I think it can do no harm, at least."

Bassinghorn frowned, stared round at the bridge personnel, meeting every eye, then turned to look down at the great gun turrets on the deck below. There was a long pause, and a total silence. Then he said, "Gunnery Lieutenant, if you please."

"Sir?"

"Number Two turret is to be laid and trained upon the bows of the *Friedrich der Grösse,* if you please. Chief Yeoman, make to the admiral: 'It is my understanding that you have a British subject aboard. If he is not immediately released and put aboard my ship, I shall open fire.'"

There was an audible gasp from Commander Percy. The captain swung round upon him, hands behind his back, jaw and beard thrust out. "Your wishes as expressed earlier have been noted, Commander, have no fear about that. But I do not propose to make myself a laughing stock for the Germans by telling them they're under arrest. Chief Yeoman, the signal quickly!"

"Aye, aye, sir."

"Mr Halfhyde, your advice is appreciated, but I believe this to be a better form of bluff. I do not think Admiral von Merkatz will wish to provoke action now that he has been firmly confronted. His patron Prince Bismarck will not wish to be pushed before he is ready."

"I trust you'll be proved right, sir."

Bassinghorn, making no reply, turned away and walked to the port wing of his bridge, watching the further exchange of signals. The grey, disturbed sea rose and fell along the plating of the ships, which were rolling heavily and would make unsteady gun platforms if action should come. As the German flagship's signal lamp, replying, made the end-of-message group, the chief yeoman came across to report.

"Captain, sir, from the admiral. 'I have aboard one British subject wishing to proceed to Germany. Your threat is impertinent and will be disregarded.'"

Bassinghorn nodded. "Thank you, Chief Yeoman. Mr Winstanley?"

Stepping forward, the gunnery lieutenant saluted. "Sir?"

"Number Two turret to open, if you please, Mr Winstanley, both guns. The shot to fall over but close."

"Aye, aye, sir."

"Carry on, if you please, Mr Winstanley." Bassinghorn turned away, avoiding all eyes, and stared across the heaving waters at the *Friedrich der Grösse*. Halfhyde, glancing at Todhunter, saw the detective inspector thrust his fingers into his ears and close his eyes tight. Shouts of command came up from the waist—the shouts of Mr Mainprice the gunner, and the captain of the gun, a three-badge leading seaman. Seconds later the ship seemed to erupt. A blaze of flame burst out, a thick pall of gun-smoke enveloped the bridge with choking fumes, and an immense roar shattered across the wind and sea. Hot air swept around Todhunter, who staggered momentarily and grasped the bridge rail to steady himself. The whole ship appeared to shudder to the immensity of the great guns' recoil, not wholly absorbed by the hydraulics. She went sideways, bodily through the water, as the mighty sixteen-inch shells winged across to take the sea in great twin spouts on the German flagship's port bow and send water cascading over her fo'c'sle. As the reverberations of the gunfire died away, Halfhyde brought up his telescope: there appeared to be consternation on the flagship's bridge, and on her decks men were doubling in all directions. Within the next second, bugles and drums sounded from all the ships of the squadron. Aboard the *Friedrich der Grösse* signal lamps began flashing messages down the line and coloured bunting crept up the signal halliards to the yards on her fore and mainmasts. A few moments later the great battle ensigns broke from each of the warships, and the gun turrets were seen to swing and bear, ready to open murderously on the word from the flag.

Chapter 17

IN A TENSE SILENCE, the seconds passed. Halfhyde said, "He's not opening, sir."

"Not yet, Mr Halfhyde, not yet. And he may not do so!"

"The bluff has worked?"

"I believe von Merkatz is perceiving the value of discretion, Mr Halfhyde." Bassinghorn turned his head. "How say you, Commander?"

"I think we are lucky, sir."

"Lucky! My assessment takes no *luck* into account! I believe von Merkatz realizes only too well that he must not allow a traitor's filth to be blazoned before the world! And while we wait upon his decision, my guns shall remain—" He broke off as a shout came from the chief yeoman.

"Flagship's signalling, sir!"

They all watched the winking lamp from von Merkatz's bridge: quickly the chief yeoman read off the signal, and reported: "From Admiral von Merkatz, sir: 'I am in position to blow you out of the water.'"

Bassinghorn's face suffused. "Is that all, Chief Yeoman?"

"Yes, sir."

"Then why in God's name does he not do so?" Bassinghorn demanded in a bellicose tone. "Mr Halfhyde?"

"What he says is true, sir. That he has not done so is perhaps due to—"

"A sudden access of discretion, as I said! I think there is still
a considerable degree of bluff, Mr Halfhyde, and I propose to
call it promptly. Chief Yeoman?"

"Sir?"

"Make to the German: 'Blow me out of the water if you wish.
I shall go down with my guns firing and your loss of men will
be heavy.'"

"Aye, aye, sir." The chief yeoman of signals returned to his
lamp and began sending. The *Prince Consort* slid on through
the rolling grey seas, keeping abeam of the *Friedrich der Grösse*
and her arrogantly flaunted standards. The silence on deck was
broken only by the sigh of the wind through the rigging and
the hiss of water along the armoured plates of the hull; and by
the clack-clack of the signal lamp as Bassinghorn's message of
possible death and destruction was flashed across the gap
between the battleships. Commander Percy's face was white, his
eyes wide, his hands thrust into the pockets of his black oilskin. In his mind's eye he saw the decks run red, the guns dis-
integrate in shattered turrets as the German shells burst upon
them, scattering flesh and steel splinters that could slice off a
man's head in an instant.

Halfhyde's thoughts ran on similar lines but were interlaced
with the deeply underlying thrill of action, that basic thrill
for which a man joined the Royal Navy, for which he went
down to the sea in ships to the uttermost ends of the earth.
The roar and thunder of the guns was ever in the mind's background, as was the satisfying feel when a well-laid broadside

raked an enemy's deck and opened up her sides like a peeled banana. Halfhyde moved to the port rail alongside the captain. Bassinghorn was as still as a statue, staring out across the sea towards the German line, his face expressionless as he strove to conceal his inner doubts. Halfhyde, who knew him well, who had been in action with him before now, understood. Bassinghorn was playing with many men's lives, and he had always had a deep concern for his ship's company; but at the same time he had a fierce regard for his duty, and this was paramount. His duty would therefore be done whatever the cost. For a moment of irony, Halfhyde found himself wondering how many men had died in past battles because a brave captain had done his duty as he saw it through his one pair of eyes, taking a possibly distorted view of that duty laid upon him by his country . . .

"Flagship signalling, sir!"

Bassinghorn swung round, but said nothing, waiting for the chief yeoman. The report came quickly: "From the admiral, sir; 'You may repair aboard in person. I shall send my sea-boat.'"

Bassinghorn stared. "A parley, by God! A parley!" He gave a cry of relief, and laughed. "It seems I was right, Mr Halfhyde, does it not?"

"It's possible, sir, but I'd not build too much on success in parleying. Have I your permission to accompany you aboard the flagship as officer of the guard, sir?"

Bassinghorn nodded. "Of course, and Todhunter also. Commander, stand by, if you please, to take the German's sea-boat alongside. Chief Yeoman, inform the admiral that I am reducing to four knots."

•　•　•

Todhunter, gibbering with terror though he was, made it manfully down the jumping-ladder, an affair of swaying rope dangling from the battleship's quarterdeck over the heaving, surging
water. Breathing prayers of thanksgiving, he thumped into the
arms of a German seaman and was deposited upon a thwart
astern of Bassinghorn and Halfhyde, his bowler hat dancing
from its toggle, wet with spray. He shook visibly. The paddle
steamer from the Clarence Pier to Ryde would never have been
like this! Almost as bad was the climb up to the German's deck,
after a terrible voyage across the sea gap, a voyage during which
almost all of Todhunter's stomach approached his mouth, but
was with a vast effort held back. As he clutched the swaying
German rope ladder and hung motionless, he heard Halfhyde's
voice beneath him, exhorting and encouraging.

"Hand by hand, Mr Todhunter, and foot by foot. Take it
slow and easy. You'll live—my word upon it!"

A low moan escaped Todhunter's lips, but he gritted his
teeth and, as Bassinghorn's rear left the ladder and disappeared
inboard, he reached up, and up again . . . and after a century
hands reached down and dragged him the rest of the way. To
be upon a solid deck was very heaven. With shaking fingers he
hove in his hat-stay and placed his bowler on his head, to
remove it again a moment later as he heard Bassinghorn's voice
introducing him to the flag captain.

"Detective Inspector Todhunter, of the Metropolitan Police."

"Ja. Welcome aboard, Herr Todhunter."

"Thank you, thank you . . ."

"If you will please to come below to the admiral's quarters,
gentlemen."

They followed. Everything was being done with punctilious

correctness. The wail of the boatswain's pipes had heralded Bassinghorn aboard, as was his double due as not only the officer commanding a seagoing ship but also as an officer of a foreign navy. There was much saluting, much bowing, much heel-clicking; also many stiff faces behind the polite formality. The British were undeniably unwelcome, and this attitude was given further evidence by Admiral von Merkatz when the procession reached his great day-cabin in the stern of the *Friedrich der Grösse*. Von Merkatz was tall and spare, as thin as a flagstaff, and had the coldest eyes Halfhyde had ever encountered. Like those of a dead fish, they were devoid of expression and humanity.

He stared at Bassinghorn, his head held back: there was as yet no invitation to sit down. In good but accented English he said, "Your actions have been unfriendly, Captain. Why is this, please?"

"Why?" Bassinghorn's temper was rising. "*Why*, my dear sir? Am I mistaken in believing you have a British subject shanghai'd aboard, or am I not?"

"No, Captain, you are not mistaken. You are mistaken only in one regard, an important one: Sir Russell Savory is aboard my ship by his own wish, and you should not seek to interfere. Your country has not, to my knowledge, closed her frontiers?"

"You talk around the point, sir, and this you know very well. I demand the immediate handing over of Sir Russell Savory."

Von Merkatz raised his eyebrows. "Upon what grounds?"

"This, also, you know. To restate it would be to waste time." Bassinghorn gestured towards Todhunter. "This is a police officer, and he is here to make an arrest."

"Of Sir Russell Savory?"

"Of a traitor, yes."

"I see. Does your country, does your queen, wish then for war?"

"Does your emperor—her grandson? I think, in family relationships, my country is the senior."

Von Merkatz made a gesture of derision. "To what effect, Captain? His Imperial Majesty has long left the nursery, and has untied the apron strings of a most tiresome grandmother given to senseless rages and autocratic demands upon such of the world as is still disposed to heed her—which His Imperial Majesty is not!"

"Sir, my Queen—"

"Pish, Captain, and pish again! Let us consider the relevant *facts* and speak no more of Queen Victoria who seeks to impose her bun and bosom where they are no longer wanted. The world has moved on, and great events are stirring beyond your British empire." Von Merkatz paused, staring at Bassinghorn with his cold gaze. "What, then, do you suppose, are the facts?"

"That you are seeking to steal secrets."

"Nonsense! Come, Captain! The secrets are being freely offered—this you know. The other fact is this: you—you, I repeat, not I—have uttered the first threat and have opened fire upon my flagship—"

"A warning shot, as is customary—"

"To pirates and such. I am no pirate, and I am not answerable to you, nor to your policeman. It is an insult to the Fatherland to confront me with your wretched policeman, and—"

"Now just a moment," Todhunter began in an official tone. The admiral rounded upon him, eyes no longer dead but full of passionate anger. "Do not be impertinent, Herr Todhunter! You shall not say 'just a moment' to me, the representative of His Imperial Majesty, nor will you attempt to execute your ridiculous and now non-existent piece of paper—your stupid so-called warrant, which I understand was destroyed in Africa!"

"Yes, just so. Another charge, sir. An act of sabotage."

Von Merkatz stared, then laughed loudly. "You English! Do you imagine you own the world, that you speak to me like this aboard my own flagship? Sabotage, pish! A wholly inappropriate word—but call it what you will, it is of no concern whatever to me, Herr Todhunter."

"I respectfully ask, sir," Todhunter went on doggedly, clutching the salty brim of his bowler hat, held before his stomach like a shield, "to be permitted to speak to Sir Russell Savory."

"No, that will *not* be permitted." Von Merkatz turned peremptorily upon Bassinghorn. "Now, Captain. I have invited you aboard in order to put the facts before you once and for all. I trust you understand them, and are prepared now to accept the situation as it is and must remain." As Bassinghorn started to speak, the admiral held up a hand. "No! You will listen. Also, you will understand—this, I *order!* I now make a request."

"What is it, sir?"

"That you shall steam your ship peacefully and offer no more threats—that you shall not fire your stupid guns again, thus inviting me to destroy you and your men. You promise this?"

Bassinghorn laughed. "I think you'll not destroy my ship! I think neither you nor your emperor nor Prince Bismarck would thank you for that, Admiral von Merkatz."

"Prince Bismarck?" The admiral seemed to start, and stared

angrily at Bassinghorn. "What is this about Prince Bismarck?"

"I think you a Bismarck's man, Admiral von Merkatz, and are firmly in his pocket. I think he is pulling you along on a string, like a puppet." Bassinghorn glanced across the cabin at Halfhyde. There was a look of pleasure in his face at the German's reaction. Halfhyde gave an almost imperceptible nod. He believed his captain had hit the nail smartly on the head, that the bluff had worked and that von Merkatz had no desire in his heart to provoke hostilities. Bassinghorn went on, "I suggest you leave Prince Bismarck to swim on his own, or sink. He is in retirement. Without your assistance, he may remain there. But your emperor is not in retirement. I think this is worth consideration."

Von Merkatz, controlling his temper, nodded and gave an icy smile. "Thank you for your exposition, Captain, which I dismiss as a typically stupid British ploy. It is not I who wish to open fire, but you. Do you give me your promise that you will not?"

Bassinghorn said calmly, "I give no promises. I shall do what my duty dictates—no more, no less."

"I see. You are honest, Captain. I give you credit for that! But I regret that I shall not now give you your freedom. You will remain aboard my flagship until I reach a German port, then you will be released—and perhaps given an opportunity of learning how angry Prince Bismarck can become! You will be well treated meanwhile, but you remain as a hostage for my safe conduct—in peace—back to port." Von Merkatz waved a hand. "I have no need for your lieutenant or your policeman. They will be taken back, to tell your ship's company that if they open fire upon me, you shall be the first to die."

• • •

More hell upon earth and sea followed for Todhunter. The voyage back was to be a repeat of the voyage out, and he almost came to grief when the crew of the sea-boat missed his descending body and he crashed to the bottom boards. Worse was to come: while they were being pulled back to the *Prince Consort*, Halfhyde uttered base things accompanied by threats.

"You are to turn liar, Mr Todhunter."

"What's that? I'm a police officer! I'm telling no lies!"

"You are, in the interest of your duty and of success." Halfhyde laughed, a cruel sound in Todhunter's ears. "A handcuffed detective, who has lost his warrant and thereby his authority! It would not be hard, I think, Mr Todhunter, to accuse you of some dereliction of your duty—"

"You wouldn't!" Todhunter was shocked, scandalized.

"I'd hate to do it. I would fall in my own estimation, and that's bad for any man. As bad for me as excess of whisky, leading to drunkenness on duty, is for you—another point to be remembered should my duty—*duty*, Mr Todhunter—force me to remark upon it later. But in case I should baulk at doing that, which frankly I doubt, I may presently ask our German crew to circle the *Prince Consort* until you change your mind." He looked out towards the horizons. "The weather, I fear, is worsening, Mr Todhunter. And we both want Savory arrested, do we not?"

Todhunter dashed water from his eyes, feeling again the dreadful surge of his stomach. "Yes, yes! What do you want of me, Mr Halfhyde?"

"As I said—lies," Halfhyde answered cheerfully. "You shall back up what I shall tell Commander Percy, and you shall back it to the hilt, for you heard the captain's last order . . . didn't you, Mr Todhunter?"

Todhunter licked his lips, stared. "What was that last order, Mr Halfhyde?"

"That, whilst obviously not giving me the command in his absence, since my rank is but lowly when compared with Commander Percy's, he ordered that my plans, yet to be propounded, are to be followed. Followed in full and without question, by Commander Percy and all officers and men. Did you not hear that said, Mr Todhunter?"

"Oh, my God . . ."

"*Did you not,* Mr Todhunter?"

Todhunter was under a tremendous and unfair disadvantage, of which he knew Halfhyde was fully aware. He was bile green and retching. He said despairingly, "Oh . . . yes, yes!"

"It should have been foreseen that they might hold the captain!" Percy snapped, his face furious and immensely worried.

"Up to a point, sir, it *was* foreseen, as you very well know. But as you also very well know, sir, the captain decided that his duty lay in going aboard, having been kindly invited. He had no choice in the circumstances. As it is, I have clear orders now, already stated. Am I not right, Mr Todhunter?" Halfhyde turned to the detective inspector, lifting an eyebrow.

"Yes, yes. Quite right."

"This is most improper," Percy said savagely. "It is I who am clearly in temporary command!"

"That is not disputed, sir. Never! But I am ordered to tell you that—"

"You needn't repeat it, Mr Halfhyde, I heard it the first time, thank you." Commander Percy stalked the bridge, embodying anger, hurt astonishment, and cast-down pride. He came back to Halfhyde and stood in front of him, trembling with his varied feelings. "No ship can have two captains. You will abide by my overall orders."

"Naturally. You, sir, are now the captain. I act merely in the role of my due appointment from Their Lordships: a lieutenant for special duties in connection solely with the pursuit and arrest of Sir Russell Savory. I trust we shall not come into conflict, sir."

"For your sake, Mr Halfhyde, so do I. If there is trouble, it will go hard for you upon our arrival at Plymouth." Percy let out a long breath of frustration. "Well? What, pray, are your *orders* now?"

"Full away for the Channel, sir! That is, of course, maintaining speed to keep in station abeam of the flagship."

"And you do not wish to open fire?" Percy asked with heavy sarcasm.

"I do not, sir. You may fall out the guns' crews and secure from quarters."

"Thank you! And when we reach the Channel—what then, may I ask?"

Halfhyde smiled and rubbed his hands together. "When we are in soundings, sir, I trust my stratagem will have completed itself in my mind. Until then, I ask your indulgence."

Percy turned on his heel and strode to the starboard side of the bridge, muttering about stupid stratagems and lieutenants who were allowed to get above themselves. Halfhyde went down the ladder with Todhunter and thence to the ward-room, where he sent for Mr Midshipman Runcorn. "A glass of sherry,

Mr Runcorn? I do not approve of midshipmen drinking gin."

"Thank you, sir."

"Mr Todhunter, a glass of whisky?"

"I think not, sir, thank you."

"H'm. Perhaps you're wise." Halfhyde gave the order to the steward. "Sherry for Mr Todhunter also. For me, whisky." When the drinks came he raised his glass towards his guests. "To Captain Bassinghorn—may he have a comfortable captivity and a speedy return. And to success!"

They drank. Todhunter said mournfully, "You sound confident, Mr Halfhyde."

"I am. Have you never been through customs, Mr Todhunter? Perhaps they don't have them at the Clarence Pier . . . but no matter. Mr Runcorn, you shall be my first lieutenant—a speedy promotion, but gained without loss to others! I've no doubt you've heard the toast of many a warship's ward-room?"

"Which is that, sir?"

"Bloody war or a sickly season, Mr Runcorn."

"Pardon?" Todhunter said.

"Each leads to speedy promotion, Mr Todhunter. In your case, when chief superintendents die, the Todhunters of this world reap their proper rewards, do they not?" He clapped the disconsolate policeman on the shoulder. "Never fear, success is coming. And now, before the watchkeepers descend upon our privacy, I shall tell you how it's going to be brought about."

The weather improved northwards. As the *Prince Consort* left the Gibraltar Strait well to starboard and headed, clear of Cape St Vincent, up the coast of Portugal, the skies were blue and flecked with scudding white cloud. Beyond Finisterre the Bay of Biscay loomed uncomfortably, but in the event proved kindly towards Todhunter's anxious stomach. Still in company with the German squadron, still with the thoughts of all aboard going across the gap towards Captain Bassinghorn, still at peace and with the guns covered, the *Prince Consort* came past Ushant and in continuing fair weather altered course, with von Merkatz, to leave Cap de la Hague well clear to starboard. By the next dawn they had the rock-bound Cornish coast in view to port, and Halfhyde, on the bridge with Commander Percy, lowered his telescope.

"Home waters, sir! Almost in soundings, I fancy." He quoted: "'From Ushant to Scilly is thirty-five leagues . . .' Is it not, sir?"

"Poets do not make seamen, Mr Halfhyde."

"True." Halfhyde brought up his glass again. "There are vessels off the Lizard, right upon our track."

"As I have already seen, Mr Halfhyde. It's by no means unusual, I would have thought. Tugs, awaiting the sailing ships from Australia and China."

Halfhyde nodded. "Precisely. Falmouth for orders, an evocative phrase. There'll be hard bargaining over the price, the first to get a line aboard having a head start over the others."

"No doubt! Mr Halfhyde, am I now under your orders to bargain for a steam tug into Falmouth?"

"By no means, sir, though I shall have a need for a steam tug presently, as you shall see."

"Will you kindly tell me what you are doing?" Percy snapped.

"A moment, sir, a moment only, and all will become clear." Halfhyde waited. Gradually they neared the first of the tugs, hovering off the Lizard like greedy hawks. Well ahead, the royal mastheads and then the topgallants of an inward-bound square-rigged ship came up, a sea-worn windjammer beating in for home. When the tug was about half a mile off on the battle-ship's starboard bow, Halfhyde leaned over the guardrail and called down. "Mr Runcorn!"

Runcorn emerged from the shelter of a gun turret, a pair of signalling flags in his hand.

"Yes, sir?"

"Action, Mr Runcorn. And take care not to let the Huns see your flag-wagging."

"Aye, aye, sir." Runcorn saluted and turned to face ahead. On the bridge, Percy loudly demanded an explanation.

"A message to the skipper of the steam tug, sir. In the name of the Board of Admiralty . . . he is to proceed with the utmost despatch into Plymouth and deliver certain requests to the commander-in-chief."

"And lose his tow?"

"I think I can promise he will be well recompensed, sir."

"That may be." Percy was almost dancing with anger and impatience, and now exploded. "God damn you, Mr Halfhyde! Will you kindly tell me what is going on in your mind, or must I—"

"A moment, sir." Halfhyde, who had been studying the lie of the German flagship as Runcorn sent his message, moved to the binnacle. "Your pardon," he said to the officer of the watch. "I shall take over now."

"Mr Halfhyde—" Commander Percy began again.

"Be silent, if you please, sir! What follows next will be dangerous in the extreme but is vital to our success. I ask your patience." Halfhyde looked ahead. The steam tug was now coming rapidly down his starboard side, funnel belching smoke already as the firemen banked up the furnaces. Halfhyde watched as the tug went on down the German line and then turned across the stern of the *Nürnberg,* heading in north-easterly for Plymouth Sound. Then he gave his first executive order.

"Mr Strawbridge," he said down the voice-pipe. "Hands to collision stations—but quietly as I told you, no pipes or bugles. You have three minutes."

"Aye, aye, sir." Sam Strawbridge's voice boomed hollowly up the voice-pipe from the wheelhouse. Percy came across, white round the gills, but Halfhyde took no notice.

"Starboard ten," he called down the voice-pipe next. "Main engines to increase forty revolutions."

The response came back: "Starboard ten, sir, main engines up forty revolutions." Then, "Ten of starboard wheel on, sir, 280 revolutions repeated, sir."

Halfhyde watched. With helm to starboard, the battleship's rudder and head came round to port, heading for the *Friedrich der Grösse,* her increasing speed carrying her a little ahead. Halfhyde bent again to the voice-pipe. "All hands clear the engine-room and fo'c'sle but remain under cover. Now, sir," he added to Percy as he straightened. "The explanation. I am about to ram Admiral von Merkatz—not to sink him, but to inca-pacitate him."

Percy raved. "My ship! You shall not hazard my ship—"

"It is not your ship, Commander. It is Captain Bassinghorn's —and mine! If there is to be blame, it shall lie with me—but there will be no blame. Hold tight for your life!"

The *Prince Consort* raced along on her closing course, the wind of her passage tugging at the ropes and wires of the standing rigging. With way enough on now, the fleet engineer, carrying out orders already given privily, shut off the steam to the main shafts before clearing the engine-room. All down the German line there was pandemonium, the ships turning this way and that to avoid ramming their next ahead up the stern when the inevitable impact came. Halfhyde, shouting aloud with laughter, ordered a signal to be made to von Merkatz, mendaciously indicating that his steering had gone. Immediately after this he ordered the bugler to sound collision stations, loud and clear, for the benefit of any of the ship's company who had not been reached by the call-less boatswain's mates. Seconds later the *Prince Consort,* huge and heavy and irresistible, her wheel now amidships and her course steadied on the flagship's forward turret as her point of aim, struck.

There was a grinding crash and a scream from tortured metal; and everywhere men went flat on their faces as they lost their grip on stanchions, stays, or other standing parts of the ship. There was an appalling racket: the cries and shouts of men, many of them injured, joined the hiss of escaping steam. Within the next few seconds, a belch of flame spurted from the broken side of the *Friedrich der Grösse.* As the embedded bows of the British battleship lurched and ground about, the damage to the flagship grew the worse, and her bows began to go down as the water flooded inboard. Men were running hither and thither, enveloped in smoke until the inrush of the English Channel doused the fire; on the bridge the furious visage of Admiral von Merkatz appeared without its halo of gold-encrusted cap, which had been danced and trampled flat as a pancake. As the German crew shut the watertight doors aft of the point of impact, the downward trend of the flagship eased, and she settled with her head inclined at an angle of some ten degrees.

Halfhyde took up a megaphone and directed it towards the German bridge, now close upon his port bow. "I apologize," he called. "It was clumsy of me. But I shall make amends. As you can see, steam tugs are already at hand, which is fortunate. It will cost your government a pretty penny in salvage or at least lost towing revenues, but you shall be taken *most* promptly into Plymouth . . ."

The *Prince Consort's* bows were badly stove in, but apart from that the damage was comparatively slight. She had struck with her watertight doors already closed, and she was still seaworthy. Using his main engines to bring her out from the German's side, Halfhyde decided to take her into Plymouth stern first and with tugs standing by. It was a lengthy business and the shades of evening were falling beneath a splendid sunset as the German Special Service Squadron came forlornly through the breakwater and entered the Sound, the admiral's flag bedraggled as it hung far above the draped collision-mats between its close escort of tugs. British sailors watched in awed astonishment from the spotless and unfractured upper-decks of the first-class cruisers of the Plymouth Command. By this time Captain Bassinghorn was back upon his own bridge: von Merkatz, bowing in the hour of his defeat to the interests of diplomacy and some salvation of his position upon his return to the Fatherland, had sent the captain across just outside the breakwater. Savory, however, remained aboard the *Friedrich der Grösse*—claiming, said Bassinghorn, political asylum from British revenge and the Old Bailey—a nice point of diplomacy to harass Admiral von

Merkatz who could well be said to have already promised him such a consideration in the very act of taking him aboard his ship in the first place. Bassinghorn himself appeared to be in a dilemma between anger at serious damage to his command, concern for his ship's company, and an awareness that Halfhyde had successfully pulled most of the chestnuts from the fire.

"Battleships are expensive to repair, Mr Halfhyde," he said. "Perhaps more expensive than a lieutenant's commission—and infinitely more so than a *lying and disobedient* lieutenant's commission!"

"Lying, yes. Not disobedient, sir, since of orders there were none!" Halfhyde lifted an eyebrow. "Anticipatory, perhaps?"

Bassinghorn laughed. "Possibly, Halfhyde, possibly! Indeed, had I thought, I might well have given those orders. I think I can promise a good word to the Board of Admiralty, though I cannot promise their attentive ear. And now, what about Sir Russell Savory, who will not budge?"

"If he will not budge, sir, then he shall *be* budged."

"There are still diplomatic considerations in regard to boarding a foreign warship, Halfhyde."

"Quite, sir. I agree." Halfhyde rubbed his hands together, his face beaming. "From now on all shall be done with due propriety and a regard for German national feelings. Admiral von Merkatz will suffer no military intrusion of the British naval command aboard his ships."

"Then?—"

"I have sent a message to the commander-in-chief, sir." Halfhyde swept a hand towards the berths in the dockyard as the ship came round Devil's Point in the care of the tugs, heading towards a mooring up the harbour to await dry docking.

Along those berths waited men, many men in uniform with gold stripes on their cuffs and keenly anticipatory looks upon their predatory faces, men whose serviceable but ill-fitting uniforms deprived them of the aspect, partly given by the gold stripes, of naval officers. Some of them were already embarking in small boats. "There are those, sir, who have enough authority to board anything that floats into a British port. The excellent rummagers of Her Majesty's Customs and Excise, sir, of the waterguard—they have a reputation for leaving nothing to chance . . . no secretive notes or documents left unturned! The search of all the German ships promises to be most thorough—and will of course not go unaccompanied!"

"You mean—"

Halfhyde pointed aft towards the quarterdeck. "Observe a happy detective inspector, sir." Bassinghorn looked. Already Mr Todhunter was waiting beneath a newly brushed bowler hat now freed of its retaining stay and toggle since his seafaring days were done, and clutching to his dark blue serge his warrantless gladstone bag, his face austerely composed to do his duty.